MADDOX

———————————

THE ITALIAN CARTEL # 5

SHANDI BOYES

Edited by
NICKY @ SWISH DESIGN & EDITING

Illustrated by
SSB COVERS & DESIGN

COPYRIGHT

Editing: *Nicky @ Swish Design & Editing*

Proofreading: *Kaylene @ Swish Design & Editing*

Alpha Reader: *Carolyn Wallace*

Cover: *SSB Covers & Design*

Photography: *Wander Aguir*

Model: *Sonny Henty*

❀ Created with Vellum

WANT TO STAY IN TOUCH?

Facebook: facebook.com/authorshandi

Instagram: instagram.com/authorshandi

Email: authorshandi@gmail.com

Reader's Group: bit.ly/ShandiBookBabes

Website: authorshandi.com

Newsletter: subscribepage.com/AuthorShandi

ALSO BY SHANDI BOYES

Denotes Standalone Books

Perception Series

Saving Noah *

Fighting Jacob *

Taming Nick *

Redeeming Slater *

Saving Emily

Wrapped Up with Rise Up

Protecting Nicole *

Enigma

Enigma

Unraveling an Enigma

Enigma The Mystery Unmasked

Enigma: The Final Chapter

Beneath The Secrets

Beneath The Sheets

Spy Thy Neighbor *

The Opposite Effect *

I Married a Mob Boss *

Second Shot *

The Way We Are

The Way We Were

Sugar and Spice *

Lady In Waiting

Man in Queue

Couple on Hold

Enigma: The Wedding

Silent Vigilante

Hushed Guardian

Quiet Protector

Enigma: An Isaac Retelling

Twisted Lies *

Bound Series

Chains

Links

Bound

Restrain

The Misfits *

Nanny Dispute *

Russian Mob Chronicles

Nikolai: A Mafia Prince Romance

Nikolai: Taking Back What's Mine

Nikolai: What's Left of Me

Nikolai: Mine to Protect

Asher: My Russian Revenge *

Nikolai: Through the Devil's Eyes

Trey *

The Italian Cartel

Dimitri

Roxanne

Reign

Mafia Ties (Novella)

Maddox

Demi

Ox

Rocco *

Clover *

Smith *

RomCom Standalones

Just Playin' *

Ain't Happenin' *

The Drop Zone *

Very Unlikely *

False Start *

Short Stories - Newsletter Downloads

Christmas Trio *

Falling For A Stranger *

One Night Only Series

Hotshot Boss *

Hotshot Neighbor *

The Bobrov Bratva Series

Wicked Intentions *

Sinful Intentions *

Devious Intentions *

Deadly Intentions *

PROLOGUE
MADDOX

Age Seven

My head cranks back when a thud booms into my ears. It sounded the same as the *oomph* that whizzed out of Landon's mouth when he beat Caidyn to the front of the line, and Caidyn showed his dislike by punching Landon in the stomach, but it was squeaky like a mouse, and it hurt my chest.

We're in line at the carpool at the front of our school. It's one of those fancy-schmancy places parents pay lots of money for their children to attend. Some students even sleep here. My brothers, sister, and I don't because we live a short drive from Seacoast Private Academy, but students like the one a bully just pushed over stay here all the time.

I don't know if their mommies and daddies can't take care of them or if they need extra help with their studies, but whatever the reason, they're here day *and* night. I like school, but if I had to be here twenty-four-seven, I'd vomit. My teachers are cranky bums. My parents are not.

"Hold my spot." My baby sister, Justine, raises her eyes to mine. She only just started at my school this year. She's a big girl now, but she doesn't need to be brave. She has four older brothers. That's all the bravery she needs. "Please make sure Mommy doesn't leave me here."

When Justine nods, promising me she won't make me sleep at the school, I race toward the little girl holding her grazed knee. She's sitting on the footpath, and big wet blobs are filling her eyes. "Are you okay?"

My heart whacks against my chest so fast I'm certain I broke something when she lifts her head to look at me. My mommy says my eyes are the color of the ocean. This little girl's pretty eyes are blue like mine, but since her hair is as dark as a starless night, they appear as big as the moon.

"Don't cry," I stammer out when a salty droplet rolls down her cheek. "If you cry, he'll think he won."

When she sucks in a shaky breath, a clear sign she's trying to be brave, I narrow my eyes like an angry bear before glaring at the boy who pushed her over. "You hurt her, you bozo!"

I'm big for my age, but I'm not as big as the grade six boy I'm yelling at. He's the size of a giant, and the fist he's racing toward my nose is bigger than a watermelon. It collides into my face with a crack and sends me tumbling backward.

I hear my older brothers shout my name as they run to protect me, but I can't see them since the girl I defended is catching the blood running out of my nose like she can't catch cooties. "Don't cry," she reminds me when silly tears prick my eyes. "If you cry, he'll think he won."

1

MADDOX

Present Day

As the bell above Stamina's door jingles in my ears, my glove-covered fist collides into Saint's nose with a thud. My older brother is usually more on the ball when it comes to deflecting the jabs I hit him with when we go a couple of rounds in the ring. He isn't quite as tall as me—Landon secured the title of being both the oldest and tallest in our family, and Caidyn, although both wiser and older than me, is a good inch shorter, but Saint knows how to command the ring.

We've been sparring together since we were kids. My dad, although a little chubby around the midsection when he sailed past fifty, always implemented a strict exercise regime for my brothers and me. At the start, I thought it was about peak physical fitness. I learned otherwise when my baby sister grew into her lanky legs and teenybopper bra.

My parents will never admit it to Justine's face, but she wasn't planned. Dad was a week out from having a vasectomy, and with four boys under the age of five, Mom had closed up shop years earlier—around the time I popped out.

Justine, as forever stubborn as she is, had other plans.

My mom was so convinced she was having another boy, she booted me out of the nursery, touched up the paint my older brothers chipped while tackling their newest sibling into submission, then chose the perfect name to go with Landon, Sebastian, Caidyn, and Maddox.

Oh, did I forget to mention Saint's real name is Sebastian? We call him Saint because he's *nothing* close to saintly. Town Stud is the only title his name will *ever* wear, and he's more than happy to keep it that way.

Justin was a tough name. It belonged to a person who wasn't to be messed with. That's why when 'Justin' came screaming into the world weighing an impressive nine pounds without any dangly bits between 'his' legs, Mom tacked an 'E' onto the end of 'his' name and went about her day.

That's very much how my parents operate. They're strict and a little unknowledgeable when it comes to electronics, but they love their kids to the core. I don't think there's anything we could do that would see us shunted out of their lives for good. Not even Justine getting 'friendly' with a boy she just met in the hot tub on her eighteenth birthday saw them giving her the cold shoulder.

They said she was an adult, and in turn, they'd treat her like one.

She didn't get off quite so easily with her older siblings.

We watched her like a hawk—we still do.

Unlike the woman responsible for the brand-new shiner forming under Saint's right eye, Justine has lived a sheltered life. She has no clue how cruel the world can be, and if I have it my way, she never will. A big brother's job is to protect his baby sister. Nothing should come before that—although I see things changing when women without our blood are thrown into the mix. We've already noticed it with Landon. I don't see Caidyn being too far behind him.

In a way, I'm lucky. With Justine having four older brothers and me being the youngest of them all, the weight on my shoulders is nowhere near as heavy as Landon's and Saint's. That doesn't mean I can get slack, though. As my father always says, "Slacking off is the quickest way to an average life."

After drifting my eyes from Demi Petretti, voted most attractive, most likely to succeed, *and* all-around badass by every male in a five-mile radius of Seacoast Private Academy senior year almost four years ago, I punish Saint's ribs with a left-right-left combination.

He groans through the pain of a possible cracked rib, but not once does he stray his eyes away from the area Demi is mingling. I can't say I blame him. That girl doesn't just have the smarts to be in the top two percent of students at our school, she also was in the top two percent in the state. Add that to the fact she's as hot as sin, and you've got a lethal combination any man would be lucky to stumble upon.

Unfortunately for me, by the time I worked up the courage to do something about an almost decade-long crush, Saint announced an interest in Demi. That put her off-limits, and the reminder she's out of reach has me punishing Saint with my fists so rebelliously, he has no choice but to man up and hit me back.

We go blow for blow for the next several minutes, only stopping when the coach from our high school wrestling team mistakes our fight as literal. "This is why I invoked the sibling code. You two will kill each other one day."

The redness lining Coach Merritt's face triples when Saint has the audacity to laugh. High school feels as if it was decades ago when you're a senior in college, but you can be assured as fuck I haven't worked up the courage to laugh in a teacher's face just yet. I'm not a coward by any means, I just know how to pick my battles. Coach Merritt isn't the wrestling coach of a state championship team for no reason. His size alone exposes he'd face no issues putting Saint on his ass, much less a cabinet full of trophies in our high school gymnasium.

"He isn't laughing at you, Coach," I push out breathlessly when the heat on Coach's face looks close to boiling over. "He's laughing at the fact he'd rather act like a pussy than eat one."

Coach chokes on his spit. It's barely heard over the warning growl rumbling up Saint's chest. He's about ready to blow his top, and I'm right there, willing to push him over the edge like all little brothers should be.

With the swagger of a man not being eyeballed as if his head is on the chopping block, I backhand Saint in the chest. "Come on, Saint, admit it. You've been drooling over the same girl for years."

"Yeah, so?"

Don't let his honesty fool you. He isn't doing it because he's a stand-up guy. Lying just isn't a Walsh forte. If you want us to sugarcoat things, you better offer one of us a scholarship in baking because that's the only way we'll sweeten things up for you.

Loud and proud isn't our motto either, but you won't ever doubt when a Walsh is in your vicinity. That's why I'm shocked about Saint's constant sitting on the fence when it comes to Demi. She's drop-dead gorgeous, smart, and witty, has never been seen with a man who isn't related to her by blood, and she forever glances his way when we're dancing in the ring like we're destined to become the next Conor McGregor. Her last name leaves a bad taste in your mouth any time you say it, but come on, doesn't the abovementioned make up for that?

When Saint remains quiet, I wordlessly demand he return his Town Stud badge with a two-finger clap. When my voiceless command doesn't have him coughing up the goods, I throw words into the mix. "You can't keep a title you're not willing to uphold."

"Fuck off, Maddox. Don't try and pin your bullshit on me." He smacks me up the side of the head before he moves to the ropes to scrub the sweat off his face with a towel hanging off the top rung. "From what Landon told me, you haven't done much... *pussy eating* yourself." A gleam I know all too well sparks through his eyes before he says, "When I was a senior in college..."

The growl that finalizes his statement pisses me off. I've been crushing on Demi for years. I'm not talking she's-real-pretty-and-I'd-like-to-get-to-know-her-some-more crush. I mean, *crush* crush. She's ruining all my hookups crush. Stick-me-with-a-fork-I'm-fucking-done crush. And they're just examples of when I've caught the occasional smile she's tossed my way the past five years.

I'm a fucking mess, and Demi Petretti is solely responsible for the carnage.

Fortunately for me, the Walsh men aren't just masters at brawling, barbecuing, and philandering, we're also really fucking good at hiding our emotions as well.

While smirking like the smug fuck I am, I add to Saint's mortification that he said 'pussy eating' in public. "As I've told you before, Saint, if your big brother is *still* chaperoning your dates, you're doing it wrong."

He hits me with an evil sideways glare, doubling my smile. "How about you be fucking honest for once? We both know why you're pushing me on this." I almost reply, *'cause you're a pussy, and it's my job as your little brother to push your buttons,* but he continues talking, foiling my endeavor. "Because you're hoping she'll reject me, then you can slot into my place." He tosses the towel back over the ropes, stands tall, then puffs his chest out. "News flash, bozo, that'll *never* happen because I've *never* been rejected."

Spit flies out of my mouth when I brush off his claims with a *pfft.* I'm one hundred percent praying like fuck Demi shoots down his signature move, then I might finally get the opportunity to prove dreams can come true, but there's no chance in hell I'll ever let Saint know that.

It's a pity for me that there are days where he knows me better than I know myself. "Now who's the fucking pussy?" With the swagger of a man aware he has the eyes of over a dozen women on him, he saunters back my way. Yes, I said saunters. The fucker is strutting like he's making his way to the octagon. "We don't travel *all the way* to Hopeton to work out for no reason, so come on, out with it. What's the real reason for the change-up?"

I give lying a shot. It isn't something I'm proud of, but when you're backed into a corner, you must come out swinging. "Our gym was remodeled."

"With better, more up-to-date equipment," Saint argues, his smirk growing. "Try again."

My back molars crunch together, hating that he read my lie so easily. I don't know why I'm shocked. I'm a shit liar. The knowledge won't stop me from giving it another whirl, though. You don't just come out swinging. You've got to have your guard up as well. "The owner doubled the membership fees."

Saint's deep exhale ruffles the reddish-blond hair stuck to my temples. "From ten dollars a week to twenty. *Jeez*. How dare he!"

Our family isn't close to being poor. Our mom works as an architect, and our father is a pilot. We're not wealthy, but my parents made a sound decision when they invested in Raven-shoe long before a multi-millionaire rocked up to glam up the place. The price tag on our family home is now in the millions, and my parents don't owe a dime on it.

Their decision many moons ago means their children didn't

have to race out and get jobs the instant they left high school. We all did, though. Landon is following in our father's footsteps, Caidyn is giving architecture a whirl, Saint has a hand in just about everything, and I'm working even while studying, just the basis of my job is kept on the down-low.

As I said earlier, my parents would never judge my decisions. However, there are some things you can't share until the time is right.

"We're here, slumming it in Hopeton because the only pussy around here is you," Saint continues, directing my focus back to him.

I roll my eyes, acting as immature as my twenty-one years on this earth. "How many times do I have to tell you, Saint? Shunting the blame for *your* lack of balls onto your baby brother won't cut the mustard. If you get out a measuring stick and the odds don't fall in your favor, only *you* are to blame for that."

Have you ever wondered what a man looks like in the seconds leading to him going into coronary failure? I had once. I'm not curious anymore. Saint alleviated my curiosity within a nanosecond of me reminding him I'm may be the youngest brother, but that's the only 'young' thing about me.

As the determination on Saint's face grows, so does the volume of his voice. "You know what, fuck it. I'll do it."

"Do what, exactly?" Coach Merritt asks on my behalf, worried Saint is about to finish what I started in this ring almost five minutes ago.

I'd like to see him try.

Saint rips off his gloves, tosses them into his gym bag at the side of the ring, then climbs through the ropes. "I'm going to prove how effective my signature move is." In a manner no man on the planet should *ever* replicate, he makes a 'V' with his index finger and middle finger, slams them against his quirked lips, then wiggles his tongue between them like he's devouring an invisible buffet of pussy.

"You're not going to do *that* here, surely," Coach Merritt blubbers out, convinced he's seconds away from witnessing Saint lift Demi onto the slushie counter at the back of the gym, then go to town on her pussy.

When Saint ignores Coach Merritt's panicked tone, he shifts on his feet to face me. "Ox..."

My eyes snap to his so fast, my head grows woozier than the anger that fused my brain while considering the possibility of Saint going through with his pledge.

I didn't think this through. That isn't uncommon for me. I did the same thing when an MC at an underground fight asked me my name. I am the first to admit I'm not overly good at thinking on the spot, so I went for something easy. Until today, no one has ever shortened my name to Ox. Well, not in this world anyway.

Although I want to ask Coach Merritt exactly how much he knows and for how fucking long he's known it, I don't have the time nor the patience to wade through that shitstorm right now. My brother is moments away from calling me out as a liar, and it's taking everything I have not to pummel his face in for outing me so cruelly.

It's not every day you encourage your big brother to hit on the girl you've been crushing on since primary school, and I had to take it one step further by forcing him to bring out his signature move.

He isn't going to simply ask Demi on a date. He's about to ignite a spark between them so furious, no amount of liquid will dose the flame, not even the blood gushing from my bleeding heart. He's about to make Demi Petretti his, and the bro-code states there isn't a single-fucking-thing I can do about it.

2

DEMI

"Oh, sweet Jesus, here he comes."

Sloane, my best friend since middle school, fluffs out her curly locks like it's perfectly acceptable for a man to waltz across the room, weave his fingers through a random stranger's hair, tilt her back, then kiss the living hell out of her.

Yes, it sounds romantic, but do you have any idea how many lawsuits Saint could face if his flirt radar was off by a measly inch? Unlike Sloane, I'm not studying law, but I imagine the penalty would be hefty—*for the average man*. I can't say the same for the men who 'work' in my uncle's industry. They don't live in the same world as you and me, and they most certainly don't follow the same set of rules.

When Saint, proverbial playboy and middle sibling of the Walsh brethren, reaches the halfway point, Sloane rams her elbow into my ribs. "Wet your lips. You don't want the zap to fall through the cracks. If there's no spark, he'll retreat as quickly as he arrived."

"What?" I crank my neck to hers so fast, I make a mental note to book an emergency appointment with a chiropractor. "Why do I need to wet my lips?"

Sloane peers at me like I'm insane. "Saint he-can-fuck-me-any-day-of-the-week Walsh is heading in this direction. We're the only females on this side of the gym, so either you or I are about to be kissed."

She tries to hold back the disdain her last sentence hit her throat with. Her efforts are borderline. The last time she looked at me as she is now was when I got the over-hyped Barbie convertible one whole week before her. She didn't care her birthday was seven days after mine. She wanted us to get it at the same time.

Sloane's narrowed eyes slant even more when my tongue instinctively delves out to moisten my lips a couple of seconds later. I'm not buttering them up so Saint can authenticate the durability of the spark he's endeavoring to ignite between us. It's because my mouth went bone-dry from catching a steely blue stare across the room.

Maddox is watching his older brother's stalk of the sweat-scented space. Unlike the numerous other gym-goers stalking Saint's prowl with the hope of witnessing his signature move be slapped back to the nineties with the crack of a palm, he looks more frustrated than hopeful.

It isn't an expression he often wears, not that I watch him or anything. He's in the general area I'm perusing, so I can't be blamed when my eyes linger on the tight bumps in his abs or the beads of sweat rolling throughout his delicious, tattooed guns. He's flaunting his assets for the world to see, and unlike his brother's nickname, I am no saint.

The Walshs have been known around this part of the state for almost as long as the Petrettis. They live in the town bordering mine, and although they have standard, everyday jobs, their family name is well-respected amongst the locals.

I can't say the same about mine.

If you believe the many reports family services have on my family, my uncle stood up to the plate to raise me when my father passed away six years ago. He paid for my education, ensured I had a roof over my head, and he even spoke with the Dean of a local college about granting me a scholarship.

Just like Saint's signature move, everything appears swell on paper. It's only once you read between the lines do you see what's truly happening.

My uncle is an abusive tyrant of a man. He pushed my father to the brink so many times, it was inevitable one day his tiptoe across the rocky cliff he forever balanced on would end badly. No one could help him, not even me, his only child.

Most children have a mother to fall back on when their father dies. I wasn't granted the same mercy. With her 'owner' dead, and her debt to my uncle unpaid, my uncle forced my mother back into the 'trade.' I haven't seen her in years. In all honesty, I don't even know if she's still alive.

Women aren't valued in my uncle's industry. More times than not, we're seen as a burden. If I don't prove to my uncle time and time again that I'm worth my weight in gold, I'll be forced into the trade like my mother. Since that scares me more than I'll ever let my uncle know, I have no choice but to play his games.

My focus shifts back to the present when the undeniable aroma of a man on the hunt streams into my nostrils. Saint has made it across the room unscathed, and unlike his younger brother's eyes that are locked on me, his baby blues are bouncing between my best friend and me.

It's wrong to admit a sigh parts my lips when Saint weaves his fingers through Sloane's hair before he dips her back and attaches their lips, so I'll keep my mouth shut. I wasn't lying when I said I didn't want to be kissed by Saint, but things would have been easier if he'd gone against the grain. Alas, life isn't easy for any of us.

With the crowd feeding off the electricity surging between Sloane and Saint, I almost slip out the back entrance unnoticed. *Almost.*

"Demi, wait up."

I recognize the voice of the man chasing me down. I heard it many times throughout my childhood and ignored how it made the fine hairs on my body bristle anytime it floated over my skin. I've even taken it in when it's on the brink of exhaustion from doing an activity someone as handsome as him shouldn't be doing.

Maddox Walsh is a beautiful canvas on the verge of being wrecked if he doesn't stop parading himself in front of numerous pairs of fists every Thursday night. From the intel my uncle has shared, Maddox is undefeated in the underground fight circuit he's been contending in the past seven months, but shouldn't the prospect that there's always someone better than you around the corner concern him?

"Hey, did the shouts back there affect your hearing?" Maddox asks after catching up with me. "I've been calling your name for half a block."

I keep my eyes fixated on the street while replying, "Yeah… ah… it was pretty crazy." I hate lying, but I'm grateful I've not yet learned how to lie to someone's face without stammering. "Sloane will be extremely happy." Since my last comment is straight-up honest, it's delivered without the slightest jitter from my vocal cords.

I stupidly drift my eyes from a stream of cars parked down one side of the street to Maddox when he asks, "Are you happy?" He nudges his head to Stamina's, a boxing gym my uncle 'claimed' as his almost four years ago. "Because you looked pretty devastated when Saint locked lips with your friend."

Hating that he read my disappointment in the wrong manner, I briskly shake my head. "Oh, no, I'm not upset about that."

Maddox slants his head in a manner that's much too adorable for a man who's been able to grow a beard since he was sixteen. "Then what are you upset about?"

Have you ever wanted to confess your heart out like they'll be no consequences to your actions? That's what I'm facing right now. I'd give anything to tell him the truth, but since I can't, I pretend I'm a perfectly stable twenty-one-year-old.

"Did you feel the spark back there?" I hook my thumb over my shoulder. "I just lost my best friend." *My only friend.*

My dropped lip lifts into a half-grin when Maddox play-fully bumps me with his elbow. "If Saint's track record is anything to go by, your best friend will need you in T minus..." He checks his watch like he can set a schedule to Saint's dating calendar. "Six days, twenty-three hours, and fifty-two minutes."

I'm a horrible person for smiling about the future heartbreak of my best friend, but it can't be helped. You didn't hear the wittiness in Maddox's tone. It truly seems as if he's happy I noticed the mammoth buzz brewing between Sloane and Saint.

We walk half a block in silence before Maddox breaks the quiet. "Come have a drink with me?"

When I suddenly stop, an old lady with purple curls and a face full of makeup bumps into me. I'm stunned by Maddox's offer but also psyched about it.

After apologizing to the lady not watching where she's going, I stammer out. "W-w-what? It's only Thursday."

"And?" Maddox asks with a laugh, killing me with his perfectly straight white teeth. His smile is one of the reasons he shouldn't be in the industry he is. It could convince you that the world is flat and my uncle is a kind man. "That means you have all of Friday, Saturday, *and* Sunday to sleep off your hangover."

I shouldn't laugh, but I do. "The fact you think I'll have a hangover means you don't really know me at all."

My eyes lower to his kissable lips when he rakes his teeth over them. "Are you sure about that, Demetria Andria Petretti?"

I slap a hand over his mouth like I didn't just imagine what his lips taste like. "Who told you my real name?" We went to the same school since the first grade, but not once was my name shared in its entirety.

It's an effort not to whack Maddox in the stomach when a string of gibberish spills through the cracks in my fingers. If he spoke normal, I'd hear him perfectly fine, but I guess that would mean I would win this round, and the Walshs don't back down when they're being haggled.

The air my fist forces out of Maddox's lungs dries the sweat on my hand. It's a pity it can't fix the sweaty mustache forming on my top lip. I've known the Walshs for years, but this is the first time I've stood across from my crush without one of his siblings chaperoning our interaction. I'm swimming in waters out of my depth, but the fear of drowning won't harness my interrogation.

"Seriously, Maddox, who told you my name?" My teeth grit when my endeavor to remove the panic from my tone fails. It weakens the chemistry brewing between Maddox and me and switches the sparkle in his eyes from playful to concerned in under a second.

Maddox removes my hand from his mouth, but he doesn't release it from his grasp. I'm twenty-one-years old. Handholding should no longer affect me, but I'd be a liar if I said zaps of electricity weren't surging up my arm.

After peering down at our hands long enough to convince me he's experiencing the same sparks, Maddox confesses, "I overheard it when your uncle was schmoozing the Dean for a scholarship. I go to STEM Academy. They have a first-class *understudy* program."

"Oh..." I could say more. I *should* say more, but I just can't. I'm too busy seeking the closest hole to bury myself in. I'm skirting the truth like it will give me rabies, yet Maddox is being as honest as it comes. 'Understudy program' is what the fighters in the college circuit call the underground fight tournament in this region. "Sorry."

He flashes me a grin that's more immoral than decent. It brings back the sexual tension tenfold and has me fighting not to squirm on the spot. "What do you have to be sorry about, *Andi?*"

I fan my spare hand across his chest, not only announcing that he needs to stop following me but also warning him I don't appreciate the nickname. Although, the spasm my briefest touch causes his pectoral muscle has me considering permitting him to call me whatever the hell he likes.

Confident he's gotten the point and needing to remove my hand from his chest before I replace it with my tongue, I tug my hand out of his grip before I continue pacing down the street.

Maddox gets the hint about my dislike of his nickname, but he doesn't quit following me. "Still not a fan of nicknames, eh?"

He'd understand my continued dislike if he knew the names tossed at me by my uncle's men. Pet. Kitty. Baby doll. They're just a few I've been hit with the past week, and they're the only ones I can repeat without vomit scorching my throat. Andi may seem the weaker of them all, but it's more than capable of destroying me.

Only one man calls me 'Andi.'

He doesn't use it affectionately.

He only brings it out when he wants to maim.

When I increase the length of my strides, eager to place distance between Maddox and me before the wrong person sees us together, Maddox jogs to catch up to me. The length of his strides is almost double mine, so he doesn't need to jog. He just wants me to know he's aware of what I'm doing and that he's refusing to let me get away as easily as he has the past four years.

Stubbornness is another well-known Walsh trait.

We walk for almost two blocks in silence before the quiet gets the better of Maddox for the second time. "Are you not a fan of talking anymore? I could barely get a word in when we were kids."

"I like talking," I snap out before I can stop myself. "Just not with you."

Jesus, Demi. Cut the guy down with an ax, why don't you.

"Ouch." His hurt would be more believable if he weren't chuckling. "Dress me up and call me Shirley, did I just get my *first* rejection?"

I roll my eyes. It's the only defense I have to hide my grin. I don't usually find cocky men endearing, but I'm seeing it in an entirely new light since it's coming from Maddox. "Let me guess, your middle name is Cocky?"

Smirking, he follows me down Westcott Lane. "Close. It's Richard." He hits me with a flirty wink that doubles the stupid smile I shouldn't be wearing. "You can call me Dick if you'd like?"

I laugh like I have the world at my feet. "So that's how you operate? I just call you up, and you'll bring dick right on over." *Oh. My. God. Who the hell am I?* I've never openly flirted like this before, much less with a man as sinfully hot as Maddox Walsh. "Not that I want your dick or anything."

Shut up, Demi. You're a sinking ship. Drown in peace.

"We'll see," Maddox mutters while jerking his chin to the left. "I've heard good things about this place, shall we test it out?"

"I'm good."

I've craved a normal existence for over a decade. Dining in my hometown with *any* man won't bring me close to the simplistic lifestyle I'm still hoping to achieve one day, but dining with Maddox would upend my plans entirely.

I make it two steps away from the Latin restaurant Maddox nudged his head at before an arm bands around my waist, and I'm yanked back. I don't put up a fight. What sane girl would? One of the most eligible bachelors this side of the country has his extremely fit body plastered against mine. Not only does it feel as wondrous as it looks, I've been dreaming about it being pressed against me since before I got my period.

"Let me try that again. I've heard good things about this place. *Let's* test it out." Maddox walks us into the restaurant like it's perfectly normal to carry a grown woman around as if she's a child. "A table for two, please. Far in the back. My girl gets randy when her tastebuds are on fire." Imagine a pro-wrestler being announced on fight night, then you'll have an indication of how dramatic Maddox's voice is during the last half of his statement.

Ignoring the plea on my face that she declare the restaurant is fully booked, the maître d peers at me as if I'm the luckiest girl on the planet before she plucks two menus from her podium, then gestures for Maddox to follow her.

"I can walk," I stammer out, not only embarrassed several eyes in the capacity-filled restaurant sling my way but still foraging a way to hatch an escape. "You just witnessed that for five blocks."

"Eh," Maddox immediately fires back, his grunt rumbling through both our chests. "I either walk you through then apologize profusely for your embarrassment during lunch, or fight off a pack of hungry middle-aged women without a taser." He peers down at me and grins. It sets my heart racing. "I left it in my bag at the gym."

When confusion pops a crinkle between my brows, Maddox rocks his hips forward. I stiffen like a board when I discover the reason he's using my body for coverage. He's hard. I'm not talking Robert Flint's reaction to our first kiss without his braces in the eleventh grade hard. I'm talking the type of stiffness a movie star would leak his dick pic on purpose hard.

The fact my closeness instigates such a fierce response out of Maddox should turn my brain to mush. Alas, you can't give up the opportunity of getting one up on your crush because of a little stiffness.

I really shouldn't say little, but you get what I mean.

"Was it calling me a man's name that got you turned on? Or the idea of dressing up like a woman?"

The longer silence stretches between us, the bigger my grin becomes. I, along with every other girl in the grades each side of mine, had massive crushes on the Walsh brothers throughout high school. They look similar, but they all have unique traits. Maddox's hair is more a reddish-blond than straight-up blond like Saint's. Landon's is burnt orange like their little sister, Justine, and Caidyn's is brown. Maddox's blue eyes have a tinge of green to them when he's moody, and unlike two out of three of his brothers, he doesn't hate the freckles dotted across his pasty white skin.

Despite having the fairest skin of them all, Caidyn skipped the freckle gene. I'm kind of disappointed for him. There's something insanely sexy about a freckle treasure hunt. Who knows where the search will take you?

"There's that sweet scent again that's got me in all types of trouble," Maddox murmurs under his breath when a shiver of excitement dashes down my spine. "At this rate, you'll have to sit on my lap while we eat."

I snatch up a used napkin from one of the tables we're veering past before tossing it into Maddox's face. "How about you mop up the mess in your pants, then we can sit down and enjoy our meal?"

He throws his head back and laughs. I really wish he wouldn't. The vibration alone has me on the verge of climax. "If you think I'm already done, I clearly have my work cut out for me this weekend."

Weekend?

I'm saved from requesting a towelette for my suddenly drenched face when we arrive at the table the maître d has assigned to us. Unlike the many dining options surrounding us, our table isn't a booth, meaning Maddox has no choice but to set me onto my feet. It presents the perfect opportunity for me to flee, but since we're at the very back of the restaurant, far from prying eyes, my feet refuse to answer the prompts of my brain— and perhaps my heart. It seems to rule the roost when it comes to anyone in the Walsh clan.

"Killjoy," Maddox whispers to the maître d, winking when she grins ear-to-ear about the mirth in his tone.

I plop into my seat before covering my flaming-with-anger face with the menu. "Is she a *friend* of yours?"

It's Mood Swing City here today. One minute I'm telling him to back off, and the next minute I'm wondering how true claims are that you can kill someone with a fork.

"Depends," Maddox replies, taking my anger in stride like it's no big deal.

He probably handles neurotic, jealous women every day. They throw themselves at him all the time. The fact I expected to be treated differently shows how stupid I am, and I'm not solely referencing accepting his invitation for lunch, either.

"Do you class Dimitri as your friend? Or do cousins not get the friend title?"

Shit.

"The maître d is your cousin?" The chirpy, she-needs-to-be-admitted-stalker, Demi is back. "That's nice."

When I sink low in my chair so the menu can cover my face, Maddox's laugh rumbles through the gilded cardboard a mere second before he plucks it out of my hand. "No hiding on me, Demi. I've been waiting for this day for years."

Years?

I begin to wonder if I said my query out loud when Maddox mumbles, "This whole time I thought you were looking at Saint. It was only when your eyes remained glued to my half of the gym during his prowl did I realize I was wrong."

The pride in his eyes almost knocks me on my ass, but it won't stop me from saying, "I wasn't looking at you."

I'm a woeful liar, and Maddox is more than happy to call me out on it. "Stalking. Eyeballing. Fucking me with your eyes. Whatever you want to call it. You were *totally* doing it."

"I wasn't *fucking* you with my eyes." I *totally was.* "I was admiring your technique." With our conversation heading in a direction I never anticipated, my next set of words come out with an edge of caution. "My uncle boards a local fighting chapter." That made it sound like a legitimate organization. Don't let me pull the wool over your eyes. "Sometimes he asks me to keep an eye on the competition for him."

"Oh." Maddox's facial expression is more reserved than I've ever seen it, and believe me, I have perused it multiple times the past thirteen plus years. "I thought maybe you were a regular at the gym because you were seeking new recruits?"

"No," I stammer out far too quickly for anyone to believe I'm being honest. "My uncle doesn't value my opinion that much." Since that's straight-up honest, it sounds that way.

I stop twisting my napkin around my fingers when Maddox says, "Perhaps he should. From what I've heard, you brought Petretti's Restaurant back to life the past three years."

My smile is genuine. I never wanted to be a cook, but Petretti's was close to my dad's heart, so I couldn't help but breathe life back into its lungs when it started to choke.

"Do you eat at Petretti's often?"

Maddox waits for the server to fill our glasses with water before responding, "Depends. Do you class every second day as regular?"

I nod like he asked if I think he's sexy. "Pretty much so."

I won't lie. I'm as smitten as a romance junkie eating breakfast at Tiffany's that he dines at Petretti's. His loyalty won't line my pockets with money, but it feels good knowing the dishes I handcrafted are being enjoyed by people not in my uncle's industry.

With my mood not as hostile as it was, we banter through three scrumptious courses, one bottle of wine, and many *many* hours of conversation. We talk about pretty much everything—school, family, and how Maddox stumbled onto the underground fight scene while endeavoring to impress a girl.

I didn't have the heart to tell him not all college-aged women want to be wooed with violence.

Some want to be saved from it.

"And that pretty much sums up the past three years," Maddox finalizes while dabbing at a chunk of guacamole stuck in the corner of his plump lips with a napkin.

I noticed it a couple of minutes ago, but since the only way my lust-filled head could conjure up a way to remove it was with my tongue, I kept my knowledge of its existence on the down-low.

I like Maddox, I have for years, but I must remain cautious. When I drag people into my life, it doesn't matter how strong they are, they get hurt. My daddy was the strongest man I knew, but not even he could survive this world, so I'm not willing to place anyone else into the fire to see if they make it out alive.

Maddox dumps his napkin onto his sauce-stained plate. "It's been a good couple of years."

"Booze, brawling, and girls. Sounds like every guy's fantasy." This isn't the first time jealousy has highlighted my tone today. It most likely won't be the last.

Ignoring Maddox's dusting of my nose like he's removing the dirt my comment sprinkled it with, I stand to my feet. "I really should head off. Sloane is probably panicked out of her mind." When Maddox screws up his face, I splay my hands across my hips. "You can't honestly believe you know my best friend better than I do. I ditched her at the gym hours ago. That kind of dumping requires more than a tub of ice cream. I'm about to go broke in the candy aisle."

He snatches up the bill wallet before my hand can get close to it, shoves it under his arm, then locks his eyes with mine. "Is Sloane spontaneous, strong-willed, and carefree?"

Confident he hit the nail on the head, I bob my chin.

"Then I have no hesitation in saying she's praying for you *not* to rock up to your apartment any time soon." Maddox pushes out with a chuckle while helming our walk to the counter to pay our bill.

I follow him like a lost puppy. Mercifully, I look like I'm begging, but my tone is far fiercer. "Once again, how would you know that? Sloane is *my* best friend. I know her better than anyone."

He pulls a wad of bills I don't want to know how he got them out of his wallet, hands them to his cousin, then shifts on his feet to face me. "Saint is my brother, so I not only know him, I know how he operates."

When I gesture for him to continue, a little confused as to

what he means, he places his hand on the small of my back before guiding me outside.

"Should you really do that?" I whisper, grinning. "I may not know how your brother operates, but if it's anything like the thread in the crotch of your gym shorts, you probably shouldn't place either of them under a magnifying glass for the second time today."

Maddox stops dead in the middle of the sidewalk. While acting oblivious to the people mingling around us, he says, "Are you saying what I think you are, Ms. Don't-Call-Me-Andi? Are you implying you'll need a magnifying glass to inspect my package?"

I wasn't, but I am now. "Uh-huh."

Maddox's mouth falls open. "Oh, that's it. This shit is about to get messy."

I scream loud enough for two blocks over to hear when he bobs down, wraps an arm around my thighs, then tosses me over his shoulder. Like all women who read far too many erotic novels, I assume he is going to race us down the alley to prove the chunk of meat that dug into my backside hours ago wasn't a footlong sub, but I'm not disappointed when he stops by an ice cream parlor a couple of minutes later.

"If leaving your best friend at the mercy of the guy she's been crushing on for years deserves a tub of ice cream, you owe me an entire fucking store. You never, I repeat, *never*, diss a guy's package on the first date. Common courtesies demand a no-package comparison clause until *at least* the third date. That way, you can kiss his *boo-boo* better when he proves you other-wise." The way he murmurs 'boo-boo' leaves no doubt as to what he's referring. "It may be the only way you can *pump* his ego back up."

His reply makes me laugh, but it won't stop me from pointing out the glitch in his grand scheme, "Date?"

Maddox places an order for two vanilla cones before replying, "Yeah, D.A.T.E. Did you not know this was a date?" When I shake my head, he mocks. "I wined you, dined you, and poked you in the ass with my dick. How could you not know this was a date?"

I accept my ice cream from the vendor before slowly pacing down the street. "I figured you'd have to ask a girl out before you could consider her your date."

"Maybe in whatever part of the world you're from, but that doesn't work around here."

His reply slackens the friction bristling between us. We're not in Ravenshoe. We are in Hopeton, the very town my uncle makes it clear women aren't just inferior, we're easily replaceable. Here, we don't get to say no. We do as we're told or die. There are no in-betweens.

After snatching his ice cream out of the store assistant's hand, Maddox jogs to catch up with me. "What did I say wrong?"

I shoo away his worry as if my stomach isn't a twisted mess of confusion. "Nothing. It's fine."

"Dem—"

"I'm fine, truly." I spin to face him, almost sighing when my eyes drift over his deliriously handsome face. A green tinge has returned to his eyes, making me wonder if there's more to their change than just a shift in moods. "But I really should go."

He almost argues, but the dumping of my barely touched ice cream into the waste bin at my side stops him. Even someone as cocky as Maddox Walsh knows turning down dessert after a date is the equivalent of snapping shut a ring box with the engagement ring still inside.

"Thank you for a fun afternoon." I can tell by the twitching of his lips when I lean in to place a kiss on his cheek that he wants to say something, but he just can't force the words out of his mouth. "I'll see you soon." *In my dreams, where you must stay.*

3

MADDOX

With my feet planted at the width of my shoulders, and my head confident I fucked up, I watch Demi's brisk retreat. I had wondered if I was coming on too strong. Can you blame me for being a little eager? For years, I've perused her big blue eyes, pouty lips, sinfully sexy face, and deadly black hair from afar because I was confident she'd forever be untouchable.

I don't give a fuck if it makes me look like a wimp, I have no shame admitting I love my family. They've had my back for years and ensured I didn't have the fucked-up childhood not many kids these days can say they went without. I'd do anything for them, anything at all. I even stood back from the girl I had a crush on for years because I'd rather endure the heartache than thrust it onto one of my siblings.

That's all done and dusted with now, though.

Saint forever peered Demi's way.

He watched her as I do when no one is paying any attention.

Well, so I thought.

After her father died, it was rare to see Demi anywhere, and anytime I was lucky enough to spot her, she wasn't without a sidekick. Even now, years after she almost became a ward of the state, if Sloane isn't at Demi's side, her uncle is.

Most people would think that's a good thing. I've not once reached the same conclusion. Col Petretti isn't a nice man. He treats his children like vermin, so I'd hate to consider what Demi has faced under his guardianship since she shares only a portion of his blood.

In public, Col portrays the role of a loving uncle well. He brings out the charm, and for the most part, his act is gobbled up by the fools hoping to live in his realm. He has everyone convinced he's a gentleman—everyone but me, and I plan to expose him for who he really is. It's taking longer than hoped, but you can only stack fraudulent chips for so long before they eventually spill. Col's day is coming, I just need to yield patience.

It isn't a known Walsh trait.

I watch Demi take a left on 22nd Street before pivoting on my heels and heading in the opposite direction. My motorbike is parked at the gym. I only walked because Demi was walking. Caidyn will chew me up and spit me out when he discovers I went on a date after a two-hour workout, but what can I say? When an opportunity presents itself, you must take it. Nothing is more expensive than a missed opportunity.

I make it to the ice cream parlor I stupidly thought I could woo Demi at with the knowledge I know her favorite flavor when a girlie tone slackens my stride. "Are you really going to end a date on a sour note? Especially with the girl you've been crushing on since primary school!"

My drooped lips morph into a grin when it dawns on me why the girlie voice is so familiar. My baby sister is in town, and although she's standing next to a man I'd rather pummel with my fists than greet with a dip of my chin, nothing can slacken my smile, especially when she says, "Even if I were still at school, I would have felt the chemistry crackling between you two. That's how intense it was."

Justine attends college a hundred miles from home. Her excuse was that there were no good architectural courses at STEM Academy. I'm calling her bluff. She doesn't want to design buildings for a living, but since she doesn't have the guts to tell our parents that, she pushed them to the brink by declaring she wanted to attend school a hundred miles from home at the tender age of eighteen. She's the youngest of our family but the first to officially move out.

"Stop it," Justine mouths when my glare focuses on her date a little longer than what can be classed as acceptable.

I don't have anything against Brax Anderson. Unlike most of the residents on his side of the tracks, he has stable employment, a roof over his head, and he's been nothing but respectful to Justine *since* they got freaky in our family hot tub two years back, but the fact he takes his dates to Hopeton for a night out reveals he isn't the right man for my baby sister. She needs someone with class. Someone who'll fight for her no matter how bad the odds. Someone who won't let her walk away when he puts his foot in his mouth.

My words trail off when the truth smacks into me. "I need to go."

"Yes, you do," Justine replies, laughing.

She knows me well enough to know where my thoughts strayed.

When she leans in to place a kiss on my cheek, I mutter in her ear, "Please don't get freaky in the hot tub with Brax again tonight, J. Dad's ticker won't survive a second massacre."

"We're *friends*. That's it." She overemphasizes the word 'friends.' "I hang out with lots of *friends* when I'm home from school."

I pull her back to an arm's length, give her a look as if to say, *no friend of mine has ever given me their virginity,* then hightail it toward the gym. My lunch should be curdling in my stomach at the recollection I know *all* aspects of my sister's love life, but for some reason, it isn't.

That isn't how our family operates.

We don't keep dark, dirty secrets from each other.

We help hide them.

Forty minutes and a near head-on later, I assure the maître d at Petretti's Restaurant for the fifth time I'm happy dining alone before she assigns me a waiter.

"Are there any tables closer to the kitchen?" I ask him when he guides me toward the front of the restaurant. I need to be near the back in the 'workers' half of the establishment.

As the waiter twists to face me, his dark brows pinch together. "There is... but they're also close to the restrooms."

"That's fine. I have no issues eating near a toilet." My last four words don't come out as strong as my first two. "It can come in handy when you're eating Italian."

Really, Maddox? I was trying to be funny. It didn't work out as planned. Now I understand why I've been dateless for so long. I thought my obsessive crush on Demi was the issue. Joke's on me.

"I don't like people."

Much better. Arrogant and only partly false. I like people, but it's rare to find good ones in Hopeton.

"Oh, okay," the waiter replies. "Me neither."

With a crass grin that reveals he's as bad at joke-telling as me, he places down a setting for one on a table that butts up with the corridor leading to the washrooms. Although I could sit out of the firing line, I take a seat in the chair that infringes the walkway. It gives me an uninterrupted view of the swinging door that separates the kitchen from the main dining area. It's the perfect spot for me to implement stage two of my ruse—woo Demi Petretti.

"Can I start you off with a drink?" the server asks, not put-off by my unusual seating request.

I issue my thanks for his coolness with a smile. "Water will be great, thank you."

He jots down my order like he'll forget it between here and the kitchen before he commences rattling off the meals customers ignore the dirtiness of the Petretti name to feast on each day.

"What is the sous-chef's special today?" I interrupt, stopping him partway through a list far too long to run through for each customer. I didn't lie when I told Demi I've dined here every second day the past two months. I'm well-rehearsed on the standard menu, but 'standard' isn't what I want. I'm here for the 'special dish' only a handful of patrons are lucky enough to secure.

"I'm not sure," the waiter replies, aware of what I'm asking but uneased by my request. "She wasn't rostered on today. She only arrived thirty minutes ago. I could ask her if you'd like?"

"If you could, that would be great." I swallow to clear the stupid-ass nerves in my throat before adding, "Or perhaps she could tell me what her creation will be... *in person?*"

"Oh." He pauses, smiles, then starts again. "I see."

He sees all right—a sucker in the making. His brow isn't cocked for no reason. I won't get anywhere near the 'Petretti special' without handing over some coin, and if the dollar signs flashing in his eyes are anything to go by, a couple of dollar bills won't cut the mustard.

While grumbling about how my glass of water better be free, I dig a twenty out of my wallet before slipping it into his hand.

"Sous-chef will be right out," he says, all pompous like.

Thirty seconds later, Demi fills his spot. "Maddox," she stammers out like I'm a mirage.

As her eyes widen in shock, they scan the restaurant. I can't confirm who she's seeking, but I can assume. The dread on her face is very telling, much less the sweat beating on her brow. It's the same expression that reflected in the Latin restaurant's door when I carried her inside, and the very reason I requested for us to be seated at the back. Even with Hopeton being her stomping ground, she isn't comfortable here. It fuels my eagerness to discover why that is.

When Demi fails to find any sign of her uncle or the men he regularly dines with, her eyes return to me. "What are you doing here? You just ate." Her dark brows pull together as an uneasy grin raises her cheeks. "And how did you know I'd be here? I wasn't rostered to work today."

"One, I'm always up for more food, especially if it is delicious as the meals you've been creating." Her ghost-like smile is potent enough to slay a man. "And two, you took a left on 22nd Street. If you were going home, you would have turned right." I shrug like it's no big deal I know all her favorite haunts. It isn't hard. She's a creature of habit. She's either at the gym, home, or here.

"*Right*." She looks torn between smiling and grimacing. "So I need to add stalking to your list of talents? Good to know."

Her facial expression settles on relieved a few seconds later. I want to say it's compliments to my undeniable charisma. Unfortunately, that would be a lie. All the credit belongs to the waiter. He didn't just fill my glass with room temperature water when he returned to my table to take my order, he also advised Demi her uncle's flight has been delayed until tomorrow, so she'll need to stay until closing tonight.

Most people scowl when lumped with the late shift. Demi almost bursts with excitement.

"Thank you, Ty." Although Ty looks on the verge of cracking a fat over Demi's gratitude, I act ignorant to the admired twinkle in his eyes. Her words may have been for him, but her eyes are solely mine. "Do you really want to know what tonight's special will be?"

I'm as stuffed as a turkey at Thanksgiving, but I'll force down anything she's offering if it keeps her looking at me the way she is.

Well, except for one thing.

"It isn't snails again, is it?"

I thought Demi's light eyes and dark hair combination was her greatest asset, but her smile makes a quick liar out of me. "Not tonight. I'm saving them for taco Tuesday. If you only want to spend two dollars on a taco, you should anticipate slugs in your meal."

"Way to ruin a good feed."

Her smile doubles. It's almost as large as mine. "They deserve it."

The mood shifts from playful to serious when I can't hold back my comment. "I'm sure they do."

Four little words shouldn't be so impacting, but they force our exchange into a prolonged stretch of silence. I wouldn't necessarily say it is uncomfortable. It's more promising than disheartening.

I'm not claiming to know all her secrets.

I am merely letting her know I'm okay with her having them.

After an additional thirty seconds of silence, Demi breaks it. "I placed a tray of homemade lasagnas in the oven when I arrived, but they need another thirty or so minutes. I could whip you up something if you have time to kill?"

I nod like she invited me to her place for a nightcap. "I've got nowhere important to be."

Her eyes fall to my watch that shows I'm due to arrive at a fight in the basement of a college library forty miles from here in a little over an hour before she returns them to my face. "Are you sure about that, Ox? From what I've heard, your Thursday nights are booked until New Year's, and your Fridays may soon follow them."

I twist my lips, not surprised she knows my fighting name and oddly turned on by it. "Who did you hear that from?"

I'm acting coy, and Demi knows it. Her cousin organizes the college circuit held every Thursday in local colleges, and he 'owns' a handful of fighters in the Friday night statewide feature his father runs each week. She knows what's been occupying my time for the past seven months because her family is very much a part of it. That's why I was hesitant with my comment earlier today. My ego wouldn't let me believe she was only glancing my way because she wanted to shift my fight schedule from Thursdays to Fridays as her cousin has been endeavoring to do the past couple of months, but it has occasionally led me astray, so I had to listen to the rational side of my brain for a change.

"No one important," Demi eventually replies, her tone honest.

When I scoot to the edge of my chair, the cuffs on the sports jacket I tossed over my gym clothes ride up past my wrists. I'm underdressed to dine in a restaurant, but I didn't want to travel home just to change my clothes. The sooner I arrived here, the faster I'd learn how badly I shoved my foot into my mouth. I can't take back what I said, but I can assure I don't make the same mistake twice.

"My schedule is set by importance." I scan Demi's beautiful face and big blue eyes while muttering, "*This* is important."

By this, I mean her.

Fortunately for me, Demi has no issues reading between the lines. With a smile that advocates my earlier stuff-up has been wiped clean, she says, "I'll be out with your meal as soon as possible."

Her steps away slow when I offer, "Then perhaps I can give you a ride home?"

The whisps of almost black hair fanning her gorgeous face slap her cheeks when she whips back around to face me. The rest of her glossy locks are pulled off her face in a high ponytail, enhancing the elegance of her long neck. "That's hours away, Maddox."

I shrug before sinking into my chair. "As I said earlier, I am *exactly* where I'm meant to be."

Demi tries to reel in the happiness beaming across her face. I hope she has no wish to become an actor. Her skills are less than impressive.

After a couple of seconds of silent deliberations, she warns, "Don't drink the water. It's most likely laced with laxatives." When my brows scrunch, her smile shines brighter than the moon on a cloudless night. "Ty can be a tad bit jealous. He'd rather you spend the night on the toilet than in my bed."

Her reply has my emotions unsure which way to swing. I

want to remove Ty's smug grin with my fists, but I'm smiling just as smugly, stoked as fuck he too could feel the sexual chemistry bristling between Demi and me even with him only being in our monarchy for a couple of seconds. It makes me confident I made the right decision putting Demi before my fight tonight.

My eyes shoot back to Demi when she says, "By the way, Ty is gay. He isn't saving me from you, Maddox. He's saving you for himself."

After hitting me with a frisky wink, loving my gaped jaw, she saunters back into the kitchen with the spring her step was missing when she left me gobsmacked only an hour ago.

4

MADDOX

"How was your meal?"

I raise my eyes from my spotlessly clean plate to Demi. Even with her spending a majority of the past two hours in the kitchen, the electricity brewing between us is at an explosive point. The restaurant is full of patrons, so the floor staff enters and exits the kitchen every couple of minutes. Without fail, my eyes forever land on Demi's between the swings of the door. She also hand-delivered my specially-crafted meal, so my stalker watch hasn't just occurred from afar. It has also been front and center for the world to see.

After propping her slim hip onto the chair across from mine, Demi says, "You'll be pleased to know it was snail free. I slipped them into Mr. Mosey's dish after he complained the tomato paste wasn't tomatoey enough for him."

After laughing at her comment, I show her my spotless plate. "I think my plate speaks on my behalf, but in case it doesn't, my meal was so delicious, I licked the fucker clean." I grimace when my swear word gains me the stink eye of a group of elderly ladies on my right. "Sorry. My mom often threatens to wash my mouth out with soap. She just can't bring herself to do it. I could be the biggest asshole in the world, but she'll *never* see it."

"If swearing is the worst thing you've done, I understand your mom's objective." After gathering up my dirty dishes like she's one of the waitstaff, Demi locks her eyes with mine. "Dessert?"

I could be completely off the mark, but I swear her question is laced with hidden innuendo.

Always willing to push the boundaries, I test the theory. "What's on the menu?"

There's no doubt about my assumption when my gravelly reply causes Demi to pull her knees together. It's the same heated, knee-knocking response she gave when I banded my arm around her waist earlier today.

After spotting my grin no amount of salt could tarnish, Demi balances my dirty dishes in one hand before she thrusts a dessert menu into my face. "You can pick something scrumptious off this..."

People who haven't watched her for as long as I have could mistake her pause as allowing me the chance to reply. I'm not close to reaching that conclusion. She wants to say more, but she's forever cautious she is about to make a mistake. It's very much a Demi trait.

Although I could let her off the hook by ordering the first

dish my eyes stumble upon, I strongly believe forcing her out of her comfort zone will do more good than harm.

"Or?" I ask like she left her comment hanging.

"Or..." she follows along nicely. "There's an ice cream parlor a couple of blocks over. I've heard their vanilla cones are to die for."

I can't hold back my smile, so I let it free. "Yeah?"

"Yeah." She bobs her head in sync with mine. "If you want. No pressure or anyth—" I steal her words by slotting the dessert menu back into its holder then standing to my feet. "Oh, I can't leave now. I have to finish my shift."

"I know." I take a moment to relish the disappointment in her tone before saying, "But I see us getting out of here a lot quicker if I take care of them for you."

When I nudge my head to the dirty dishes in her hand, her cheeks glow. "I can't let you wash the dishes, Maddox."

"Why not?" I ask while transferring the mess from her hands to mine. "If it's good for you, it's good for me."

Demi doesn't just cook here. She waits the tables, cleans the dishes, and turns a blind eye to the many shady deals that occur here every weekend, yet I've not once seen her accept a tip. Even the ones from the patrons who can't take no for an answer are placed into the tip jar at the front of the bar.

With Demi too stunned to talk, I steer our walk into the industrial kitchen. Some of the waiters eyeball me with confusion. The twinkle in their narrowed gazes switches to amused when I fill the stainless-steel sink at the side of the large space with soapy water. They think I can't afford the bill for my one-of-a-kind meal. If it keeps news of my backstage tour from

Demi's uncle's ears, I'm more than happy for them to believe I'm poor.

"Is that it?"

"I think so." Demi swings her eyes around the sparkling clean and empty kitchen before returning them to me. Even donning the apron she handed me partway through my new career as a dishwasher hasn't stopped the front of my gym shorts from being soaked.

I take a couple of seconds to relish her hidden smile before asking, "It looks like I pissed my pants, doesn't it?"

"No," she replies while nodding, incapable of lying directly to my face.

When I arch a brow at her, calling out her deceit, she sets her smile free. It's her biggest one tonight. "Okay, maybe a little."

I whip her backside with the tea towel I haven't been without for the past three hours. When it cracks on her backside, she squeals before darting to the other side of the kitchen. "Your secret is safe with me. I won't tell a soul. I promise."

"It's not a secret if it's untrue." I follow her around the kitchen, playfully whipping her another two times before my campaign to whip her into line is ended by her splatting a handful of bubbles in my face.

When my exhale replicates a bubble machine on the brink of running out of detergent, the happy gleam in Demi's eyes the past six hours amplifies. I haven't seen her wear this look in years, and it's taking everything I have not to ask her exactly how long it's been. I wouldn't hesitate if tonight were about re-hatching old memories, but I want us to create new ones.

"You know I'm going to need to retaliate, right?" I speak through the ghastly smelling bubbles coating my lips. I've got enough suds on my face to scrub my mind clean of the many inappropriate thoughts I'm currently having. In case you're wondering, every one of them features Demi. "It's a Walsh trait. We don't let anything slide."

Sparks of the girl I knew before her father died fire in Demi's eyes when she takes three giant steps back. "You can retaliate... *if* you can catch me."

When she spins and bolts, I scoop up a huge handful of the bubbles in the sink before chasing her down. I'm on her heels in an instant, and even faster than that, I have her pinned to the industrial refrigerator with my crotch and am holding a suds-soaked hand in front of her face as if it is a cream pie.

Our closeness shifts the tension from playful to lusty in an instant, and the struggle to keep things friendly is heard in my voice when I ask, "What are you going to give me to keep these bubbles to myself?"

Demi runs her finger down my sudsy nose like I did hers earlier tonight before she shrugs. "Is a free meal not enough for you?"

When I shake my head, she angles hers to the side, better aligning our lips. I've been waiting for this moment for years, so you can imagine my utter disgust when the only thing landing on my lips is the bubbles Demi stole from my hand when my concentration diverted to ensuring my mouth wasn't as dry as a desert.

"It takes more than scrubbing a mountain load of dirty dishes to be in my *favor*, Maddox." While giggling about my uncomfortable grab of my crotch from her husky deliverance of the word 'favor,' she bobs under my arm, snatches up her purse from beneath the massive stainless-steel counter in the middle of the kitchen, then struts toward the exit.

Yep, you once again heard me right. Hips swinging, tits bouncing, I'm-going-to-come-in-my-pants-like-a-dweeb strut.

For years, I've wondered if Demi Petretti was a tease or a straight-up pleaser. I had no clue she was a bit of both. Don't misunderstand I'm stoked the years she spent under her uncle's care hasn't altered her personality. I'm just praying like fuck her slide from teaser to pleaser isn't a month-long slip. My gym shorts don't have a zipper. However, my cock is aching as if it does.

I push off my feet like the man at the start line fired his gun when Demi warns, "If you want dessert, Maddox, you better hurry. The ice cream parlor closes in ten minutes."

"You've never seen snow?"

Demi giggles at the eccentrics in my tone before shaking her head. "It doesn't snow around these parts, and I've never left the state."

"Fuck." I should have a better reply, but I'm truly shocked. Our state is decent in size, but come on, there's a ton more of them for her to explore. "All right. I don't think my shock can get any higher, but I'll give it a shot." I take a moment to pick my next question in our game of twenty questions. "What is the smelliest thing you've ever smelled?"

Demi screws up her nose while contemplating a reply. We consumed our ice cream, talked more than we did at lunch earlier today, and have taken the longest route possible to her apartment building by foot just to force our date into the mandatory overtime every world's best date demands, and now we're on the final stretch. The sun is beginning to rise, and my eyelids are drooping with tiredness, yet the ache of my cheeks is by far the most obvious sign of how much fun I've had the past fifteen-plus hours. I haven't smiled this wide in a long time, and my life is fucking awesome, so kudos to Demi. She not only blew my expectations on dating out of the water, one night with her made up for years of missed opportunities.

I hope she's just as smitten, or I'm about to make an ass out of myself.

I stop summarizing the best way to guarantee a kiss after a first date when Demi answers my question. It doesn't go in the direction I'm hoping but proves, without a doubt, her uncle is as shady as fuck. "There's a room in the basement of my uncle's warehouse. I've never been inside, and the smell that creeps underneath the door when I dash by ensures it will remain *off* my itinerary for eternity."

Not even wearing the jacket I draped over her shoulders two hours ago weakens the brutal shiver jolting down her spine.

She's quick to brush off her disgust, but I can still see the turmoil in her eyes when she locks them with mine. "You?"

"Uh..." I pretend like I need a few seconds to formulate a response. In reality, I'm drinking in all the gorgeous features of her face before it's too late. We're walking up the footpath of her apartment building. Our date is coming to an end. "It's a tie between the locker room at Seacoast and Landon's socks."

Demi's hand shoots up to cover her mouth when her laugh comes out with a snort. "From what I've heard, your gym socks aren't much better."

"*Ohhh,* so you not only eye-fuck me in the gym, you take sneaky whiffs of my socks as well."

"What? No!" When she drops her hand from her mouth to my stomach, she steals some of my laughter with a playful two-finger jab to the bottom of my ribcage. "Hopeton is small. Rumors circulate."

My teeth grit when jealousy flares through her impressive eyes. My ex-girlfriend, Harlow, always jokes that we're not together because of my stinky gym socks. Truth be told, we were kickass friends, but we didn't have the spark needed to make us a long-term couple. We ended things mutually, and we're still friends to this day, although we may not be if she ruins my chance of a sunrise kiss.

Even though I'm only holding a pair of twos, I aim to end our game with a royal flush. "Same time tomorrow?"

"I'm working the lunch shift tomorrow," Demi replies, assuming I'm referencing the meal we shared at lunch.

"I know." I smirk at the shock on her face before hitting her with a playful wink. "But a guy has got to eat."

I think I have her, my cockiness won't allow another response to formulate in my head, so I try not to pout like a soft cock when she says, "Let me think about it." My life stops circling the drain when she leans in to press a kiss to my cheek. Her lips aren't where I want them, but the words she whispers in my ear makes up for their detour. "They say breakfast is the most important meal of the day, and the Petretti's torte makes the need for sleep unnecessary."

When she pulls back, I ask, "What time do they start serving that?"

Please say 'now.'

Please say 'now.'

My prayers don't get answered, but considering the early hour, it's pretty damn close. "Around ten."

Demi's eyes still expose her weariness.

It's a pity for her I can't see it past the hope.

"I guess I could swing by at ten to test its sleep deprivation reversal capabilities for myself."

After dragging my index finger down her nose still crinkled with her earlier jealousy, I hit her with a frisky wink before I spin on my heels and walk away.

I only make it to the sidewalk before my naturally engrained cockiness kicks in.

When I turn to face Demi, I smile when the heat of her gaze is authenticated from it landing on my face. My ass was on fire a couple of seconds ago. "If I misread the whole brunch thing, please put me out of my misery. I'm already walking funny, so I doubt wedging a tail between my legs before rejoining you on the porch will make much difference."

Her smile makes the sun irreverent. She's as smitten as me. I'd put money on it.

"Good night, Maddox Walsh."

"It was," I agree, laughing when she rolls her eyes at my corniness. "Now scoot before I conjure up a way to make it even better."

Her hesitation thickens my cock. It's got nothing on the smile she flashes my way before she darts through the front entry door of her building, though. It's the smile a man would go to the ends of the earth to see day in and day out. A smile I'd kill for to keep it on her face.

I've schmoozed thousands of people in my lifetime, gained the respect of almost just as many, but nothing compares to the number of times I made Demi smile tonight. There are billions of smiles in the world, but hers are the hardest to earn, and by far, my most favorite.

5

DEMI

"Whoa... shit... dammit."

As my hands shoot up to cover my eyes, my cheeks turn the color of beets. I guess this is what Maddox meant when he said Sloane wouldn't be waiting for me to arrive with an angry scowl and the expectance of a bag full of sugar. She's mad, all right, but it has nothing to do with me ditching her at my uncle's gym yesterday afternoon.

She's pissed I walked in on her and Saint getting freaky in the kitchen.

The *kitchen* of all places!

I eat in there.

"I'll... umm... go... ah... to my room."

Why do I sound like I'm twelve? I've seen women naked before—many of them thanks to the ones forced to prance around my uncle's house like his wrinkled face doesn't make them want to barf. I've just never faced the jungle-like vine Saint is swinging around like Tarzan.

Don't read that the wrong way. I've seen penises before, nearly as many as I have vaginas. They just weren't as long as Saint's and nowhere near as handsome.

Wind it back in, Demi, you're getting off track.

The size of the guy's penis I lost my virginity to made it seem as if I didn't lose my virginity. The *one* man I've been with since could have fixed the injustice if he had come *after* removing his penis from his trunks.

There, now you know *all* my sexual history.

I bet you're feeling sorry for me, aren't you?

It's okay. I'd rather your pity than share a story similar to how many women in my uncle's industry lose their virginities. My sexual escapades have been via my choice. Many others, including my mother's, were not. I don't know about you, but I'd rather face a dud in the bedroom than a man who paid for the privilege.

I've barely released a frustrated sob into my pillow when the patter of tiny feet filters into my ears. I'm not angry about Sloane's adventurous locations to have sex. I'm annoyed that the first thought that popped into my head when I stumbled onto their antics was that I could have been doing that with Maddox right now if I weren't such a chicken. I've never wanted something more in my life, yet I left him standing on the footpath like a loser.

I'd hate myself if my dislike of my uncle left any room for self-loathing.

Mistaking my sob as annoyance about her sexual exploits, Sloane asks, "*Exactly* how much did you see?"

When I sling my eyes to my door, she props her shoulder on the doorjamb. She's wearing more clothes than she was moments ago, but nowhere near enough to be classed as decent.

A grin tugs my lips higher when my stink eye causes her to forcefully swallow. "*That* much?"

I prop myself onto my elbows before increasing my glare. It's all an act, but I'm happy for her to think otherwise. "Let me be clear. I'm. Never. Eating. Cucumber. Again."

"With your mouth or *other parts of your body*?" Her last five words fly out of her kiss-swollen lips with a girlie, high-pitched laugh.

When I gag, she pushes off her feet and races my way. The smell of sweat-slicked hair and skin teems into my nose when she swan dives onto my mattress like she's diving into the pool at her family mansion. "Saint is—"

"Inventive with salad, pegs, and... was that your nanna's scarf I saw?"

Sloane barges me with her shoulder. "It was." After waggling her brows long enough to award herself a brand-new wrinkle, she asks, "So how about you? How was Maddox?"

I stiffen like a board. "Umm..."

In less than a nanosecond, her face goes from playful to stern. "Don't play Ms. Innocent Act with me, missy. Everyone was talking about how he raced out after you. I wouldn't be surprised if your cousins in New York have heard about it by now."

She's being playful.

Unfortunately, I'm not close to laughing.

"Everyone saw me with Maddox?"

Her anger is pushed aside for fret, the panic in my voice the sole cause of her worry. "Not everyone. They just heard him call your name." Her eyes bounce between mine. They're full of panic. "Why would it matter if anyone saw you with him?"

I swallow to soothe my burning throat before replying, "It wouldn't. I just don't want to get a name, that's all."

Sloane's brow gets lost in her curly blonde hair. "A name for bedding one of the most eligible bachelors this side of the country? *Girl*, that's a badge you should wear with honor."

I agree with her, but not only do I like to argue, she has it all wrong. "We didn't do anything." I internally battle myself for nearly twenty seconds before blurting out, "I kind of ditched him on the sidewalk."

"He came all the way here, and you didn't invite him in?" When I nod, Sloane slaps me up the back of the head. "Demi!"

"I know," I say with a groan. "I suck."

I whack her in the arm when she gabbles out, "If you did, we wouldn't be having this conversation." After joining me lying on my bed, she peers up at the ceiling then asks, "You've had a crush on Maddox since the fifth grade, so why did you bolt as soon as the fireworks started?"

She's a little off with her dates, but since that's more my fault than hers, I let it slide.

"It's complicated," I murmur, incapable of lying to my best friend.

She rolls onto her side before hooking an arm around my waist. "Too complicated to halve the burden with your best friend?"

My sigh is packed with so much disappointment, it rustles one of her springy curls. That's rare. They're so thick and dense that usually nothing unkinks them. "Unfortunately, yes."

I've kept her off my family's radar as much as I can. She's never invited to family functions, the only place her contact details are stored are in my head, and even with her paying half the rent on our apartment, her name isn't on the lease.

If my uncle can't threaten me to do what he wants, he will shift his focus to those around me. Sloane is all I have. I can't bear the thought of losing her.

The abovementioned exposes how foolish I was to invite Maddox to Petretti's for brunch tomorrow. My uncle has been conducting business in Italy the past two months, so I'm confident his flight won't land until well after midday, and Petretti's is the only establishment he owns that doesn't have surveillance cameras, but still, I'm taking risks that could end fatally.

I want to be happy. I just refuse for it to be siphoned from those I love.

The feeling that I'm drowning on land evades me when Sloane gabbers out, "Five minutes." When I peer at her, stunned by the sudden flip in our conversation, she winks, then rolls off my bed. "Five minutes of wallowing, then you'll need to pop your headphones on. The sun is rising, and I've only orgasmed three times. It's time to add some bass to the tingles in my pussy."

While doing the worst Beyoncé booty shake I've ever seen, she shimmies out the door, closing it behind her. Although I'm in desperate need of a shower, I roll onto my side, hug my pillow, then shut my eyes, where I spend the next four hours pretending I can have both my crush and a life without misery.

6

MADDOX

I wake up startled when the buzz of my cell phone vibrates across the coffee table of my friend's crash pad. He's out of town, and I promised to water his plants. I wasn't meant to fall asleep. When I'm dog tired, I usually pass out for a solid eight hours. Since I didn't have eight hours to burn between 'dates' with Demi, I put *Diehard* on Netflix, pumped up the volume, then guzzled down three cans of energy drinks like they don't have the ability to kill me.

That should have kept me awake until next Thanksgiving.

As luck would have it, my brain is far more brilliant than me. I not only got four hours of sleep, but I also dreamed about Demi the entire time.

It's been an awesome twenty-plus hours.

While scrubbing a hand over my eyes, I use the other to snatch up my cell phone from the coffee table. I'm not shocked when I unearth the identity of my caller. Justine snoops into her brothers' lives as much as we interfere in hers.

> **JUSTINE:**
>
> Caidyn said you didn't come home last night. Is there something you need to share?

As I pace toward the shower, I type out a reply.

> **ME:**
>
> Depends? How high do dirty dishes rate on your naughty scale?

I add a heap of horned devil emojis to my message.
Her reply arrives at the same time I reach the bathroom.

> **JUSTINE:**
>
> Aww... you washed dishes for her. Mom will be so proud!

The rest of my message screen is filled with sickening heart emojis.

Even while giving myself a mental pat on the back, I roll my eyes like we're talking in real-time instead of over the phone.

> **ME:**
>
> I'm about to have a shower. Need to wash the stickiness off my skin. I'll buzz you later.

As three dots trickle across the screen, I remove my gym shorts, t-shirt, and trunks.

Just as I flick on the faucet for the shower, Justine's next message pops up.

JUSTINE:

Way TMI... but I still expect to be updated on all the deets later.

I hit the thumbs up button before sliding into the shower, praying like fuck I'll have more to share than an innocent peck on my cheek after a second date.

My bristle-covered jaw is drenched with cologne, my outfit is more suitable for a man planning to dine at a high-priced restaurant, and my hair is combed back from my face. I don't give a fuck what Caidyn says, my suaveness smashed it out of the park this morning.

After hooking a leg over my bike, I push out the kickstart lever. I'm about to fire her up, but a snarky voice stops me in my tracks. "You should stick with the brooding act. She seemed to favor it over the college jock you played yesterday."

Agent Arrow Moses steps out of the shadow of an apartment building's low-hanging frontage. He's dressed like we're not in winter. I guess his moody FBI demeanor makes a coat unnecessary, so I won't mention the fact he's peeved as fuck I was a no-show to my fight last night.

"You know what they say, Ox, the good guys always come last."

"I wasn't playing," I respond, even with my head

demanding for me to keep my mouth shut. "Not with her and not when I tell you if you keep following me like you fucking own me, I'll be forced to show you otherwise with more than words." I ball my hands into fists in case the snarl of my words didn't get my point across.

Agent Moses whips his sunglasses off his face to ensure I can't miss the disdain in his slit gaze. "You're threatening me? A federal agent. I could have you put away for life."

"I'm not threatening you." I smirk when he can't hold back the bob of his Adam's apple. "I'm *telling* you how it is. That's all you ask of me, isn't it, *Agent* Moses? My brutal honesty."

Those were the words he used when he encouraged me to accept an underworld associate's invitation to fight in an illegal circuit. He said I'd have a chance to clean up the streets I grew up on and that women like Demi and my sister wouldn't have to constantly look over their shoulders when they go out dancing with their girlfriends. Since that's all Demi does day and night —*the looking over her shoulder part of my comment, not the dancing part*—I jumped at the opportunity to do some good.

All I've done the past seven months is triple Agent Moses's investment each fight night. We haven't schmoozed the men who organize the events without the Florida State Athletics Commission's approval, nor have we accepted their offer to double our involvement in their organization. I turn up, fight, win, then go home with a measly share of the prize money.

The first couple of months, I let the money side of our arrangement brush off my concern. I was making enough coin to pay my college tuition, which removed the burden from my parents, and had plenty left over for the fun and finer things in life—like taking a beautiful raven-haired woman to an exorbitantly priced Latin restaurant for lunch.

I would have continued ignoring the obvious if Agent Moses hadn't started riding my ass. He doesn't just want to control what I do in the ring, he wants to govern *all* aspects of my life. He spoke to the Dean at my college about shortening my classes so I can slot in more hours at the gym, shifted my study schedule without seeking permission, and he even rocked up at my family home unannounced last week like we're best mates.

In all honesty, I can't stand the prick. He's arrogant, temperamental, and when things don't go his way, he chucks a hissy fit worse than any tantrum Justine has ever pulled. He's a loose-fucking-cannon, and I'm done putting up with his shit.

"I don't think I can make next week's fight, either. I need to wash my hair or some shit." While fighting the urge not to farewell him with a two-finger salute, I dip my chin, mentally flip him off, then kick over my bike's engine. My father didn't just teach us how to protect ourselves, he taught us values as well, and Agent Moses isn't enough of a man for me to lose my morals over.

The healthy revs of my custom Triumph Bobber should drown out Agent Moses. Unfortunately for me, he raises his voice to ensure it can't. "Do you really think she arrived at *that* gym at the exact time she did for no reason?"

He doesn't need to say Demi's name for me to know who he's talking about, and I don't need to nibble at the bait he's throwing out to announce that. Demi's uncle owns the gym I work out at. I knew that when I drove the forty miles from my local gym to Stamina, and I knew it when I signed up for a year-long membership.

My bond with my brothers meant I couldn't make a move on Demi, but not a single thing in the rulebook said I couldn't torture myself by admiring her from a distance.

Mistaking my quiet as deliberating, Agent Moses attempts to stack more wood on the inferno he's hoping to instigate. "She's playing you, Ox, but unlike the last guys she fooled, you have the means to fight back."

My brain screams at me to pull back on the throttle, to get the fuck away from Agent Moses before his vileness rubs off on me, but my heart demands otherwise. As I've said earlier, I've been crushing on Demi for years. Just the thought she could be playing me isn't something I can ignore. I'd donate a lung to see her smile one more time, but I don't want it costing me everything.

I work my jaw side to side before killing my bike's engine. "You have five minutes."

Agent Moses splatters, coughs, and gargles before he finally pushes out, "Only yesterday, Demi was seen approaching four men at three separate gyms."

When he tosses his briefcase onto the trunk of the car parked in front of my bike, he bumps into an elderly gent enjoying a morning stroll. Unlike Demi's collision when she endeavored to get away from me yesterday afternoon, Agent Moses doesn't apologize to the gray-haired man. He stares at him as if he's worthless before he thrusts an unmarked envelope my way.

"The statistics in this file reveal only forty percent of her recruits make it out of the carnage unscathed."

I shouldn't fall for his tricks, but what can I say? Curiosity killed the cat, but satisfaction brought it back.

When I rip open the envelope as if I'm unaware there are confidential files inside, Agent Moses discloses, "Intel suggests Demi has been recruiting for her uncle's fighting syndicate the past three years. At the start, she merely pointed out fighters he may be interested in, but when her knowledge of the industry grew, her involvement in *all* aspects of it evolved."

I have no reason to disbelieve him. Not only is it printed in black and white as clear as day for all to see in the file in my hand, Demi mentioned at the start of lunch yesterday that she wasn't eye-fucking me. She tried to fawn off her gawk as an appreciation for my technique.

"Two years in, Col changed things up. The crowd grew bored with standard fights. They pay top dollar for ringside seats, so they felt they had the right to demand a level of entertainment that suited them." Agent Moses flips over a handful of pages in the document in my hand, stopping once he reaches a bunch of glossy photographs. "The first change-up was the right of the fighter's owner not to throw in the towel. As long as his fighter was standing, he could demand that he stay in the ring."

If the timeline of the snapshots in front of me is anything to go by, the longer Col's new rules went on, the more regularly fighters were stretchered out of the ring.

After plucking a single surveillance image out of the pile, Agent Moses says, "The new rules kept the spectators happy for months. Profits were good, Col had owners arriving with new fighters every week, and although illegal, his fight circuit remained off the FBI's watch list."

"What changed?" I ask, aware the FBI isn't merely watching Col's underground fighting syndicate. They have eyes on his entire family.

"This." He places down the image he plucked from the stack onto the gas tank of my bike. As per the previous images, the boxing ring's mat is coated with blood. There's just one difference, this one has a body bag hanging over the frayed ropes. "There's no throwing in the towel. No referee interference. In this circuit, they fight to the death."

"No fucking way," I mutter under my breath, my shock incapable of being harnessed.

The fight syndicate ran in the basement of STEM Academy is tame compared to the one Agent Moses warned me about when he demanded I put more hours in at the gym, but still, this is beyond belief.

Although it has nothing on the shock that pummels into me when Agent Moses uses the handlebars on my bike to produce a sickening timeline. In the first lot of images, smiling, sweaty gym junkies are seen talking to the woman who occupies my mind even when I'm sleeping. In the second lot of stills, the same men are either lying lifeless on the floor in pools of blood or standing over a deceased man.

Confident I have the gist of what he's saying, Agent Moses gathers up the surveillance images, stuffs them into his briefcase, then locks his eyes with mine. "She's sentencing these men to death, then enjoying Latin cuisine as if their *murders* aren't her fault."

"She didn't kill them."

He *tsks* me as if I'm blinded by Demi's oceanic eyes and cock-thickening body. I probably am, but he doesn't need to spell it out for me.

"She may as well have, Ox. She knows of her uncle's plan when she recruits these men. She knows the torture they'll endure under his watch, and if she has it her way, you're her next victim. I have all the proof you need in my office." His lips once again curl into a pompous, arrogant smirk before he says with a breathy chuckle, "Unless you have somewhere more important to be, *Agent* Walsh?"

7

DEMI

"Not those ones."

Millie, a second-year apprentice chef, moves away from the oven keeping the last two tortes warm with her hands held in the air like she's about to be arrested. "Are they not for sale?"

Considering it is almost noon, it's stupid for me to shake my head, but I can't hold back. Maddox could still be sleeping. We ended things very late last night. Not everyone is accustomed to lagging sleep schedules.

Millie looks torn between wanting to comfort or strangle me when I say, "They were preordered last night. The customers wanting them will have to order something else."

Stealing her chance to reply, I continue kneading the dough for today's lunch special, acting as if a two-hour delay is perfectly acceptable. I've never been on an official date, so for all I know, it could be.

"Jesus! Shit. Sorry," I push out in a hurry when my storm into the kitchen causes the swinging door to crash into one of the waiters exiting from the other side. Creamy ricotta spaghetti and baked ziti sail into the air before they land on the floor with a flop and a crash. "I'll prepare them again now. Please tell the customer their bill is on the house. I'll pay for it."

Ty halts my blubbering by curling his hand over mine. "It's fine. I'm sure the bills you sneak into the waitstaff's jar each night will more than cover the bill." After removing a cracked plate from my hand, he nudges his head to the back entrance. "Go have a breather for a couple of minutes."

I'm so dead on my feet, I'd donate a lung for a nap, but that isn't possible. There's no rest for the wicked. "I can't. I have three orders waiting, need to prep tonight's special, and I now need to remake two dishes."

"And you've also been working for over seven hours without a break." Ty forcefully stands me to my feet before he hip-barges me toward the exit. "Go call him and ask him where he is before I do, then maybe you'll survive the next five hours of your shift."

"I don't have his number." That was harder to articulate than it should have been. I'm not just embarrassed admitting I didn't exchange numbers with the man I had a marathon date with. I hate that Maddox's no-show has me so out of sorts, almost-strangers are noticing a change in my demeanor. Ty is great but other than the occasional chit-chat at work, he doesn't know me at all.

Nobody knows of my struggles because they know it is the best way to stay out of trouble.

Ty's eyes dilate with desire when the new head chef my cousin, Dimitri, hired last month, joins our conversation. Jude's facial structure is as scrumptious as the Walsh brothers. He just prefers for it to be admired by men. "What time did you leave last night, Demi?"

After whispering a silent apology to the waitstaff I've left to clean up the mess, I pace closer to Jude. He's preparing a Florentina steak on the grill. "A little before one. The late rush was crazy for a Thursday, but I had help." Even with us being run off our feet the past several hours, the kitchen still gleams in several places. Maddox has a way of making filthy, used things feel shiny and new. And no, I'm not solely referencing Petretti's.

"Then I not only agree with Ty's suggestion for you to take a breather." Ty almost melts to the floor at the knowledge Jude knows his name. "I'm telling you to take one for the rest of the day. I'll see you tomorrow afternoon."

"I can't leave. I still have three—"

"Meals to make and preparation to do for tonight? I've heard it all before. I'm not buying it. You're dismissed from my kitchen."

"Jude—"

A man with a face as sinfully sexy as his shouldn't be able to scowl like he does. It would have the brawliest man retreating like his momma took off her shoe.

"Yes, Chef. Thank you, Chef."

"Will you please do wicked things to me, Chef?" Ty whispers under his breath.

I untie my apron and toss it into Ty's face before gathering my belongings from under the counter, then spin to face Jude. "Are you su—"

"Yes. Go." He shoos me away with a wave of his hand before he browns chunks of ground beef in a wok to replace the baked ziti I ruined.

The cool afternoon air of a fall breeze smacks into me when I push through the double doors at the back of Petretti's. I stand in the alleyway for a couple of minutes, perplexed about what to do. Four in the afternoon is a little late for most people to make plans, but it's rare for me to walk out those doors before midnight.

After sucking down a lung-filling gulp of air, I head toward my apartment building. I have several series on Netflix I've been meaning to binge-watch. Now is as good a time as any. I'll steer clear of the romance series, though. The last thing I want to do is remind myself how much I suck.

The truth smacks into me hard and fast when I arrive at my apartment building in under twenty minutes. The same walk took Maddox and me two hours last night.

I sigh out my disappointment, jab my key into the front door of my apartment, push it open by a measly inch, then call out Sloane's name. Just because there's no noise projecting from our apartment doesn't mean it's safe to enter. Sloane's quietness is usually the first indicator she's up to no good.

When I fail to get a response after several shouts, I hook my coat over Maddox's jacket he lent me last night, dump my keys and cell phone onto the entryway table, then flop onto the couch.

I'm only planning to hide from reality for a couple of seconds but soon discover my weary head needed hours when Sloane charges into the space like a bat out of hell. It's dark outside, and there's enough drool on the couch cushion to reveal I was out for a couple of hours. I have a problem with excess saliva when I sleep.

"Should I go for fuck-me-slowly pink or fuck-me-fast red?" Sloane holds up the two lipstick suggestions she wants me to pick from. "I want to be fucked fast, but that doesn't mean I want it to be quick."

Her facial expression replicates the time she had to put her beloved dog down when I mumble, "It's called hard and fast for a reason, Sloane."

"True, but..." When she fails to find an excuse, she dramatically tosses her hand to her forehead. "Just choose a goddamn color. I've been staring at them for ages."

With my lips twisted in pure concentration, I take in the two unique colors before blurting out, "Pink."

"*Pink?*" Sloane appears as if she wants to vomit. "I was leaning toward the red."

I roll my eyes. "Red, then."

I stare her deadpanned in the face when she mumbles, "But the pink is *really* cute." When the painful bite to the inside of my cheek makes blush unnecessary, she finally concedes, "Fine. Pink it is." She pivots away, struts two steps, then jackknifes back. I check my face for drool when she runs her eyes up and down my body. Nothing seems out of place, except what Sloane says next, "You're not wearing *that* out, are you?" She nudges her head to my plain black trousers and white polo shirt. "Your boobs look great in anything, but a girl has to occasionally let her hair down."

Confusion is heard in my tone when I ask, "Are we going somewhere?"

For a woman smarter than *all* the men in her pre-law class, she looks really stupid when she answers, "Dancing. Remember? I told you this morning."

"Was this before or after I had my morning coffee?"

Sloane taps the pink lipstick tube against her unpainted lips. "I think it was before. Saint needed whipped cream. I went to the kitchen to fetch it..." Her eyes brighten like a light inside her head switched on. "It was before because you dumped your full mug into the sink when I asked if you wanted cream in your coffee before we used it all."

"That's right," I reply, suddenly clicking on. "You stole my right of an early morning pick-me-up. No wonder I've been so dead on my feet today."

Sloane smiles like I'm praising her. I'm not. She's grinning because she knows I never back out of an agreement—*unlike Maddox Walsh.*

"How long do I have to get ready?"

She twists her lips while mentally calculating if I have enough time to go from dishwasher sleek to nightclub ready. "Saint left around ten minutes ago, so he should be here in around thirty?"

After putting two and two together remarkably quick for how woozy my head is, I ask, "Saint is coming clubbing with us?" I don't know why I'm shocked. Sloane has no issues getting friendly on a first date, but she never 'dates' more than one guy per weekend.

Sloane pulls a 'duh' face. "How do you think we're getting to Ravenshoe?"

"We're going to Ravenshoe?" That was articulated as loud as you're thinking. We make trips to Ravenshoe all the time. It has better shopping than Hopeton, better restaurants, and far sexier men. I just wasn't anticipating a trip so soon after being 'ditched' by one of Ravenshoe's most eligible bachelors. "Will Saint be the only Walsh in attendance?"

It's an effort to keep my shoulders square when Sloane answers, "Maybe." She saunters back into the living room before flattening her hands on my shoulders. "Why? Are you hoping for another run-in with bachelor number four?"

"No." Her brow doesn't even arch halfway before I withdraw my lie. "He was a lot of fun to be around yesterday. I didn't realize he had such a cheeky personality. He always seemed a bit standoffish when we were in high school, but he was nothing like that last night. It was a magical seventeen hours, then he went and ruined it all by standing me up."

Forever the romantic, moisture glistens in Sloane's eyes when she slots the final piece of the puzzle into place. "He didn't turn up for brunch?"

Unable to speak for the fear my voice will crack, I shake my head.

"Aww, honey." Sloane plops her backside in the seat next to me before slinging her arm around my shoulders. "I don't have an excuse for his actions today, but I know why he took so long to make the first move." When my begging eyes lock with hers, she spills the beans. "Years ago, Saint made out he had a crush on you. Since he staked a claim first, Maddox couldn't make a move. Saint said it's in the bro-code."

Snubbing my skyrocketing excitement that Maddox's comment yesterday about our date being years in the making was accurate, I gabber out, "One, why would Saint do that? And two, *staked a claim*? What century are we in again?"

Sloane almost sends me flying to the opposite end of the couch with a playful hip bump. She's a lot stronger than she looks. "The same century your panties moistened at the thought of being claimed by a Walsh."

I gag at both her comment and her use of the word 'moistened.' "I don't want to be claimed."

"Then what do you want, Demi?" She asks her question as sincerely as Maddox did when he queried why I was upset when I fled the gym. She isn't angry or snooping. She's genuinely interested in my reply.

I mull over her question for a couple of seconds before asking, "Do I need to give you an answer right now?"

Springy curls fly in all directions when Sloane shakes her head. "But I'd love some kind of idea within the next decade." Any unease melding in my veins evaporates when she adds, "I can't help you reach your goals if I have no idea what they are."

After sucking in the scent of my overpriced shampoo, she nudges her head to the door in my room. "Come on. Let's add some whipped cream to your strawberry scented hair." When I attempt to tell her whipped cream won't be on the menu for a few weeks, she pushes her finger to my lips. "You said no to salads. Sugary treats were *not* mentioned."

She misses the roll of my eyes. She isn't just racing away before she can be subjected to my wrath, she's on a mission to find the sluttiest, raunchiest, most immodest dress in my wardrobe. And for once in my life, I'm not cringing at the idea of being beautified by her.

Maddox's attention made me hopeful for a future. I just need to determine who gets to be a part of it. A night out dancing won't help me achieve that but neither will wallowing.

"I've got it," I assure Sloane when the toot of a horn at the front of our building has her dashing out into the cold without her jacket. It's the least I can do since she spent the last thirty minutes glamming me up like a Barbie doll. If Mattel ever makes a Cleopatra doll, I could be the prototype. That's how exotic and glamorous I feel.

After slinging Sloane's winter coat over my arm, I gallop down the front stairs of our building. This is one of the perks of having a ground floor apartment. Sloane can greet our collector with a kiss within seconds of racing out the front door, leaving me plenty of time to take in his flashy ride.

Saint's car would have you believing the Walsh's are mafia royalty, not the woman leaving a ground floor apartment in designer heels she bought at a goodwill store for twenty dollars.

When I arrive at Saint and Sloane's side, it takes almost a crane to winch Sloane off Saint's lips. Once Saint has her wrangled into submission—*barely!*—he slings his eyes to me. "Hey, Demi, nice to see you again." The cockier his smirk becomes, the more my cheeks bloom. "What? No return greeting. I can take off my shirt if it'll make things more comfortable for you."

"Leave her alone, Saint." That deep, thick, gravelly tone didn't come from Sloane. It came from the back seat of Saint's pricy ride—from the direction Maddox is seated. I didn't notice him during my walk because the tint on the retro-curved windows of Saint's car is very dark, and the sun went down hours ago.

After shimming off the panic warning me I'm walking head-first into a disaster, I slip through the door Saint is holding open for me. Since his car is a coupé, my tumble through the tight confines almost has me landing in Maddox's lap.

"Sorry," I stammer out a mere inch from his crotch. "At least he's de-mast this time around. I might have lost an eye."

When nothing but dead quiet comes from Maddox's side of the cab, I sink in my seat with a sigh. I'm not overly good with banter, but I was anticipating a breathy chuckle. I didn't even get half a snicker.

Once my belt is fastened, I greet Maddox with a smile. It's the least I can do after shoving my face into his crotch. He returns my non-verbal greeting with a dip of his chin, however, not a word seeps from his lips. His second rejection in less than twenty-four hours would be harder to swallow if his greeting wasn't chased by him dragging his eyes down my body. It's a little chilly, but there's no taking from his heated gawk. I'm wearing a dress—a very fitted dress that leaves *nothing* to the imagination. So as much as Maddox wants to act as if I'm not in his realm, not even he can hold back the second look a dress this breathtaking demands.

"It's vintage couture." Not that the sale stockiest at a local thrift shop knew that. She had no clue of its value when I bargained her down to ten dollars. "It's not really nightclub appropriate, but it's okay to change things up occasionally, right?"

The breathy chuckle I was seeking earlier finally arrives, but it's more a huff than a laugh.

While Saint helps Sloane into the passenger seat, I scoot closer to Maddox, suddenly fretful I almost mashed my face into the wrong Walsh brother's crotch. It's dark, and they do have similar features, so I could be mistaken.

Nope! There's no mistaking the eyes glaring at me beneath hooded lids. Apart from Justine, Maddox is the only Walsh sibling with greenish-blue eyes, and if the amount of green in them is anything to go by, he's really mad.

Great. I had more patience for brooding jerks when I was in high school. Now, I don't have the time nor the patience for them. We all wise up eventually.

After jogging to the hanging-open driver's side door, Saint slips behind the steering wheel, fastens his belt, then fires up the engine. The vibrations of his powerful motor are felt through the seat. It has nothing on the zap that roars through me when Maddox's thigh brushes mine, though. He may be angrier than a bull with a cowboy strapped to his back, but he looks scrumptious enough to eat. His black slacks and button-up shirt give him a casual yet sophisticated look. The sleeves of his dress shirt are rolled to his elbows, and the top three buttons of the dark, pinstriped material are undone. With his hair wet from a recent shower and combed back, it's not flopped in his face like it usually is. He has the sexy, casual look down pat, and it's setting my pulse alight.

"Where to?" Saint asks, encouraging my focus to him. He's dressed similarly to his brother, but his shirt is a couple of shades lighter. It makes the brightness of his blond locks even more noticeable, and they take the focus off his kiss-swollen lips.

When awkward tension fills the air for the next several seconds, Saint bounces his eyes between the three pairs staring at him. "I was thinking we could grab a bite to eat before hitting the nightclub scene?"

I vomit a little when Sloane purrs, "Did I not satisfy your palette this morning?"

Maddox maintains his quiet front.

The closeness of the Walsh siblings is well documented, so I'm confident every sordid detail would have been shared with Maddox by Saint this afternoon, so why isn't he responding with a morsel of disgust?

As put off by Maddox's quiet as me, Sloane tiptoes her fingers up the buttons in Saint's shirt. "I'm just playing. I'm famished. Food sounds divine." She twists her torso to face the silent party for two in the back. "You guys?"

"I could eat," I reply, ignoring the twisted knot in my stomach saying otherwise. "You?" I shift my eyes to Maddox, who is acting *nothing* like the man I dined with yesterday. When silence is the only reply I get, I whisper, "I can go if you'd like?"

Not giving him the chance to answer, I request for Sloane to drag her seat forward so I can climb out the way I entered. Her knees brace the glove compartment before Maddox's hand shoots out to grip mine, halting my exit. Although he doesn't say anything, he must non-verbally announce to Saint he's happy with his plans because I'm thrust into my seat by Saint planting his foot on the gas pedal.

I would have preferred for Maddox to straight-up say he's fine with me being a tagalong, but I guess beggars can't be choosers, and I've been a beggar longer than I've been a woman.

8

DEMI

"The cucumber was wrapped, so why is it no longer consumable?"

I peg an uneaten portion of a breadstick at Sloane. "It was wrapped in a condom."

Maddox remains quiet—as he has for the past two hours—but I hear Saint choke on his whiskey when Sloane says, "And? Latex will preserve it better than plastic ever would."

"Sloane..." Needing backup, I swing my eyes to Maddox. "Will you help a girl out? *Please.*"

Steam almost billows from my ears when he shrugs instead of speaking. He hasn't spoken a word to me all night. Not one. He flirted with the waitresses, smiled at the women making gaga eyes with him in the booth across from ours, and even stopped to chat to a random stranger when he escaped my clutch for a thirty-minute bathroom break. He's being a dick, and I'm about ready to call him out on it.

"What's with you tonight, Maddox? You've barely spoken a word, and not one of them has been directed at me, but when I tried to out-talk you yesterday, you beat me three words to one."

Frustrated and perhaps a little upset about his second nonchalant shrug, I toss my napkin into his face before sliding out of the booth. I understand his ego was stung when I left him high and dry in the wee hours of this morning, but that doesn't give him the right to be an ass. Call me a cock tease, tell your friends I'm a bitch, but don't take me out in public then make me feel worthless. If I wanted to be treated like scum for the world to see, I would have accepted my uncle's offer of a last-minute invitation to dinner. He doesn't care if I'm circled by Buddhists on sabbatical or being hungrily eyeballed by the men in his crew, he disrespects me as often as possible.

I have to put up with his crap because he's my uncle.

I don't need to take it from Maddox.

"I'll come with you."

I stop Sloane's exit of the booth by pushing down on her shoulder. "I'm fine. I can find my way home. Enjoy the rest of your night." I shift my eyes to Maddox. Just like every other time I've glanced at him tonight, his eyes aren't on me. That won't harness my retaliation, though. "I hope she chokes on your smelly gym socks, dick."

I miss the spray of whiskey spurting out of Saint's mouth since I sprint for the exit. I refuse to hang around and watch Sloane and Saint convince Maddox he should go after me. I'd rather they let bygones be bygones because if I get any angrier, I may not keep Maddox off my uncle's radar as I have the past two years.

My uncle's business needs fighters, and the main part of my job being his 'personal assistant' is to locate the best fighters in the area. I make the gig sound as unappealing as possible when I approach the top contenders at local boxing gyms. I tell them the conditions are atrocious, that the boss is an ass, and ramble on about how they could face charges if they accept my uncle's offer, but the instant they scan a couple of thousand per fight on the contract I'm forced to present to them, they act as if my warnings have no steam.

I don't know what happens to the men once they're umbrellaed under my uncle's wing. I've heard rumors some of them have gone pro, but since those claims are mostly issued by my uncle, I don't give them much credit. I just know that no matter what, being in favor to my uncle always ends poorly. You'll be lucky to escape with your life.

I increase the length of my strides when my name comes tumbling out of the asshole's mouth who refused to talk to me all night. I'm tempted to rile him that my storm out forced him to interact with me, but he isn't the only one immature enough to give someone the silent treatment.

It only takes half a dozen strides for Maddox's anger to get the better of him. I'm not surprised by his short fuse. All the males in his family are known for being hotheads. "If you're planning to walk back to Hopeton, you're walking in the wrong-fucking-direction."

After folding my arms under my chest, I take a sharp right, then continue on. We walked for hours last night when we had nowhere to go, so I'm sure my legs are up to the task when my stomps have purpose.

"Try again," Maddox barks out in a dull, angry tone.

I peer up at the sky before cursing my uncle's name in vain. He blew up my phone so effectively the first hour of my 'double date,' my cell phone battery died almost forty minutes ago, so I can't access Google Maps. Considering I'm shit at paying attention to my surroundings, I have no clue which part of Ravenshoe I'm in.

I could have sent my uncle's calls to voicemail, saving me some charge, but since that would lead him to believe I was purposely avoiding him, I didn't. It'll be easier for all involved if he believes I left my cell phone at home. Less lethal.

"Now keep going straight for another forty miles," Maddox says when I take another sharp right. "Or better yet, swallow your stubbornness and accept my offer of a ride home."

When he nudges his head to his motorbike, it takes everything I have not to scream. I don't know what's worse, the fact he's demanding I go *anywhere* with him or that he prearranged an exit strategy like he knew this is how our night would end. Whatever it is, he isn't the boss of me.

"Dem—"

I cut off his growly delivery of my name with an evil glare and flaring nostrils.

He finds it more amusing than scary. "It will take hours to walk to Hopeton. You can be rid of me in under thirty minutes if you'll just get your ass on my bike."

I keep walking. Unlike the song, my shoes weren't made for walking, but that's what they're going to do.

"For fuck's sake. You really will be the death of me, won't you?" With an agility that proves why he's undefeated in the circuit he's been fighting in the past couple of months, Maddox sneaks up on me unaware, wraps his arm around my waist, then hoists me back.

Unlike yesterday when I stiffened like a virgin feeling her first cock braced against her ass, I fight him with everything I have, hurt enough to give as good as I'm getting.

When the whacks of my arms and legs do little to slow Maddox down, I use my voice. "Help me!" I shout into the street, confident one of the many people milling on the sidewalk will come to my rescue. This isn't Hopeton. Surely, the people of Ravenshoe have some type of morality. "I'm being assaulted. Please help me!"

My last three words come out muffled when Maddox clamps his hand over my mouth. That should shut me up in an instant. My uncle values silence, and he puts measures in place to ensure he can have it no matter what. Duct tape. Gags made from used socks. He's even gone as far as sitting on my chest and clamping his hands over my mouth when my teenage rebellion went one step too far.

Unfortunately for Maddox, the memory he forced into my head also reminds me of the pledge I made when the screams of my lungs were finally granted.

Fight to live or not fight and still die. They're my only options.

"Jesus Christ, Demi! You drew blood," Maddox roars when my teeth sink into the fleshy part of his palm.

You'd think his battle wound would have him dropping me like a bag of manure. Regretfully, Maddox is as stubborn as a mule. He continues dragging me away from the people watching me be assaulted but do *nothing* to come to my aid.

I assume he's going to straddle his bike with me strapped to his front, so you can imagine my shock when he pays off the doorman of a nightclub half a block up from the restaurant we ate at—*it was chosen for a reason*—then he walks me through the thrumming space.

When the bass out of the speakers above my head booms through my ears, I immediately stop screaming. I can barely hear Maddox telling me to behave, and his lips are right near my ear, so there's no use subjecting my lungs to more torture than necessary.

The prickles on Maddox's jaw create havoc with my skin more than my fight to get away from him. So I won't mention the controversy I face when our arrival to the middle of the dance floor is followed by him splaying his hand across my stomach, then stepping me back until our bodies are intimately pressed together.

I begin to wonder if I tripped and hit my head when he commences swinging his hips. He refused to speak to me all night, yet I'm supposed to believe he wants to get down and dirty with me on a dance floor.

I'm a little naïve when it comes to aspects of my family's 'businesses,' but I've matured a lot since high school.

Brooding? Yes.

A little rough around the edges? Another yes.

Straight-up asshole? Hell to the fucking no.

I don't believe in the motto 'treat them mean to keep them

keen.' If you want me to treat you like a king, you sure as hell need to think of me as your queen.

What's good for one is good for all.

"Nuh-uh," Maddox growls in my ear when I attempt to pull away from him.

After readjusting his grip on my waist, he grinds his crotch into my ass, leaving me no choice but to pay attention. He isn't hard like he was yesterday. He doesn't need to be for my deviant mind. Even soft, he has more under the trunk than the fool I gave my virginity to.

Confident I'm seconds from eating out of the palm of his hand, Maddox presses his lips to the shell of my ear and says, "Look to your right. Just beyond the bar."

I'm unsure if his gravelly tone is responsible for the prickling of the hairs on my nape or spotting the narrowed watch of a man I'd guess to be mid-thirties. He's dressed oddly for a nightclub. Don't get me wrong, the women surrounding him seem to appreciate his brooding demeanor and all-black outfit. He also has a handsome face. It's just so constricted with annoyance, it makes him unapproachable.

"Do you see him?" Maddox asks, his tone reserved.

While swinging my hips in beat to the *doof doof doof* music pumping around us, I inconspicuously nod. It looks like we're getting caught up in the music. Only Maddox and I know different. The tension is so thick between us, it's almost at the point it was when Maddox interrupted my homecoming dance kiss with Robert Flint. His unexpected arrival meant we never went past first base. I was fine with that. Robert was not.

Upon spotting the bob of my head, Maddox confesses, "He's a federal agent." When I stiffen, shocked I've caught the eye of a law enforcement officer, Maddox drags his teeth over the shell of my ear. "Keep moving. As far as he is concerned, we're two friends from high school reminiscing about our teen years."

When I follow his instructions to the wire, Maddox advises why I've gained the devotion of the dark-haired agent's eyes. Even with his body plastered to mine, and his lips replicating a man hoping to devour me instead of shattering my very existence, it's a terrifying few minutes, and the tragedy deepens when the reason for Maddox's earlier quiet steamrolls into me.

"You believe him. You think I *knowingly* sent those men to their deaths?"

I shiver through the sting of Maddox's teeth sinking into my shoulder, then I shake some more when he breathes out a husky, "No."

He's lying. I don't know how I know. I just do.

"If you leave now, he'll most likely arrest you," Maddox pushes out in a hurry when I attempt to break away from him. "Is that what you want, Demi? Do you want to face prosecution?"

I whip around so fast my hair slaps the faces of several club goers surrounding us. I wore it down tonight. That's a rarity for me. Usually, I have it up and out of the way, so it can't be used against me as it was in my teens.

"Haven't I already been prosecuted?" I fire back, too worked up to let it go. "You *think* I'm guilty. That's all I need to be convicted, isn't it? A jury of my peers to believe I'm a heartless bitch who sends men to slaughter with a smile on her face." I thrust my hand at him, calling him out as my judge, jury, and executioner. "Stuff the truth. Don't let that be shared because God forbid anyone in this town should be given a fair trial!"

I'm shouting at the wrong person, and I am lumping all my anger on the wrong person, but I can't hold back. I thought Maddox's sneaky glances the past three-plus years was because he found me attractive. I had no clue he was striving to unearth my hideous insides.

"I need to go." I almost make a dash for it, but morals my father instilled in me before he died stop me. "I'm sorry for biting your hand, ruining your night out, and for anything else you seem to think I've done but most likely haven't." Okay, I'll admit, the last part wasn't needed, but I have a hard time being amicable when I'm unfairly judged. "Enjoy the rest of your night."

Maddox doesn't shout my name like he did earlier, but I know he's shadowing my walk. Not only does his gasp hit my neck when an Audi A4 pulls up to the nightclub's back exit doors within a second of me bursting through them, but his eyes also shoot to the agent he pointed out as fast as mine.

I don't want to be witnessed sliding into my uncle's car by a federal agent. I'm aware of the many reasons he's being tailed by the FBI, but the silent opening of the back-passenger door doesn't give me any other option. Col never sits in the front. He feels superior when he's in the back. It's where he wheels and deals, and more times than I care admit, where he punishes me for being disobedient.

Mercifully, only my ego has been walloped into submission since I reached womanhood.

Cheek slaps are reserved for special occasions.

"Demi..." Maddox whispers in warning when I step toward my uncle's idling vehicle.

I keep my eyes forward, but I direct my voice in Maddox's direction. "I'm fine," I force out, issuing my go-to reply anytime I feel snowed under. "Innocent until proven guilty, right?"

The thud of my pulse in my ears could have me mistaken, but I swear Maddox gabbles out, "Not in his fucking realm," a mere second before I slip into the back of my uncle's car and am driven away for my second trial tonight.

9

DEMI

"It went flat a little over an hour ago."

Ignoring me, my uncle snatches my cell phone out of my hand before he plugs it into the charging cable dangling out of the door of his pricy vehicle. He may have stained our family name in dirt multiple times the past four decades, but that doesn't mean he's struggling to make ends meet. That hustle is left to the people below him—the shitkickers, as he likes to call them. The people like me who do everything he asks but get paid a pittance for it. I could earn more in hell than I ever will from him. It's why I'm so generous with the tips I receive. Not one of the staff at Petretti's is there because they want to be. They all owe my uncle in some way.

"Was that before or after I called?" my uncle asks, shifting his focus back to me.

I smile at him like a brainless idiot. Unlike the Walsh brothers, my uncle prefers docile, submissive women. "Was what before or after you called—"

He steals my words with a vicious backhanded slap. It reddens my cheek in an instant and has my molars crunching together, but since it was an open-hand hit, I act as if not even the faintest sting is creeping across my face.

"It was in my purse, so I'm unsure. P-perhaps it was after."

The quick balling of his hands warns me he's bordering on retaliating with more than a slap. I'd be worried if all my concentration wasn't focused on the frustrating stutter of my words. Furthermore, I deserve to be punished. Maddox said half the men I've recruited into my uncle's fighting syndicate were murdered within weeks of them signing the dotted line. *Half.*

I deserve so much more than an open-hand slap.

I should be hung.

When my uncle growls at me in warning, my lips get flapping. "I attended the gyms you requested yesterday morning. I signed another three recruits. I did as you asked."

"But you *haven't* secured the man I want!" he interrupts, yelling. "You had orders to bring me the best. You're *not* bringing me the best!"

With two fights already under my belt this weekend, I pray like hell the third time really is the charm. "Because he doesn't want to fight for you. That isn't my fault—"

I should have paid more attention to his balled fists. They hurt more than any slap ever could. The hit he splits my cheek with juts my head back so far, the back of my skull comes close to shattering the glass next to my head. I feel instantly woozy, and the tangy taste of blood has me forgetting the amount of garlic my dinner was laced in.

I want to say I'm surprised he hit me, but in all honesty, I'm not. He's wanted Maddox fighting under him for even longer than Maddox has been contending in the underground circuit at his university. It's why I bolted when Maddox caught my relieved sigh from Saint kissing Sloane, and it's why I acted like I had no interest in him even with my crush being borderline psychotic.

While rubbing away a smear of blood from his hand like it isn't from his niece, my uncle sinks into his seat. "If he isn't interested in fighting for me, what was tonight's date about?"

"It wasn't a date." The brutal shudder of my lips chops up my words. "He... umm..." I'm usually more on the ball with thinking on the spot, but since my brain was just rattled against my skull, I'm a little slow off the mark. "He needed help with a paper."

He *tsks* me as if I'm a child. "You didn't go to college, so how could you possibly help him?"

I didn't go to college because I didn't want to owe you anything, is what I want to reply, but since I can't, I continue with my ploy to pull the wool over his eyes. "His paper was based on an experiment we did at Seacoast Private. I supplied him the evidence, so he supplied me a free meal."

I thought he'd appreciate my wheeling and dealing—he'd sell my lung on the black market for a free meal—so you can picture my shock when disdain hardens his features instead of anger. "A man doesn't buy a woman steak unless he wants to fuck her." My skin crawls when he unlatches his seat belt so he can scoot to my side of the cabin. "But you wouldn't know that, would you, sweet innocent Demi?" I can't see my face, but when he drags the back of his index finger down my cheek, I know the exact area that's starting to welt. It whitens along with the rest of my skin when the reasoning behind his gentleness comes to light. "You have so many of your father's features, I often forget you're as pretty as your mother."

I want to scream at him that I'm his niece when his finger drops to my collarbone before it moves to the neckline of my dress, but no matter how loud the words are shouted in my head, I can't force them out of my mouth.

Denying him only ends one way.

Death.

While he traces the outline of my strapless bra through the thin material of my dress, he mutters, "I was disappointed when you failed to answer my calls tonight. When word got out you were seen dining with *Ravenshoe* royalty yesterday..." he spits out Ravenshoe like it scorched his throat, "... I thought you had *finally* done as asked." He *tsks* me again. "Should have known better. You're just like your father. Stupid and incapable. You'd be more useful to me dead. Alas..." he sighs like he's doing me a favor, "... I promised your mother I'd take care of you." I've seen men almost beaten to death, yet it has nothing on the smirk my uncle releases while saying, "She paid very well to ensure your safety. Perhaps I should make you do the same?"

When he reaches for his belt, I sneak a hand around my back to secure a firm grip on the door handle. Rolling onto asphalt at seventy miles an hour will hurt, but I doubt it'll be as painful as discovering there was a reason for the horrified gleam in my cousin's eyes anytime she begged to have a sleepover. Ophelia only ever pleaded to stay the night when her father returned from 'business' trips. It was rare for her request to be granted since my uncle refused to let her go on the basis he had barely seen her the months prior.

After wetting his lips, my uncle whispers, "Do you want to play a game, Andi?" He only ever calls me Andi when he's up to no good. My father was so desperate to please him, he christened me with the female version of his beloved son's name. He can't use that when he wants to forget we're related by blood.

When he glares at me, demanding an answer, I tug on the door latch. No matter how I answer him, my response will produce the same result. I'll either die from colliding with the pavement, too ashamed to remain living, or be strangled by the belt now hanging loosely down his splayed thighs when I tell him no.

My grip on the door handle loosens when my uncle's temper gets the better of him. He lunges for me, his grip on my hair enough to spring tears to my eyes. "I asked you a question!"

The hand he raises to strike me across my cheek suspends midair when the revs of a motorbike sound over the roar of his words.

When my uncle jackknifes to investigate where the disturbance is coming from, he rips a chunk of hair out of my head. This is the exact reason I usually wear it up.

"What did I tell you, Andi? He wants to fuck you. Enough

to risk his life for the chance? I'm not sure." After returning his eyes from Maddox tailing us on his motorbike to me, he sneers a snarling grin. "But I'm always willing to push the boundaries." He sleazily winks so I can't miss the double meaning of his comment.

I breathe for the first time in what feels like minutes when he signals to his driver to pull over. Once he has his belt looped back around his waist and his zipper sitting in its original spot, he dismisses me with a wave of his hand through the air.

I have my seat belt off and my door flung open in under a second, but I'm far from free of additional controversy.

"Are you forgetting something, Andi?" my uncle asks, his tone laced with an equal amount of humor and superiority. When I crank my neck to face him, he taps his cheek like I'm unaware of what he's asking. "Did your father not teach you any manners?" The gleam his eyes held when he undid his belt returns full force when he mutters, "Perhaps I should spend the weekend teaching you? Sometimes the only way a child can learn respect is by having theirs stripped."

"You can't," I stammer out, too frightened to care he's using my ultimate fear against me. I've done everything he's asked of me because I don't want to end up like my mother. I gave him my soul, yet it still isn't enough. I have to give him the one thing I've wanted for over half my life. I have to throw Maddox into the fire with me. "I have a fighter to sign."

My reply pleases my uncle more than my fear of his threat. "That you do."

When he taps his cheek for the second time, I tilt across to his side of the cabin. Kissing his cheek already makes me want to vomit, and doing it under Maddox's watch is even worse, but it has nothing on the disgust that rains down on me when my uncle twists his head a mere nanosecond before my lips land on his cheek, forcing them onto his open mouth.

The growl that rumbles up his chest is horrific, much less what he says next, "Almost as sweet as your mother's cunt."

10

MADDOX

I've seen some sick-fucking-shit in my life. Men fighting after they've had digits removed by their 'owners' for disobedience, my sister half-naked in the hot tub with a townie, one of my brothers balls-deep in his college professor, but the gleam in Col's eyes when he forces his niece's lips to land on his mouth cuts the fucking cake.

Ophelia was more friendly with the seniors at our high school than her female counterparts, but since it was brushed off as her wanting to gain their approval than her being too sexually advanced for her age, I didn't think much of it.

I am now, though, and the thoughts are as ugly as I'm about to make Col Petretti's face.

He wants to see me fight. Who am I to deny his every wish?

I'll give him a front-row seat to the festivities, bloody nose and all.

At the same time I throw my leg over the leather seat of my

motorbike, Demi stumbles out of the back of her uncle's Audi. Her lips are cracked and dry, her eyes are brimming with tears, and blood is dribbling from both her nose and a cut in her cheek, yet her attention is far from herself. It isn't even on her uncle. It's solely devoted to me.

"Turn around, Maddox. This isn't your fight."

"Like fucking hell it isn't." My words sound as if they were delivered straight from the fiery underground I referenced, fueled by the annoyance Col is even more of a coward than predicted.

He's such a weak prick when I climb into his car to drag him out by the lapels of his fancy suit, he doesn't draw his gun on his niece. He orders one of his goons in the front seat to jab it under her ribs instead.

"One more crinkle to my suit will see you spending the weekend scraping her body parts off the asphalt so you'll have something to bury."

The brutal heave of my lungs is heard in my reply when I yell in his face, "She's your fucking blood, you sick prick."

His laugh is as evil as his soul. Unfortunately, it isn't loud enough to drain out the sob that escapes from Demi's mouth when she's brutally clutched by Col's head goon. Since I didn't immediately jump to Col's demand, Demi is being forced to endure the punishment of my disobedience. That's almost as bad as me believing a single thing Agent Moses said about her. Deep down, I knew she wouldn't have done the things he said, I was just worried my years' long obsession had me refusing to absorb the truth.

That's done with now.

After fixing Col's crumpled suit in a manner that reveals I look forward to fucking it over more ways than Sunday once his niece is far from his reach, I climb out of the cabin of his car, then sling my narrowed eyes to the man fisting Demi's hair so firmly, she has to balance on her tippy toes to save her glossy locks from being ripped from her scalp. "Let her go."

The dumb fuck acts as if I didn't speak. He maintains his arrogant stance, his grip on Demi's hair only weakening when Col signals for him to stand down.

After watching me pull Demi behind me in a protective manner, Col clicks his fingers at the man seated behind the steering wheel. Two clicks and a business card is thrust over the privacy petition separating him from the two men in the front seat.

"Meet me at this address tomorrow night at nine o'clock sharp."

Col jots down an address on the back of his business card before he passes it to a shuddering Demi peering at him over my shoulder. He's smart. Even though the card is for me, he hands it to Demi because he knows not even the threat of being shot will stop me from getting in a punch when he's within striking distance. That's how much I despise this prick. I've never wanted to kill a man until now, and a quick, painless death isn't at the top of my wish list.

I want to torture this fucker and smile while doing it.

After drinking in the pure rage reddening my face, Col says, "Wear white. The more blood, the more money you'll pocket—"

"I'm not fighting for you," I interrupt, my voice almost a growl. "I'd rather starve."

"Okay." I stare at him, stunned as fuck he gave in so quickly. He's a coward, but he is usually more on the ball when it comes to threats. "If he doesn't show up, I'll finish what I started before *I* decide where we go next." He isn't looking at me. His eyes are locked with Demi's. "Do you understand, Andi?"

The quiver wreaking havoc with Demi's tiny body exposes why she reacted so fiercely when I shortened her middle name yesterday. I did it in jest because her christened name is so similar to her male cousin, it felt odd expressing it while having improper thoughts about how sugary her mouth most likely tastes. I had no clue it had been used against her before, and Col's seedy delivery guarantees I'll never use it again.

When Demi nods, albeit sheepishly, Col grins a victorious smirk. "Good." He shifts his eyes to the dark pair watching him in the rearview mirror. "We're good to go." As the driver seeks an opening in traffic, Col issues one final warning. "Tomorrow, Andi. Don't let me down."

Instincts tell me to go after him, but my head is so fucking messed up right now, I doubt my legs would move even if demanded. There are a million questions I need to ask, and only one person who can answer them.

"What did he mean he'd finish what he started? What did he start, Demi?" I almost choke on my last question when my eyes land on her face. It's more fucked up than first realized. The graze across her cheek is deep enough she'll most likely need stitches, and the red welt on her cheek is now purple. "What the fuck did he do to you?"

Demi waits until her uncle's car is lost in a stream of traffic before she shifts her focus to me. Even then, she isn't really with me. Her eyes are wide and terrified, her lips are trembling so much every time her tongue delves out to replenish them with moisture, I'm afraid she'll gnaw it off, and the dams in her eyes are close to spilling over. She's petrified, so you can imagine my utter shock when she steps back before murmuring, "You can go. I'm fine."

With her words impacting my heart more than any punch I've endured, I almost fold in two. "I'm not going anywhere." When I take a step closer to her, her dilated gaze bounces between mine. "Except here..." I tap the card she's holding so tightly, a large crease careens down the middle of it. "So you don't have to face whatever he's holding over your head."

She shakes her head so fiercely, I'm shocked big salty blobs don't topple down her cheeks. "You can't fight for him, Maddox."

"Why not? I'm a good fighter. I'll win."

"It's not about winning," she screams like our freeway confrontation isn't being live-streamed on Facebook by the dick-heads causing the bumper-to-bumper traffic creeping past us to back up further than needed. "The underground fight circuit he runs is *always* held on a Friday. Tomorrow is Saturday."

Oh fuck.

"Exactly," Demi says on a sob. "He doesn't want you to fight in the normal circuit, Maddox. He wants you in the... the..."

She can't finalize her sentence, and neither the fuck can I.

The brutality that comes with boxing has never bothered me. You show up, fight, and the stronger competitor leaves victorious. From what Agent Moses told me, that doesn't happen in

Col's new monthly circuit. If you don't win, you don't leave the ring breathing.

Although I'm cocky about my winning streak, nobody wants to be undefeated in a syndicate that ranks victories by how many men you kill. I'm not a killer. I'm just a man who wants to do a bit of good for his community.

"That's why you need to go home, Maddox," Demi says when she reads the horrified expression on my face. "You don't want to do this anymore than I don't want you to do it."

I want to tell her she doesn't know me well enough to know what I'm thinking, but since that would be a lie, I go a different route. "How bad will your punishment be if I don't show up?"

"It doesn't matter," she replies while shooing away my concern as if it's inconsequential.

"It does matter. *You* fuckin' matter, Demi."

Who knew four little words could break someone's heart? She's as brave as a soldier on the front line and ten times prettier, but it takes everything she has not to let the tears in her eyes spill from my comment, even more so when she asks, "Do I matter more than your family, Maddox? Am I more important than them?"

I don't know how to answer her question, so I don't.

My lack of reply doesn't harness Demi's campaign. If anything, it doubles her determination. "That's why you need to walk away. This isn't just about you and me. He will drag your entire family into this mess." When her voice cracks during the last half of her statement, she grits her teeth before heading toward the stream of traffic to hail a taxi.

"You can't take a taxi home, Demi, and act as if what just happened didn't."

"Why not, Maddox?" she screams after whipping back around. "Why can't I look out for myself for a change? Why can't I put myself first?"

"Because that isn't who you are! You're not him, Demi." I point in the direction her uncle's car just traveled. "You're not a selfish prick." I'm a fucking asshole for using her fears against her, but if it's the only way I can get her to see sense through the madness, so fucking be it. I'll accept the label and wear it with pride. "What do you think Sloane will do when you turn up looking like that? She saw you get into your uncle's car. She and Saint were standing outside the restaurant. The only reason she stopped ordering for Saint to follow you was because I promised I would."

That isn't a total lie. Sloane and Saint did witness her getting into her uncle's Audi, they just assumed it was an Uber I hired for her. I followed her because the knot in my gut wouldn't stop twisting until I caught up with Col's Audi. Now I'm so fucking glad I trusted my intuition.

I might have found her in a ditch if I hadn't gone off-script.

Agent Moses wanted me to step back and see how things played out. I told him to shove the badge he keeps promising me up his ass before I hot-footed it to my bike.

"Sloane is probably blowing up your cell now. Who knows what else she'll blow up when she sees what he did to your face?"

I want to start a war. Sloane's family has the capital to fund one.

Demi curses under her breath. "He has my cell." She twists to face the traffic. "My uncle has my cell phone." When she fails to locate his Audi, she rejoins me in the emergency lane. "Where's your phone? I need to borrow your phone."

She snatches my phone out of my hand when I dig it out of my pocket. Although she immediately logs into my phone app, it takes her a few seconds to dial a number she must know by heart. She could blame a technology-dependent world for her slow response time. I'm placing the burden on the frantic throb of the vein in her neck. She's aching all over, and the knowledge has me struggling not to track down Col Petretti to wring his fucking neck.

"Sloane... hey." Demi stops, peers up at me, then nods. "Yeah, he found me." She licks her lips before lowering her eyes to my midsection. "Things got a little heated on the side of the freeway."

Don't misconstrue her words. She isn't confessing to neither her physical altercation with her uncle nor our verbal one. She's making it seem as if we're about to get down and dirty.

"I was thinking about taking things back to our apartment. You were right, this has been years in the making, so why not scratch it off my list?" In between the screeches bellowing down the line, Sloane must alter Demi's plan of attack. "Oh... you're heading back there now? C-can you not go to Saint's house tonight?" Her eyes snap to my lips when they curve into a grin from her verifying, "He still lives with his parents? Oh, okay... umm..."

Some of the fear in her eyes shifts to pleading when I remove my phone from her ear and squash it to mine. Sloane stops rambling about how it's fine Saint hasn't cut the apron strings yet when I say, "It's okay, you guys continue on course. I'll take Demi back to my place."

"You don't live with your parents?" Sloane doesn't wait for me to answer her. She directs her focus to my brother, who I can't see but can imagine him wringing the steering wheel when she asks, "Maddox is younger than you, so why are you the only sibling still living at home?"

I miss Saint's reply since I pull my phone down from my ear before hitting the disconnect button. "Then, I guess it's sorted. You're staying at mine for the night."

While acting as if the pulsating of my veins is adrenaline instead of the desire to kill, I head for my bike, punching out a quick message on my way. I technically live out of home, but it isn't *exactly* how I implied when I told Sloane Demi can stay with me.

I remove a second helmet from a saddlebag on my bike, straddle the leather seat, clear the pleading from my eyes with a handful of blinks, then raise them to Demi. She's standing almost in the exact spot her uncle left her. Her eyes are still wide and terrified, but the blood dribbling down her nose has cleared away, and the swelling of her cheek has almost closed the gash under her right eye. If I were unaware of what she faced tonight, I could almost pretend the coloring under her eye is from a lack of sleep. Unfortunately for Demi, I'm not willing to do that. I let her leave with Col, so I'm partly responsible for the pain she's enduring.

"Please," I silently beg, knowing I'll never leave her here, but praying like fuck I don't have to fear her into doing as I'm asking. She's scared enough. I don't want to add to the terror she was forced to endure tonight.

My silent prayers are answered when Demi stuffs her purse under her arm, then pushes off her feet a couple of seconds later. Her steps are shaky, and not an ounce of trust is seen in her eyes, but she took a leap of faith. I can help her regain the rest.

"Lift your chin for me."

When she does as requested, I place my spare helmet on her head, then tighten the straps under her chin before holding out my hand to help her onto the back of my bike.

"Have you ever ridden on a bike before?" I feel the shake of her head more than I see it. "The sissy bar will ensure you won't slide off, but if you're worried, you can hold onto my waist."

I stop imagining Col gargling in a pool of his own blood when Demi's arms slip around my waist, and her unbruised cheek presses against my back.

After squeezing her hands, wordlessly ensuring her I've got her, I kick over my bike, then merge into traffic. Even with the hour late, traffic is thick. The cars that forever clog the streets of Ravenshoe are one of the reasons I got my bike license. I can whip in and out of traffic with ease, meaning our twenty-mile commute is done in less than fifteen minutes. It would take more than three times that in a car.

I park my bike at the side of a set of stairs before helping Demi off the back. Our ride through the hilly streets soothed her shakes as well as it dampened my anger. I'm still on the brink of blowing my top, but since I'd rather make sure Demi is okay than go on a murderous rampage, it isn't as obvious.

After dragging her eyes over a wooden cabin nestled in the foothills of a national park, Demi asks, "Is this—"

"The Walsh family cabin *everyone* this side of the country has partied in at least once in their life? Yes, it is."

While handing me her helmet, Demi mumbles, "Not everyone. I've never been here."

"You were invited. *Many* times." I know this for a fact because it was a lakeside party five years ago that had me pushing on the brakes. Demi's name was the first one Saint scribbled at the top of the invite list that year. That spot is only ever reserved for the girls he's interested in. Usually, if his invitation went unopened, he scratched her name off the list, then moved on to another wannabee conquest. Demi's name is the only one that's remained at the top of the list for as long as it has.

Considering the circumstances of her visit, this isn't a conversation we should be having, but since it will keep her focus off her swollen eye, I continue guiding us down the slippery slope. "If I recall correctly, one year you had to wash your hair, the next year your grandmother died, and the year following that—"

"My grandmother actually *did* die." I can't tell if it's remorse dangling off Demi's vocal cords or guilt. It may be a combination of both. "I wanted to come, Maddox. I just... *couldn't.*"

"I know," I reply, weakening the groove between her dark brows. "But you're here now, and that's all that matters."

As she follows me up the marble-clad staircase, she chews on her bottom lip. I really wish she wouldn't. I'm not a teen boy who can't control his cock. I'm afraid she'll inflict more damage to her delectable mouth. It's not split like her cheek, but it's pretty damn close.

I've barely worked my jaw side to side two times when a gruff voice says, "Hot-fuckin'-damn. I can finally scratch your name off the list. Demi she's-so-pretty Petretti, the holy grail of Seacoast Private Academy, has *finally* rocked up to a Walsh get-together. My every desire has now been catered to. I can die a happy man."

After rolling her eyes at Caidyn's dramatics, Demi gallops up the stairs to throw her arms around his neck. Caidyn is the Mr. Popularity of our family. The girls love his 'sensitive' side, the boys want to learn his ways, and more than once, I've strived to emulate him, although that's far from my mind when I realize what he's wearing. He's shirtless and almost fucking pantless. Nothing but a super-thin pair of boxer shorts are between Demi and his cock.

I'm seconds from knocking out some of his teeth, but the panic in his eyes when he locks them with mine over Demi's shoulder stops me. *"What the fuck happened to her face?"* The redness on his face matches mine to a T. As does the murderous gleam in his blue eyes.

"I'll tell you later," I mouth back before I pretend Demi is here under an entirely different set of circumstances. "I texted that we were coming, Caidyn, so why the fuck aren't you wearing pants?"

Caidyn's laugh reveals he understands my ruse, but Demi is utterly oblivious. She whispers an apology to Caidyn when I remove her arms from his shoulders, spin her away from his buff body, then whack him in the stomach. "Go to bed, grandpa.

Everyone knows you haven't been up this late since high school."

I jerk up my chin to Caidyn's unvoiced request for us to have a word once Demi is settled before guiding her into the bathroom attached to the master suite. I'm not a paramedic, but I've got to do something to lessen the chance the split in her cheek will scar. Her eyes are so mesmerizing, I doubt anything could steal their devotion. I just don't want to pop into her thoughts anytime she sees her scar. I want to be there for far better reasons than that.

"Holy shit," Demi murmurs when our entrance into the bathroom has her spotting her reflection.

"It's okay," I assure her when she pivots away from herself, too horrified to look at the damage a member of her family did to her. "You don't need to look. I just want to clean it up a little."

To back up my pledge, I grab one of the king-size towels off the rack, then curl it over the mirror's frame. Once it's covered, I snag the first-aid kit out of the cupboard before placing it onto the vanity. Demi watches me with her arms curled around her midsection and her eyes fixed on the floor. When I nudge my head to the first-aid kit, she sheepishly shakes her head.

"I don't care what I look like. I just don't want you seeing me like this."

Her eyes float up from the floor when I ask, "See you like what? Brave? Fucking strong?" I pull her arms down from her waist before carefully tugging her toward me. "I've seen grown men go down crying after one hit. You've yet to release a single tear."

Her lips quiver as she struggles not to respond to the pride in my voice. I'd be a lying prick if I said her unshed tears aren't cutting through me like a knife. I'd give anything to stop them from occurring, but since I know that will hurt her more in the long run, I have no choice but to encourage them.

I lift her to sit on the counter before saying, "While I get you cleaned up, why don't you tell me about the time you made Robert Flint come in his pants with only a peck kiss."

Demi waits for me to soak a handful of cotton balls in iodine before replying, "I'm not telling you about that."

"Why not? It's a funny story."

"It is," she agrees, smiling even with the gentle dabs of a cotton ball causing her pain. "But I don't need to tell you what happened because you were right there, stalking me like you always were."

Once I have the dried blood under her nose taken care of, I shift my focus to the gash in her cheek. "I wasn't stalking. I was..." I've got fucking nothing. "Fine. I *was* stalking, but it wasn't for me. I might have been pissed as hell that Saint showed an interest in you first, but that doesn't mean I'd let any random guy mosey in on his turf."

Demi hisses. I assume it's from the iodine swab inching close to the gash in her cheek. I couldn't be farther from the truth. "*His turf?* Jesus, Maddox. I'm not a piece of property."

Since her voice doesn't have an ounce of humor in it, I lower the cotton ball from her face, then lock my eyes with hers, ensuring she can see the truth in them when I say, "I know that. That wasn't what I meant."

"Then what did you mean?"

With her mood not as hostile as it was moments ago, I give

her the straight-up honesty she deserves. "I love my brother, so I didn't want him gutted like I was when I realized I had blown my chance with you."

Her drenched eyes bounce between mine for several long seconds before she whispers my name in a husky tone, "Maddox?"

"Yeah?"

After wetting her suddenly bone-dry lips, she asks, "Can you dab my cut with the iodine, so I have an excuse for my tears?"

I'd rather kiss her until crying is the last thing on her mind, but as my mother likes to say, crying is how your heart speaks.

"I could." My response is short and direct but impacting. "Or you could let them fall and trust me to take care of you while they do."

When she shakes her head, the first tear splashes onto her cheek. "I don't want to cry."

"Why not, Demi?" I ask while brushing away the salty blob sitting high on her cheek as if it's insignificant.

She loses her battle to hold in her second and third tear when she replies, "Because if I cry, he'll think he won."

I'm as stoked as fuck she remembers the time I defended her in the second grade, but I keep my excitement on the down-low. This bully is worse than any we'll face, and he's related to her by blood.

After dumping the dirty cotton ball into the bin, I press my hands to each side of her thighs, then lower my head so we're eye to eye. "I was wrong back then, Demi. Crying isn't a sign of weakness. It usually only happens when you've been strong for too long."

"Are you sure?" she asks through a sob.

I nod. "And if it isn't, he'll never know he won because I'll *never* tell him you cried." I brush my hand across her cheeks, being extra careful with her bruised one before lifting her into my arms and carrying her into my room. "I won't tell anyone. It'll stay with me until the day I die." *As I hope you will too.*

11

MADDOX

"What do you mean there isn't enough evidence?" I shout down the line, frustrated as fuck. "You saw her face at the restaurant. You know it wasn't marked. Now fucking look at it." I thrust my hand to the screen of my laptop as if Agent Moses can see the images I forwarded to him through my eyes. "Her eye is almost swollen shut."

He huffs like I'm being unreasonable. "His legal counsel could argue the puffiness was from crying."

"It wasn't from crying." I strangle the cabin's landline phone as if it's his neck. If I truly believed none of his annoyance centered around me not arriving for my fight Thursday night, I'd listen to what he has to say. But since I know more than half his grouchy attitude is because Dimitri, my part owner, would have chewed his ass out for my no-show, I'll continue pushing until he gives me the answers I want. "She was assaulted on your fucking watch, Arrow. You could lose your badge over this."

When Caidyn suggests that I lower my voice, I jerk up my chin before moving into the kitchen. It's the furthest room away from the one Demi is sleeping in. The cabin has been through four remodels since my family has owned it, but it still has its original super long springy cable my mom twisted around her fingers while talking to our dad during their courtship.

Although Demi did cry last night—more than I ever wanted to witness—Agent Moses is wrong. The marks and cuts on her face I photographed an hour ago have nothing to do with the number of tears she shed. They were there long before the first tear spilled down her cheek, and to my fucking disgust, they'll still be there days after her final tears.

"Col didn't just slap Demi, Arrow. He hit her, closed fist."

An undeniable urge to go on a murderous rampage slams back into me when Agent Moses murmurs, "According to Demi. This is a she-said-he-said case, but even if it weren't, domestic altercations aren't the Bureau's field of expertise. We—"

"Chase mass murders, terrorist cells, and cybercriminals. I've heard it all before. It's the same fucking shit every time we talk."

His sigh agitates me to no end. "If you know this, why are you bringing this matter to me?"

"Because Col has more of Ravenshoe PD on his payroll than the fucking state." I rake my fingers through my hair before hitting him with the real reason for my call. "I also wanted to prove Demi isn't a part of Col's operation. She's being forced to participate."

I want to ram my hands through the phone and wring his scrawny neck when he mutters, "Nobody held a gun to her head when she went on recruiting drives at local gyms."

My words are forced through a tight jaw. "No, they didn't, but they have no issues shoving one under her ribs when she doesn't jump on command."

I hear Agent Moses's chair click into place. Considering it is almost two in the morning, I'm shocked to discover he's still at the office. He doesn't seem like the type of agent to hang around after everyone else clocks off. "You saw that? You witnessed someone pull a gun on her?"

"Yes!" I answer, a little too loudly. "In the second lot of photos, you can see where the muzzle of the gun bruised her rib." That evidence was harder to amass without Demi's knowledge, but since she's sleeping in only a pair of panties and my gym shirts, the loose fit helped me gather sneaky snaps of her injuries.

Don't misread what I'm saying. We didn't do anything last night. I'm not a complete-fucking-asshole. I slipped my shirt over her head while she was still dressed, then she shimmied out of her dress under the bedding. I'm not entirely sure when her bra was removed. She was wearing it when I snuck out to speak with Caidyn. It was gone when I went back to document evidence of her abuse.

Yes, I noticed things other men think are unimportant. I also liked the fact she felt comfortable enough to sleep in my bed as if it's hers.

The click of a mouse sounds down the line a mere second before Agent Moses's indecisive sigh. "There's no doubt that's a muzzle indent."

"But?" I ask when I hear one hanging in the air.

"But... I don't know if it'll be enough to convince my supervisor to take on this case." He sounds as disappointed as I feel. I understand the Bureau wants to get Col on more than a battery charge, but something is always better than nothing, right? "With more credible evidence, we could get him on attempted murder."

"But..." I repeat when it continues to linger like a bad smell.

"But..." He leaves me hanging longer this time around. "What you've given me is nowhere near enough. I'll need a lot more to take this to the head of my department."

"More what? More bruises? More abuse? Exactly how much torture does she have to endure before you'll do something to help her? Does he have to kill her, Arrow? Does she have to lose more than she already has?"

Mistaking the annoyance in my tone as me being so desperate I'll do anything he asks, Agent Moses replies, "Video footage would be great. Or catching him in the act. That could work, too."

"So you want to put her back in the line of fire to secure more evidence?" He can shove his next 'but' where the sun doesn't shine. There's no fucking chance in hell I'll place Demi undercover with anyone, much less someone as incompetent as him. "That damage you see, those bruises, cuts, and grazes, they occurred in under five minutes. Five fucking minutes, Arrow. Yet you want to throw her into shark-infested waters without so much as an oar for protection. Fuck that. I ain't doing that. If that's all you've got up your sleeve to keep her safe, I'll take the matter elsewhere."

His sigh this time around represents a dismayed man instead of an annoyed one. "How long do I have?"

I stray my eyes to the grandfather clock next to the refrigerator. It reveals it's precisely two in the morning. "Seventeen hours." If you're a kid counting down the hours until the fat man in the red suit arrives, seventeen hours seems like a lifetime. Now it feels as if I only have seconds left on the clock.

"Give me until midday to work out a plan of attack." When I attempt a rebuttal, Agent Moses talks faster. "I need time, Ox. Nothing happens in an instant."

I could call him out as a liar. It only took me looking into Demi's eyes once when I was seven to be a goner, but I keep my mouth shut. Not even my mom could understand my immediate fascination, so why the fuck should I expect any different from a weasel of a man like Arrow Moses?

"Keep me updated."

"I will," he promises like his pledges are worth something. "And I expect you to do the same."

He can't see me, but I jerk up my chin as if he can before I disconnect our call.

"No good?" Caidyn asks almost immediately, exposing he was eavesdropping on my conversation. I can't blame him. It took me promising to keep him informed on *all* aspects of Demi's case before he would hand me the keys to his Jeep. He wanted to pummel Col into his grave just for backhanding

Demi, so I'd hate to think how far he'll go now he knows one of Col's hits was with a closed fist.

"He doesn't believe there's enough evidence for a conviction."

Caidyn rounds the island in the kitchen before he props his hip against it. "How isn't there enough evidence? You saw her assault."

"I only witnessed the tail end of it." I swish my tongue around my mouth to ensure my next lot of words can make it through the carnage unscathed. "And him forcing her to kiss him." The swish of moisture did little to lessen the scorn of my tone. It's as furious now as the anger that pumped through me last night. "What do you think that was about? That isn't normal, right?" We've kissed our aunts on the lips before, but that all ended when our top lips grew as hairy as theirs.

"If the look on your face is anything to go by, it was far from normal." Caidyn moves to a stack of drawers before pulling out his wallet. "Ask Avery to have a word with her. If anyone can get her to open up, Avery will be that person."

"She's talking to me."

He squeezes my shoulder more in support than to maim. "I'm not saying you can't be there for her, Maddox. I'm just asking you to step back a wee bit so she can get *all* the help she needs." My brows furrow when he adds, "You don't want Saint and Landon conspiring against you again, do you?"

"What the fuck are you on about?"

It's rare for Caidyn to show fear, but I'm confident that's what he's expressing now. "I thought Saint told you."

"Told me what?" His lips hadn't stopped moving. I'm just too damn impatient to wait.

He takes a moment to consider how best to tell me his news before he rips off the Band-Aid in one fell swoop. "Saint wasn't crushing on Sloane all these years. He just veered for her when Demi freaked about his approach."

"What are you saying, Caidyn? Are you saying he wanted Demi? Are you telling me I'm in the process of mowing my bro's turf?"

In all honesty, I don't know how I'll respond if he answers with anything but a stern no. I don't want to hurt my brother, but I sure as fuck don't want to step back from Demi. She cried in my arms for hours last night. She's sleeping in my bed right now. Even despite the fucked-up mess her uncle forced us to endure, we've bonded. I feel closer to her than my own blood. I can't give that up.

"No, that's not what I'm saying, Maddox." The relieved breath I push out is sucked back in when he adds, "I'm saying he cares about you so much, he wanted to save you from this." The back of his hand barely touches my chest, but it feels like he sucker-punched me. "When you went against a bully double your age to protect Demi, your chivalry was awarded with a broken nose. How much worse would it have been if that bully was the same one you're facing now."

I understand what he's saying, and I get where his worry comes from, but I don't have to fucking agree with it. "So I should just step back and let the bullies win?"

Caidyn shakes his head. "That's why Saint altered the direction of his course. He saw the fear in Demi's eyes when he approached her, and he realized he'd fucked up. He wasn't saving you from a bully. He was being a bully... to Demi." He snags an apple out of the fruit bowl on the island, then tosses it in the air like our conversation isn't half as serious as it is. "We all make mistakes, Ox. Even you."

After winking at my gaped jaw, he crunches his teeth through the apple before he walks away. I should go after him, his unusual use of a nickname is a sure-fire indication he's on to me, but when his dramatic exit is quickly followed by Demi's arrival, I can only get my feet to move in one direction.

"Hey. How are you feeling?"

Demi drags her teeth over her lower lip to lessen the size of her smile from the fumble of my words. I'm not known for being a jittering imbecile. It just appears as if I have no control over anything when Demi is in the picture. Can you blame me? Even with her face bruised and swollen, she'd still take out Seacoast Private's most attractive senior title. "Good. I'm not sure what was in the pain medication you gave me, but it knocked me out for a good..."

When she strays her eyes around the cabin, seeking a clock, I lower my eyes to my watch. "Almost a whole four hours. Not a bad effort for a first-time sleepover." I hit her with a frisky wink, lowering the panic in her eyes before pledging, "I'll aim for eight next time."

My reply has a double meaning, and if the heat on Demi's cheeks is anything to go by, she knows it.

I relish her bloomed face for a couple of seconds before guiding her deeper into the kitchen. "Are you hungry?" She ordered an entrée last night, but since I was being an ass, she more picked at it than devoured it. She must be starved.

With a shrug, Demi replies, "I could eat."

I send a silent prayer to heaven when my briefest touch causes her voice to come out higher than normal before saying, "Great, because I'm starved, and I have no fucking clue how any of this shit works." I wave my hand over the six-burner gas stovetop my parents had installed after one of the infamous Walsh parties ended with a kitchen fire. It isn't what you're thinking. No one was cooking. Saint was just seeking a new term for Fireball whiskey. "If you promise not to tell anyone how bad of a cook I am, I promise to make your super early breakfast half-edible."

"You're going to cook for me?" I realize food is the way to her heart when the highness of her tone has me convinced someone put a helium tank in the air vents.

I drag my finger down her nose that looks like a slippery slide since she has to crank her neck to peer at me. She's a good foot shorter than me. "Under your supervision, of course. We may end up dead if you don't guide me."

I'm lying. It isn't my specialty, but I can see my skills flourishing if it maintains the smile Demi is wearing now. It isn't a full grin, the busted lump on the side of her face won't allow a full smile, but it's clear she's content.

"Are you sure you have time for this now? It's pretty early."

I do a singular dip of my chin. "I have all the time in the world." *For you.*

Her smile would have you convinced she heard my

unspoken words. As would what she says next, "Then, I guess I better cook. I don't want you dying on me."

———————

Three empty plates of egg benedict and many, *many* flirty touches later, I test the authenticity of the zap buzzing between Demi and me.

Get your mind out of the gutter. My lips aren't going anywhere near Demi's *unless* she forces them together. Then, all bets are off. I'm merely verifying she's as strong as the little girl who kneeled on a fresh wound to comfort the boy hurt while sticking up for her.

"Demi, can I ask a favor?"

She stiffens for a mere second before she stacks the final plate into the dishwasher like she never froze. "Sure." Her short reply can't weaken the obvious. She's never been given anything without expecting something in return for it. Not even a shoulder to cry on.

Although the knowledge has me wanting to backtrack, I can't. If I don't do this, everything I've done the past six months is pointless, and her bully wins.

"Will you let me photograph your bruises?" When fret fills her face quicker than fear, I talk faster. "If you want to hold your uncle responsible for what he did, you'll need evidence to back up your claims." I drift my eyes over her face that will heal but is far from healed. "If we don't give them proof, it'll be our word against his." I have the proof I need. I just want to gather it without a heap of lies. A lie can't hide the truth, but it can change the truth.

Demi's mouth remains shut, but I see her working the 'our' part of my statement through her head on repeat. Once she has it decompartmentalized, she strays her eyes in the direction Caidyn walked after devouring the meal we made together like I'm a sous-chef in the making.

"He'll be dead to the world the instant his head hits the pillow. Food comas do that to people." If he isn't, I'll knock him the fuck out if it's the only way I can get her to agree to this. "If you're not comfortable with me doing it, I could ask my mom or Justine to come over later today?"

She shakes her head so fast, I'm confident her eyes feel like balls in a pinball machine. I assume her denial centers around her not wanting more people to see her banged up than necessary but am proven wrong when she stutters out, "I'm fine with you doing it."

"You'll let me take them?" I sound like a prepubescent teen instead of an almost twenty-two-year-old.

Demi's head shake switches to a nod. "You can't beat bullies with silence."

That's what my mom said when she was called to the principal's office the afternoon my nose was broken. She wasn't mad all four of her sons were being suspended for fighting, she was proud they stood up for what they believed in. She would have just preferred if it weren't four against one. It wouldn't have been if Glen's friends hadn't bolted the instant Landon and Caidyn showed up with their school blazers pushed up to their elbows. Saint was close behind, he just had to detour past the crossing lady, so he could borrow her stop sign. He always brings a bat to every game we play. It's just rare for it to be shaped like a bat since we've never played baseball.

I'm bad at shoving my foot in my mouth, and it's showcased in the worst way when I snatch my phone up from the counter before nudging my head to my bedroom. "We should do it now while they're fresh."

Fresh? Seriously, Maddox! That's the best you could come up with?

"I'm sorry. That didn't come out right."

"It's fine," Demi murmurs before adding on a set of words that reveals she's anything but. "I'm fine."

12

DEMI

I contemplated suicide by rolling out of a vehicle driving over seventy miles an hour, was almost sexually assaulted by my uncle, had my hair wrenched from my scalp by one of his hired goons, and cried in the chest of a man I've had a crush on longer than I've been a woman, yet my knees are wobbling more now than they did last night when I stumbled out of my uncle's Audi.

I'm not scared.

I'm stupidly nervous.

And perhaps a tad bit excited.

I thought Maddox would look at me differently. My stomach convulsed when I caught my reflection in the mirror last night, but for some insane reason, the way Maddox stares at me would have you convinced my face isn't as battered as it feels.

Don't get me wrong, the uncontrollable tick his jaw gets

every time his hooded eyes float over my face indicates it's pretty messed up, but I'll take that response over the one I was anticipating. I'd even accept the look of disgust if it keeps him here with me instead of seeking my uncle in the shady shadows of the underworld.

The Walsh brothers aren't solely known for their good looks and player ways. Their fierce protection of those they love is also blatantly obvious. That's why I'm so shocked Justine is attending a university over a hundred miles from here. I didn't think her brothers' tethers extended that far.

"Did you want to do it here or in the bathroom?" I spin to face Maddox, almost stumbling when I realize just how close his stalk is. My lips are mere inches from his, although nowhere near as close as they are to his chest. This is the annoying part of being a short-ass. I'd have a better chance of 'accidentally' sucking his nipple into my mouth than his tongue. I'd take either, but since I'm unsure if that is what he wants, I have to act nonchalant. "The lighting in the bathroom is probably better."

"Sounds good," Maddox replies, his voice throaty and deep. "I'll take you any way I can get you."

Excitement blisters through my veins until it dawns on me what he's doing. Flirting is his go-to emotion when he feels snowed under. Mine is pretending I'm fine.

"Can you spin around for a tick?" I sheepishly wave my hand at my bra dumped at the foot of Maddox's bed. "I need to put my bra back on."

His eyes drop to my now-budded nipples before he curses, then turns around. "Sorry. Bad habit I don't *ever* see me giving up."

The gash in my cheek burns when I smile. I'll suffer the injustice because that wasn't a preplanned slide into seduction mode. It was a genuine slip-up.

"Okay. You're good to go," I announce once I have my strapless bra in place.

Maddox spins around for barely a second before he snaps his eyes shut, and the veins weaved throughout his tattooed arms pulsate as furiously as the throb between my legs. He's shirtless, and I can no longer act as if I haven't noticed the fact.

"Are you sure you're good to go because, to me, it looks like you're not wearing a shirt." He pops open one of his eyes, does the quickest scan of my body, then closes it tight again. "Or pants. You're either standing in front of me in a pair of teeny tiny I-really-fucking-hope-I'm-not- dreaming panties and bra, or I'm dreaming. Please tell me I'm not dreaming."

"You're not dreaming."

"Are you sure?" I giggle like a schoolgirl when he drags his hand across the front of his low-riding sleeping pants that show off every spectacular inch of his 'V' muscle. "Because I'd rather blame a wet dream for the mess in my pants than the removal of dental braces." When his fingertips come up free of carnage, he sighs heavily. "Jesus, Demi. You can't scare a man like that. I was certain I had done a Flint."

Still laughing, I pace into the bathroom. "If you had, the entire Walsh reputation would have been voided by default."

"I know," he replies, following after me. "Why do you think I was so worried?" He doesn't wait for me to answer him, he simply requests me to stand in front of the tiled wall next to the freestanding shower. "Although I now feel a little guilty about what Robert went through." He grabs at his crotch, returning my smile. "He had a reason for his boner. Do you remember the dress you wore to the homecoming dance?"

I shake my head, truly forgetful.

Maddox doesn't seem as absentminded as me. "The midsection was cut out in a crisscross design. If you squinted your eyes the right way, you could almost pretend you were wearing a bikini top." He moves my hair to one side of my neck before tilting my chin, so the bruise my uncle's goon inflicted when he grabbed ahold of me is front and center. "It didn't seem like your style. It was nice and all, just—"

"More something Ophelia would have worn?"

He snaps my profile two times before he lowers his iPhone from his face, so I can't miss the lift of his chin. "Do you miss her?"

Ophelia died in a traffic accident over four years ago. I want to say her death was the commencement of my uncle's downfall, but that would be a lie. Dying was the only way Ophelia was guaranteed any peace, so although I do miss her, I believe she's better off where she is.

"You don't have to explain your motives to me, Demi," Maddox assures when my quiet causes an awkward stretch of silence to extend between us. "Nobody can judge your life because they've never walked a day in your shoes."

The same blue eyes that peered down at me fourteen years ago watch me now, but there's just not an ounce of green to them, freeing me from the worry I'm about to make a fool of myself.

The scent of the homemade hollandaise sauce Maddox

burned to the bottom of the pan an hour ago fans my lips when I balance on my tippy toes and plant my mouth on his. He doesn't weave his fingers through my hair like I'm hoping, nor does he band his arms around my back to draw me closer, he merely murmurs a prayer against my lips loud enough for me to hear. "Please, God, forgive me for what I'm about to do."

I assume he's begging for forgiveness because he's about to reject me. I've never been happier to be wrong in my life. He doesn't pull back like he begs himself to do two times. He kisses me—once. It's a frugal yet carnal embrace that has me craving so much more.

"Don't. Fuck. I can't," Maddox murmurs against my mouth when I do the movement I wanted his fingers to do twenty seconds ago. I weave them through his reddish-blond locks before tilting my mouth so we're better aligned. "You're hurt and vulnerable. I don't want to take advantage of you." He peppers my lips, jaw, and neck with kisses with each word he speaks. He even adds a little nibble to his longer sentence. "Caidyn will fucking kill me if he walks in on us now."

"Then maybe you should lock the door?"

Maddox shakes his head while slamming shut his bathroom door and fixing the lock into place.

"Stop me. Tell me to stop," he begs when he returns to my side of the bathroom.

He doesn't stand as close as he was when I kissed him. There's a massive barrier between us, a barrier that ensures I'll never concede to his demand. He's hard, and the button on his sleeping pants doesn't look capable of containing his erection for much longer.

"No."

He kisses my non-bruised cheek, my jaw, then one side of my mouth. "No, you want me to stop? Or no, don't stop?"

"Don't stop."

When he pulls back to make sure he heard me correctly, I slant my head to the side so the bruised half of my face is shadowed by the unflattering light above our head.

"Don't hide from me, Demi." His voice is a whisper but as powerful as a roar. "Don't *ever* fucking hide from me."

After kissing the welt on my right cheek and the cut a bucket-load of tears washed out last night, he returns my kiss. Gently, ever so gently, he tastes my lips, glides them along his, and draws in the shuddering breaths his awe-inspiring kiss instigates.

It's an all-encompassing embrace that sees me kissing him back as if our lives aren't precariously dangling in the breeze. Tongues, lips, teeth, they all get in on the act. Even my nipples can't be held back from the festivities. They bud against Maddox's chest, encouraging him to cup my thighs and guide my legs around his waist.

Our kiss goes on and on and on, and the entire time, Maddox keeps one hand on my ass and the other lodged halfway between my nape and the now-drenched roots of my hair.

I thought he would have pulled out his cock by now, pushed aside my panties, and driven home. He hasn't even cupped my breasts, which are begging for his attention. He merely kisses me like this is enough. Like his every desire is being satisfied.

"Not yet," he forces out with a groan when my needs get the

better of me. After grinding his thick cock into the hand I lowered to his crotch, assuring me he's as into this as me, he says, "I've been dreaming about kissing you for years. I'm nowhere near done with this stage yet."

Years?

I shudder through the thrill his confession awarded my body, then pretend as if I didn't. "We can kiss while doing other things. I'm good at multitasking."

I feel Maddox's smile more than I see it. "You might be skilled in multitasking, but I most certainly am not." His throaty voice does naughty things to my panties. "Well, I am, just not when I want to be greedy."

"Greedy?" I ask, a little lost.

"I've not yet found a way to kiss..." He swipes his tongue across my lips. "Eat..." He feels the mess he made of my panties when the hand gripping my neck lowers to the soaked-through material. "And fuck at the same time."

O. M. G. Maddox Walsh has a filthy mouth in the bedroom, and I'm obsessed with it.

"So, until I work out how I can do all of the above at the same time, we'll need to take things one step at a time."

"Is there a rule that says kissing has to be first?" I blurt out before I can stop myself.

A mini orgasm tightens my core when he throws his head back and laughs. Our bodies are intimately joined. I feel every vibration of his chuckles. They have me fighting like crazy not to throw my head back and moan through the sensation awakening within me.

I shouldn't have bothered holding back. Maddox seems to

know all my inner-workings. "Jesus, Demi. Did you just come? Are you coming right now?" Although he's asking questions, he doesn't give me the chance to deny his accurate claims. "Oh, fuck this, I need in on that."

After reattaching our lips, he walks us into the main part of his room. We kiss the entire trip, and the head of his fat cock rubs the buzzing nub between my legs with every step he takes.

When we reach his bed, I'm anticipating for him to place me down before he drops his lips several inches lower, so you can picture my shock when he spins around, plants his backside on the edge of the bed, then flops back, leaving me seated in his lap.

The veins feeding his magnificent cock could easily get me off, but Maddox has other ideas. "Bring it to me." Shock must register on my face as he's quick to alleviate my confusion. "Your pussy. If you want me to kiss it, you're gonna need to bring it to me."

When he licks his lips, I shudder. Maddox Walsh wants me to ride his face, and I'm horny enough to do it. "I've not... I'm not..."

"You've never sat on a guy's face before?"

I wouldn't have worded it that way, but he's on the money.

When I nod, he licks his lips again before he stretches them into an insanely sexy grin.

Fuck sanity.

I'd rather endure a six-year stint in a mental hospital than give this up.

"That's it," Maddox encourages when I shimmy up his body. "Put your knees on each side of my head." You have no idea how hard it is not to immediately sink onto his face. His voice is gravelly and thick, and it carries through every inch of me. "Now pull those panties to the side." His growl when I do as asked causes my knees to hug his head. It's deliciously rough. "You'll want to watch this," he grunts out when I take a minute to gather my bearings.

I'm not in shock.

Well, I kind of am.

In all honesty, I never thought this day would arrive, not to mention after he placed his life on the line for me.

When Maddox gets my eyes, he curls his arms around my legs, spreads them wider, then asks me to drop. I'm certain he's on the verge of being suffocated when he drags the tip of his nose through the crevice in my pussy to suck in the smell of my arousal. The thrill of anticipation it scuttles through my veins is enough to pull my knees out from beneath me.

Fortunately for me, Maddox thinks it's all part of my brilliant plan to seduce him.

He moans a husky, "Yes," into my pussy before he wholly devours it.

Just like our kiss, the movements of his mouth and the sweeps of his tongue are gentle and sweet, but as the tension grows between us, so does his pace.

A strangled noise leaves my throat when he sucks my clit into his mouth a couple of licks later. I'm so sensitive, it takes me concentrating on one of the freckles dotted across his nose not to come after one tug.

His skin has a golden hue from spending hours in the sun, so his freckles are harder to spot now than they were when I searched for them as a child. They are great orgasm blockers. Not because they're not sexy—they increase Maddox's appeal, not decrease it—but because I'm so immersed in my treasure hunt, I can keep my focus on anything but Maddox going to town on my pussy.

"I see how it is," Maddox mumbles a couple of seconds later. "I need to work for your climax, not have it gifted to me on a silver platter." After playfully biting the inside of my thigh, he blows a hot breath over my super sensitive pussy. "I washed dishes for hours and went home content with a peck kiss on my cheek, so I think I'm up for the challenge."

"Sweet mother of God," I murmur to myself when he pokes his tongue inside of me.

I've been eaten out before, but it was with the guy who took my virginity without breaking the seal, and it was nothing like this. This feels so good, I rock back and forth instead of being embarrassed the first time Maddox saw my pussy was from me shoving it in his face.

My cheeks grow warm as the panties I'm holding to the side slip in the damp conditions. My self-control is running out. I'm about to come.

"Do it, Demi," Maddox suggests like he's truly tapped into my inner-workings. "Come hard and fast on my face."

The gravelly deliverance of his words forces me to grip the headboard in a white-knuckled hold. Maddox keeps my soaked panties in place with one hand before he uses the other to pull me down lower on his face. I almost vault off the bed when his teeth graze my clit. He eats me like he's starved, and after several perfectly placed licks, jabs, and tugs, I have no choice but to respond to the intensity brewing in my stomach.

When I come with a mangled groan, I try to close my legs, but since Maddox's head is wedged between them, I can't. The knowledge has me shrieking even louder. I arch my back as tingle after tingle hits my pussy. The crush of my senses is almost overwhelming. I shudder and shake and chant Maddox's name in a high-pitch, desperate scream as if he's a god. And he laps up every damn scream with big, hearty licks before he makes me come all over again.

13

MADDOX

I went into the bathroom with good intentions and high morals. When I carried Demi out, I thought I had left them sitting in the toilet. I should have trusted Demi more than that. She isn't riding my face because she feels obligated, she's doing it because she wants to, it feels good, and she's forgotten all about the shitstorm that rained down on her last night.

She may even be doing it because she's wanted this for as long as I have.

It's amazing how free you feel when you stop leaving things to chance.

"Nuh-uh," I murmur against Demi's swollen clit when she attempts to hook one of her wobbly legs over my head. I've made her come twice, beads of sweat are rolling down her chest, but I'm not close to being finished. "I'm not done with you yet."

I'm not a religious man, but I have words with God for the

second time tonight when Demi replies, "I want to return the favor."

"Return the favor? *Nah.* You've contributed *more* than your share." I'm not lying. I am so desperate to taste her again, I'm clawing at her thighs in desperation, hating that her delectable pussy is inches above me instead of being squashed against my mouth. "How about you respread those legs and let go again?"

When her thighs stop hugging my ears, a confident sign she's happy with my plan, I bunch her soaked panties in my hand, then tug them away from her sinfully sexy body.

"I'll buy you another pair," I grunt in confirmation when her moan comes out strangled. She could be turned on by my aggression, but I don't want to risk the chance the thud of my pulse in my ears has me mistaking an annoyed groan as a moan.

After dumping the cotton material on top of the dress that almost caused me to have a coronary last night, I say, "Lower onto my mouth again. Bring that sweet pussy to my lips."

My thick voice exposes how badly I'm dying to feast on her again. It would be quicker if I rolled her over, spread her thighs, then delved my head between her legs, but that also means I'd be taking all the control.

I can't do that.

I need to know Demi is here because she wants to be. A woman not in control of her life wouldn't straddle my head as if it was a seat.

"That's it. Right fucking there."

As a smell I can see me becoming obsessed with fills my nostrils, I curl my arms around Demi's ass, kneed the bouncing globes of flesh with my hands, then tug her forward so I don't have to kink my neck to spear my tongue inside her pussy.

I fuck her with my tongue, grind the tip of my nose into her clit, and double the buzzes hitting the nervy bud with my teeth for the next several minutes.

She's so fucking sensitive, her third orgasm arrives even quicker than her first two.

As a simpering growl rolls through her, she tries to burrow her dripping pussy into my face. She makes the cutest sounds when she comes. They're not quite grunts, but they're a step or two above wanton moans.

When she says my name in a husky grunt, announcing her climax is coming to an end, the room commences spinning. I'd give anything to keep her pussy attached to my mouth for eternity, but the amount of time we spend in our blissful bubble isn't up to me. Col hung a bomb above Demi's head. The timer is ticking down, and I have no fucking clue where he's hidden the detonator. If I want to eat Demi's pussy more than once, I need to man the fuck up and protect her how she deserves to be protected.

After rolling off my sweat-slicked body, Demi flops onto a set of pillows I'll never look at without smiling. She's exhausted, but her eyes remain on me when I enter the bathroom to gather a washcloth and towel.

"Did I hurt you?" I ask while placing a warm washcloth between her legs. My hunger to eat her had the prickles on my chin scratching the sensitive parts of her body. The skin between her pussy and her ass is almost raw.

Demi smiles in a way I'll never forget. "No. It was perfect."

When her twinkling eyes lower to the monster dick in my sleeping pants, I give it a hard squeeze, begging for him to calm down. I already took it one step too far tonight. I can't take another. Not only would I be lectured by my parents for the next six years, I'm reasonably sure my siblings would teach me a lesson with their fists.

I can hold my own, but it's always harder when it's four against one.

Glen learned that the hard way.

Once I have the smears of arousal cleared from Demi's wickedly sexy pussy, I nudge my head to the bathroom. "Do you want to shower before you sleep? Or are you good to wait until daylight hours to scrub my aftershave from your skin?"

"Shower?" Demi asks, clearly confused. "I thought we were going to... you know."

Fuck me, this woman is adorable when she's nervous. Not even her battered face can detract from that. She's pure fucking dynamite. Small yet explosive, and oh-so-fucking sexy.

After wiping the hope from my tone, I reply, "You thought we were gonna fuck?"

I'm a prick for smiling when she bobs her head, but I can't help it. It's either smile or bang my chest like a neanderthal. I went for the one that wouldn't make me look like a dickhead.

The worry in Demi's eyes clears away when I say, "I wasn't lying when I said I can't multitask. The whole time I was kissing your pussy, I was thinking about how it tastes as sweet as your mouth, so what will happen when I stuff my cock inside of you..." I don't give her a chance to answer. "I'll be thinking about the time my mouth was on your pussy. I don't know if I'm ready for that just yet. The first time I put my dick inside of you, his undivided attention *needs* to be on the task at hand. I don't want to do a Flint."

"Or a Ramsey," Demi gabbles out with a giggle.

"Who?" I ask, certain she didn't just mention another man's name after riding my face like a carousel at the fair—over and *over* again.

Conscious the snip of anger in my tone isn't in malice, she drags her teeth over her kiss- swollen lips before saying, "Robert Flint came in his pants. Luke Ramsey came while removing his cock from his pants."

I angle my head to the side before arching a brow. "You did it twice?"

When she nods, gone is the sheepish woman who slowly climbed up my body to straddle my face, replaced with a woman who looks like she eats men for breakfast.

"That makes you proud, doesn't it? You fuckin' love that you have men making a mess in their pants from doing something as simple as looking at your sinfully sexy face." I say my comment as if the face peering back at me isn't messed-up compliments to a man's hand.

Please note, I use the term 'man' loosely *anytime* I'm referencing Col Petretti.

"It's not my fault they have no clue what they're doing," Demi fires back, still giggling.

"Oh... burn," I bark out with a laugh, not the slightest bit confronted we're having this conversation in my bed of all places. Friends become lovers even quicker than strangers, and I want that for us more than anything. "I promise when we reach *that* stage, I won't leave you hanging like those dweebs. I've got you."

Demi's laughter immediately ends. After licking her lips that were more parched from her erotic screams than her uncle's knuckles, she lowers her eyes to the crotch of my sleeping pants —the *extended* crotch of my sleeping pants. "Until then, are you sure there isn't anything I can do to help your *situation?*"

Please, God, let me be a decent man for once. I believe in Karma, so I sure as hell believe she'll gnaw the fuck out of my ass if I answer *any* of the pleas my cock is currently dishing out. He begged to sink into Demi before we entered the bathroom. Now he's straight-up demanding I get the job done.

"Not tonight." I hate myself. I truly, madly, fucking deeply hate myself. "But how about we reconvene in the morning and reassess the situation?"

I'll be dead in the morning due to a lack of blood supply to my brain!

I'm sentenced to an eternity in hell when I raise my eyes to the ceiling and whisper a stern, *"fuck you,"* to God when I spot Demi's destroyed panties on the floor. I'm not really mad at him. I'm angry at myself. I'm the one who tugged Demi's panties off so aggressively there's no chance in hell they're wearable, so I'm the one who should face the consequences of my actions when she slips beneath the sheets I'm holding open for her and shimmies to my side of the mattress in nothing but a bra.

"Are you sure there isn't something I can do to relieve the pressure?" Demi asks when the throbbing rod of flesh between us digs into her naked backside.

I slam my fist into my thigh, wordlessly warning my cock

he's next on my hitlist before I draw Demi back as if I have no clue what she's talking about.

Spooning will take care of my erection. It will have my cock slouching against my thigh like my nanna walked in on me masturbating. I'm not a snuggling type of guy. I can't recall a single time I've hung around to cuddle after a hook-up, which most likely means it's never occurred.

Unfortunately for me, emasculating moments of endearment don't deflate my monster cock. He remains firm and erect, his throb growing more urgent when Demi asks, "Do you want me to switch off the light?"

Not once since the nineties has a man begged for clap lights as I am now.

"No. I'll get it," I reply when my pleas aren't granted by an invisible genie.

With the light switch above Demi's head closer than the one by the door, I stretch across her body to reach it. I'm almost there. My fingertip is a mere inch from the gleaming, plastic material—an inch I gain when I jerk my hips forward to fill the gap.

It's the same inch that sees my cock popping the button in my sleeping pants.

The same inch that delves between Demi's thigh gap in hunt for the wetness I'm struggling like fuck to ignore.

The same inch that causes Demi to moan like she's on the brink of climax again.

And the same fucking inch that reminds me sometimes adulthood doesn't start for men until they're thirty.

I'm not strong enough for this.

He-Man wouldn't be strong enough for this, and he kicks all the other superheroes' asses.

After rolling Demi onto her back, I fill the gap between her splayed thighs with my body, then lower my mouth to hers. I don't kiss her straight away. I peer into her eyes, acting oblivious to the fact her right one is nearly sealed shut.

"Are you sure this is what you want? I'll stop right now if you ask me to, and I'll *never* mention it again." Her half-smirk exposes that she understands the last part of my statement. I won't keep quiet for her reputation. I'll do it to save face. A man's ego can only take so many hits, and her rejection would be by far the most painful. "This isn't why I brought you here. I want to take care of—"

Demi forces my words back into my mouth with her tongue, curls both her legs around my hips, yanks down my sleeping pants like my dick isn't already hanging out, then intimately joins us in a way there's no doubt I'd kill for her.

14

DEMI

I pushed down Maddox's sleeping pants, I led his thick cock to the crest of my pussy, then I curled my legs around his fantastic ass to join us in a way I always hoped we'd do but never truly believed would occur, but the last forty minutes of pure bliss has all been Maddox's doing.

He readjusted my hips so he could take me deeper than I've ever been taken. He found the proverbial G-spot everyone knows about, but not many men endeavor to find, and he brought me to climax so hard, the slickness between my legs ensures not an ounce of friction can be felt between us.

It's been a glorious forty minutes that grows more blistering when Maddox drags his teeth over the shell of my ear. "In case you're wondering, both your pussy and your mouth are on my mind right now." I shudder when he sucks my earlobe into his mouth to soothe the sting of his bite before he releases it with a pop. "I could come right now just recalling how delicious they taste."

A moan rumbles in my chest when his cock throbs during his confession. He couldn't possibly get any thicker, he's already stretching me wide, but somehow, he does.

"Oh, God. Yes." I raise my leg higher on his sweaty waist, relishing a sensation that should be painful but is much more pleasurable. I'm so full—so gloriously full—and my clit is being awarded the undivided attention of Maddox's pelvis with every thrust he does.

Each perfect pump hazes my mind. I'm floating amongst the clouds, clawing, moaning, and oh so very close to orgasming again.

"Let go, Demi," Maddox purrs into my ear as his perfectly structured pumps fail to relent. He grinds into me on repeat, taking me deeper and deeper with every controlled jerk of his hips. "Trust me to catch you. I've got you. I'm right fucking here."

He cups my ass in his big hand before he lifts it from the sticky bedding. His movements are effortless like he was built for fucking. He knows the exact pace to drive me wild. My erotic screams leave no uncertainty of this, and neither does the tremoring orgasm that blindsides me out of nowhere.

"Yes," Maddox hisses into my ear when my pussy tightens around his fat cock. I shudder and shake while chanting his name on repeat. "That's it. Right-fucking-there. Grip my cock with your tight little pussy like your lips will when you suck me off for the first time."

His dirty mouth turns me on more than I ever thought possible. It extends my orgasm, dragging it out from a three-second shudder to a thirty-second shake.

"Oh... ah... I need... a minute," I breathe through the brutal tremors lighting up every inch of my skin.

"All right." Not speaking another word, Maddox rolls us over until I'm straddling his lap, and his back is resting on the headboard I pierced my nails through earlier.

Having his deliriously handsome face directly in front of me doubles the tingles low in my stomach. His hair is flopped to one side, his cheeks are red from the brutal fucking he's hit me with the past forty minutes, and the bumps in his midsection are more noticeable since he's panting as hard as me. He's downright sexy, and I could climax from just looking at him.

Maddox waits for my eyes to return to his face before he says with a grin, "Show me what you've got. Wow me with that fantastic body of yours."

The unwanted attention I got throughout high school reveals I didn't miss out in the looks department, but I've never felt as sexy as I do right now. Maddox is looking at me like he can't see the marks on my face. Like I'm beautiful, unflawed, and very much craved.

His admiration pushes me out of my comfort zone. It has me rising to my knees until the tip of his erect cock nestles in the folds of my drenched vagina and has me watching every thought that passes through his head when I slowly sink back down.

I'm raw and open, emotional and moved, and smiling like a naïve fool, and so is Maddox.

We gel together so well. I feel closer to him now than I did when he held me while I cried. It's a beautiful moment I'll cherish for a lifetime.

I rise and fall on Maddox's impressive cock another three times before he grips my hips to stabilize my sways. That's how much his heated watch shatters my resistance. I'm on the verge of climax again after only a handful of grinds.

"Take your time, Demi," Maddox pushes out with a moan when the clenching of my cervix demands me to go faster. "There ain't nowhere more important we need to be right now than here."

I nod slowly, my breathing shallow. "It feels so good."

"It does," Maddox agrees after adjusting the girth of his thighs so I can sink even lower. I take him to the very root, moaning when my low grind causes our pelvises to touch. The buzz it bestows on my clit is dangerously delicious.

"Good. So, so good. More." Full sentences are beyond me right now. I can barely breathe, let alone hold a conversation.

Bursts of pleasure shoot through me when Maddox follows my husky command by cupping one of my breasts in his hand. When he tweaks my nipple, it sends delightful zaps straight to my clit. The moans they produce convince me I'm having an out-of-body experience. You can't logically feel this good and not be floating toward heaven.

We're not fucking. Our pace is much slower. More controlled. I'm not being pushed toward the edge of insanity with the brutality I'm accustomed to. I'm being cherished. Loved. I've never felt more wanted and protected in my life.

I've also never been so sated.

When I bite my lip, struggling to keep my expression

neutral, Maddox gently tugs it free from my teeth. "You're going to hurt yourself if you don't be careful."

While rocking against him, I moan out the reply I was meant to keep in my head. "Too late."

Something flares through Maddox's eyes. It isn't lust, covetousness, or any of those other things you'd expect to see while making love. It's protective, materialistic, and proves, without a doubt, he doesn't just want to save me from my uncle, he's willing to become him if it's the only way he can keep me safe.

15

MADDOX

Have you ever smoked a joint laced with so much shit, the toxins have you believing your high will never end? You're up there, lounging on a cloud, certain you're destined for better things, then you start freefalling back to earth without warning. The crash is fucking brutal. It swears you off drugs for weeks and has you considering enrolling in Sunday school.

That's kind of how I feel now.

Last night was—I don't have words to explain it. It exceeded anything I could have imagined. We didn't fuck until the spark between us simmered to a respectable level. We threw a ton of gasoline on it and turned it into an inferno. We made love. Kissed. Groped. Fucked. We did it all. Then, just as exhaustion started to hit, we went back for round two.

It was perfect. Demi was perfect, but now I'm sitting here, glaring at the landline phone, willing it to ring. Agent Moses said he needed until midday to work out a solution for Demi's predicament. It's now 1:14 p.m.

Since he's as old school as they come, some shit about not being able to pinpoint landline calls as easily as cell phones, I'm in the living room of the cabin instead of catching up on missed sleep with Demi in my room.

I won't lie. Not all my swollen chest is compliments to how well Demi and I meshed beneath the sheets. I'm also smug as fuck I exhausted her to the point she's sleeping in today of all days. There's a big-ass clock above her head. We only have hours until it detonates, yet she's in my bed, faintly snoring like she has the world at her feet.

I love that I've given her that small moment of peace. I doubt she's had one in a while.

"Still nothing?" Caidyn walks into the living room like he hasn't been eyeballing me like a freak for the past hour and fifteen minutes.

I shake my head. "Do you think I should call him? Push him along?" This is just like Agent Moses. If you don't constantly prod him, he gets nothing done.

"From what you've told me, it couldn't hurt," Caidyn answers with a shrug.

I tried to keep things basic between us when we spoke last night. I wanted his focus on Demi, not me, but Caidyn is smarter than he looks. He told me I was playing with fire, explicitly stated not to cry to him when I get burned, then shifted his focus back to Demi. He isn't awarded *all* the girls' attention because he's a tyrant. They love his sensitive side, and taking care of a beaten woman brings it out tenfold.

"What are you looking for?" he asks when my hunt for my phone and wallet comes up empty-handed. I could have sworn I left them on the side table next to the sofa.

"I don't have Agent Moses's number memorized. He changes it more often than Saint pulls his signature move." I groan about how much of an idiot I am before I crank my neck to the hallway leading to my room. "I left my wallet in my trousers. His new number is in there."

"I'll grab it," Caidyn says, believing he's being helpful. "Then you can maintain your stalk of the landline."

"Ah... that's not a good idea." I jump up from the single sofa. "Demi *isn't wearing any pants*." My last four words are barely whispers.

"What did you say?"

Caidyn's death stare reveals he heard what I said. He just wants me to repeat it.

"I said Demi *isn't wearing any pants*." My second attempt isn't any better than my first.

"Maddox—"

I cut him off only a second into one of his infamously long lectures. "It isn't what you're thinking. She came on to me."

Not entirely true, but mainly.

Caidyn whacks me up the back of the head. It's an old-style Dad move, and since my undercut was recently clipped, it makes the impressive *crack* noise our father always sought after our mother trimmed our hair when we were kids. "That shouldn't have mattered. Last night, Demi needed a friend, not a one-off fuck buddy."

"It wasn't a one-off." I sure-fucking-hope it wasn't. "And we're both adults who consented to *every single thing* we did."

My tone is way too cocky for Caidyn's liking. He slaps me again, except this time, he puts some *oomph* into his swing. "Go get your wallet, dickhead." I charge for the hallway, more than eager to skip his three-hour-long lecture on treating ladies right. My brisk strides slow when he adds, "But don't think this is the end of this. We'll have words about this later."

Great.

When I round the corner of the hall my room branches off, I lessen the thumps of my feet. Not a sound is projecting from my bedroom, so I don't want to wake Demi if she's still sleeping.

With the curtains closed and the light switched off, it takes me longer than I care to admit to realize the lump in the middle of my bed is the bedding.

"Demi?"

After scanning my room to ensure she isn't hiding in the shadows, I head for the bathroom.

"Demi, are you showering?"

I tap two times on the glossy white door before entering the bathroom. I can't hear the shower running, but that doesn't mean she isn't in here. When you have four siblings, you soon realize silence isn't always a good indicator that things are swell.

"Are you decent?" *I fucking hope not.* Her body isn't just dynamite, it's downright explosive.

When my search of the bathroom comes up empty-handed, I race back into the main part of my room. Unwilling to leave anything to chance, I switch on the light this time around. It reveals most things are where I left them. My watch and cell phone are on the bedside table, but my wallet is no longer in my trouser pocket, and Demi's ruined panties aren't on the floor.

With the removal of my wallet the most obvious sign something is amiss, I snatch it up from the bedside table, then search for any clues as to what Demi was seeking when she removed it from my pants. I gave her unlimited access to it only hours ago, so I'm a little perplexed as to why she needed to go through it a second time.

My wad of bills is untouched as is the piece of paper Agent Moses's latest cell phone number is scribbled on, but the card Col handed Demi yesterday is gone.

Fuck it!

"She's gone," I announce after returning to the living room, my steps slow and weighed down.

Sleeping with Demi doesn't grant me the knowledge of all her inner-workings, but watching her from afar for years most certainly does. Her disappearance is very unlike her. The only time she vanished without a trace was when her father died. I thought she was grieving. It turns out, she was being bounced from foster home to foster home.

"What do you mean she's gone? Where the fuck could she go? We're in the middle of nowhere, and she doesn't know how to ride a motorbike..." Caidyn's words trail off when he leans to the side to peer out the big French doors that lead to the patio. His Jeep is usually parked a few spots up. It isn't there today.

"Fuck!" I curse out loud this time around. "I hid your car keys in my room—"

Confirmation Demi has done a runner doesn't steal my words. Caidyn's fist does. "I thought you said last night was consensual."

"It was," I fire back, more panicked than annoyed at his assumption I'd ever hurt Demi like that. I wasn't lying when I said last night was years in the making. I've been dreaming about last night for ages, and it was better than I could have imagined.

It also assures me I'm on the money with my assumption Demi didn't take Col's card for no reason. She did it because she experienced the same sensation that hit me when I sunk into her last night. There's just one difference. She'd rather be assaulted by her uncle than see me become him.

"Then why did she leave?" Caidyn asks, averting my focus back to him.

I breathe out the heaviness on my chest before answering, "Things are more complicated than you realize."

He points to the sofa my ass was planted on while Demi hatched her escape plan. "Then you need to sit the fuck down and explain yourself."

I'd laugh about how much he emulates our father when he's stressed if I had the time. "Call Saint. Sloane may know where Demi has gone."

Although he looks like he wants to argue, Caidyn jerks up his chin before pulling his phone out of his pocket. "If he's not with Sloane?"

"He'll be with her." Saint's eyes were gleaming last night when Sloane galloped down the stairs of her building. More than his signature move was placed on the cooktop the past couple of days. I'm certain of it.

While Caidyn does as requested, I tug on a pair of jeans over my boxers, cover my plain white T-shirt with a jacket, snatch up my bike keys from the kitchen counter, then rejoin Caidyn in the living room. "Anything?"

He shakes his head. "My calls are going straight to voice-mail." He angles his head to the side when I fail to keep my expression neutral. Saint *always* answers his phone. Even when he's balls deep in a female, he forever takes his brothers' calls. "What?"

"Nothing," I reply, denying the knot in my stomach its chance to speak. "Keep trying. If you get anything, come back to me."

"I'm coming with you," he announces while shadowing my sprint to the front door.

"How, Caidyn? Are you gonna ride bitch on the back of my bike?" When he makes a face like vomit is scorching his throat, I arch a brow. "Exactly. Besides, you're better off staying here. If Demi has popped down to the market to gather supplies, who will let her in if we both leave?"

"True." His reply is as unconvincing as my piss-poor excuse for Demi's unexpected disappearance. My mom stacked our fridge only yesterday. There are enough supplies in the kitchen to feed an army.

"Keep me updated," Caidyn requests while tossing me my cell.

After lifting my chin, I stuff my phone into the front pocket of my jeans, then gallop down the porch stairs, praying like fuck my intuition is way off base due to a lack of sleep the past forty-eight hours. As I hook my leg over my bike, I push down on the kickstart lever at the same time. Since I'm also twisting the throttle, I rocket out of the dusty driveway before my ass is fully in my seat. I don't even have my helmet on, but I don't give a fuck. Nothing I said or did last night was fraudulent. I would kill for Demi. I'd even send myself to slaughter if it guaranteed she'd leave the massacre uninjured.

———

Because I thrash the living shit out of my motorbike, I skid to a stop at the front of Demi's building a record-breaking twenty minutes later. Although my phone hasn't buzzed, I'm confident Caidyn got ahold of Saint. He isn't wrestling Sloane into submission in the kitchen of her modest apartment. He's dragging her away from her sports car like she isn't scratching, kicking, and screaming at him.

"Let me go!" she repeats before she slings her begging, wet eyes to me. "Tell him to let me go!"

My father taught me to protect any woman in need, but I can't this time around. Saint isn't hurting Sloane. He's trying to keep her safe.

"Do you know where she is?"

When Sloane shakes her head, salty blobs splash onto her cheeks. "No, but she wouldn't just pack up and leave unless something bad happened."

"She packed?" The shortness of my question can't hide how airless her reply made my lungs. I feel like I'm being suffocated.

I suck in a relieved breath when Sloane shakes her head.

My reprieve doesn't last long.

"But she left a check on the entryway table for three months' rent and gave notice at Petretti's." More tears plop down her face when she mutters, "When we moved in together, we made an agreement that if either of us were *permanently* leaving, we were to pay three months' rent, so the other half wasn't burdened with the full amount. I agreed because I would *never* abandon her, but I also didn't think she'd ever amass the funds to leave me." She scrubs a hand over her wet cheeks. "If she was leaving for better things, why wouldn't she take her belongings? She didn't even pack her coat. It's cold today." She hiccups through her last couple of words.

She is so devastated, Saint wordlessly pleads for me to end my interrogation. I can't. If anyone knows where Demi is, it will be Sloane.

"She isn't leaving via her choice, Sloane. She's being forced out."

"What do you mean?" As her drenched eyes bounce between mine, her lips quiver. "She could have come home last night. I didn't mean she had to stay away, and certainly not forever."

"That isn't what I meant." She stops thrashing against Saint when I add, "You're not forcing her out. Her—"

"Uncle is?" The redness on her face goes from devastated to murderous in under two heart-thrashing seconds, and just as quickly, she recommences her campaign to get out of Saint's grip. She fights him with everything she has, her battle coming with a ton of words I'm certain she'll regret within the hour.

It takes Saint lowering Sloane to the ground and hooking one of his legs around her waist to keep her contained. He'd rather face the battery charge she threatens him with than see her go against a man as evil as Col Petretti.

"A quarter a mile out of Hopeton, take a left on Sandy Plains Road. Halfway down, you'll find a mansion hidden by tall hedges." Saint's words are chopped up by the brutal pounding Sloane is hitting his ribs with. She can't punch him since he has her wrapped up tight, but she has no issues ramming her elbows into his ribs. "If anyone has the means to find Demi, the men inside that compound will."

After lifting my chin in thanks, I hotfoot it to my bike. "Once things settle down, call Caidyn."

Saint replies, but the revs of my bike's engine gobble up what he says.

With traffic light and my love of the throttle at a pinnacle, I make it to Sandy Plains Road in under three minutes. I lower the revs of my motorbike long before I spot the hedges Saint mentioned. Stumbling upon two men with machine guns strapped to their chests is enough incentive to slow any man down.

"If you know what's good for you, turn around and pretend you never took this route," says goon number one while the sight on goon number two's gun adds a Hindi bindi to the crease between my brows.

"I was sent here—"

"By whom?" goon number one interrupts before I get out half my sentence.

I curse Saint like I'm not about to put his life on the line before muttering, "Saint Walsh."

The seemingly higher-ranked foot soldier pushes two fingers to his ear for barely a second before disappointment crosses his features. "Welcome to our humble abode." He steps back, then fans out his arm like he's inviting me to curtsey before the Queen. "We hope your stay is pleasant."

Not having neither the time nor the care to work out his riddle, I glide my bike down the asphalt driveway he motioned at with his finger. "Jesus-fucking-Christ," I murmur under my breath when the mansion in its entirety comes into view.

Calling this place a mansion is an understatement. It's more like a palace.

A tattered-up man with a cropped beard, green eyes, and a shit-eating grin meets me at the stairs at the front of the thirty-plus room mansion. "The day has finally arrived. All the Walshs are falling into line."

It takes me a couple of seconds to place him, but when I do, my plan of attack alters in an instant. You never stumble across Rocco Shay without laying eyes on Dimitri Petretti. They're joined at the hip.

"What are you doing here, Ox? Dimitri ain't got time for your family's shit today."

He stops rubbing his hands together like a man perusing a buffet of pussy when I say, "What about his family? Does he have time for that?"

"Fien?"

I don't know who the fuck Fien is, and in a way, I'm glad. Rocco looks seconds from murdering me where I stand.

"Demi." I articulate her name as roughly as Rocco did Fien's.

When Rocco's dark brows pull together, I use his confusion to my advantage. "Does he have time for her? She *is* his family, after all."

He waits a beat before lifting his chin. When he spins on his heels, I dismount my bike and follow him inside.

"Wipe your fucking feet," he says after splaying a tattooed hand across my chest, stopping me on what must be an invisible welcome mat since there's not a single bristle to be seen. "Does this look like a barn?"

While I scrub my boots on the cobbled porch, I stare at Rocco like he has rocks in his head. He's having a full-blown conversation, but not one of his words are directed at me. He's talking about me, not to me.

"This way," he says a couple of seconds later. "Dimitri is working out of his downstairs office today." He shakes his head before adding, "Nah, don't tell him. Let me surprise him."

Once again, he isn't talking to me.

One of his multiple personalities must give him the go-ahead because our arrival at a large office in the lower level of the mansion is met with a surly and aggressive Dimitri Petretti. "I said I didn't want to be interrupted."

He was a grouchy bastard when he was a teen, and it seems as if age made him even grumpier. Other than handing a wad of cash to Agent Moses after each of my fights, I barely see Dimitri. He wasn't interested in a conversation, and I preferred saving my suaveness for his cousin.

"You always say you don't want to be interrupted," Rocco

pushes out with a laugh. "But I know you're full of shit. The *only* time you say you don't want to be interrupted is when you're getting lost in a hooker, which we *all* know you haven't done since..." He stops talking at the same time Dimitri's growl thunders across the room.

While smiling like Dimitri fell right into his trap, Rocco says matter-of-factly, "Maddox is here about Demi. Shall I leave? Or can I join in on his beatdown?"

I give Rocco a look as if to say *I'd like to see you try*, before I move closer to the desk Dimitri is seated behind. I know who he is, what he's associated with, and just how fucking dirty his hands are, but I'm praying like fuck his parents instilled *some* kind of values into him.

My strides slacken when it dawns on me how stupid I'm being.

Col Petretti isn't just Dimitri's uncle. He's his father. He *raised* him.

The return of my smarts has me switching things up. "I'm here to get your permission—"

"To date my cousin? No fucking chance." I assume Dimitri is taking the high road. I should have known better. That isn't how his family operates. "Who she dates isn't up to me. She isn't on my payroll." A glint darts through his eyes, but he's quick to shut it down. "If that's all." He nudges his head to the door I just walked through, wordlessly giving me my marching orders.

"It isn't."

I step closer to him, grinning when Rocco announces his dislike at me not accepting no as an answer by ramming his gun into the back of my head. "The man said no, Ox. Don't make me splatter my new shoes with your brain matter. I only bought them last week."

I act as if he never spoke. "I wasn't asking permission to date your cousin. I was approached by a fight promoter." That's a stretch, to say the least, but when you've got nothing, you must work with what you have. "A high-profile event is coming up. I want permission to fight at the event." When confusion darkens Dimitri's eyes, I pretend he takes more than a share of my profits each month. "If I get injured, I can't fight for you. Figured you wouldn't take too kindly to that, so I thought it would be best to seek permission instead of assuming."

Dimitri drops his pen onto the paperwork in front of him before he slouches low into his chair. I'm confident he's calling my bluff, so you can imagine my shock when he asks, "Who's the promoter?"

"Your father," I answer without pause for thought. I don't have time to pussyfoot around, and in all honesty, I'm reasonably sure Dimitri would see through any bullshit I attempt to dangle in front of him.

Dimitri shakes his head. "You can't fight for him *and* me on the same night. You might be good, Ox, but you're not *that* good."

"That's the thing," I reply, stepping even closer. "His fight is tonight." Dimitri's fights are held on Thursdays and Fridays. Today is Saturday.

"Tonight?" When I jerk up my chin, Dimitri snaps out, "Smith..."

I peer past my shoulder, anticipating for someone other than Rocco to be standing behind me. I'm shit out of luck.

There's only one fool with his gun directed at my head. That fool is Rocco.

After a couple of seconds staring into thin air, Dimitri locks his icy blue eyes with mine. "Where is the fight scheduled to take place?"

"That's another thing." I swallow to eradicate the annoying nerves in my voice before saying, "I lost the card he printed the details on." When Dimitri's jaw grits, I talk faster, "I know it is in Hopeton and that I have to arrive at nine o'clock sharp." Rocco snickers when I add, "I was hoping you could fill in the blanks."

Dimitri leans forward until his elbows are propped on his desk. "Let me check if I have this right. You want me to grant you permission to fight *after* I unearth the location where the event is taking place, even with you being a no-show at *my* events both Thursday *and* last night? Is that right?"

Rocco calls me a fucking idiot under his breath when I lift my chin. "You need to learn the art of ass-kissing, my friend," he suggests at the same time Dimitri says, "Not interested."

"I'm willing to negotiate. State your terms." When he orders Rocco to remove me from his office, I shrug out of his hold. He may have a gun, but I have unquenched desperation. There's nothing more potent than that. "I'll do anything. I'll give you a bigger cut of the proceeds. I'll even compete in your Friday night schedule if that's what it will take for you to help me. State your terms, and I'll agree with them."

Dimitri slices his hand through the air, wordlessly requesting for Rocco to stop hauling me out of his office. "You want her *that* bad?"

Some may call me a fool for immediately nodding, but I can't help it.

Lying isn't my forte.

"All right," Dimitri breathes out many prolonged seconds later. "But it'll cost you more than a bigger slice of the pie."

Having nothing to lose, I once again nod.

16

DEMI

"Beggars can't be choosers," I murmur to my reflection in the mirror.

I've scrubbed my face clean, filled in the gash under my right eye with liquid foundation, and done up my face as if I'm about to spend the night on the town, yet, only now is the real show about to begin.

I had hoped my life would never reach this stage, but I can no longer walk around wearing a blindfold. Everyone knew my life would eventually take this path, even Maddox. That's why he fought so hard to make me forget last night, and it's the very reason I fled the instant he snuck out of his room this morning.

My uncle's monarch sucks the blood out of the veins of the heirs born to rule it, so imagine the damage it will cause a man not programmed to jump on cue. Maddox may last a couple of months in this realm, perhaps even a year, but eventually, it would wear him down as it has me.

I refuse to let that happen.

I swung the bat.

I missed the ball.

Now I'm hoping like hell I don't punch out.

After ensuring my face is half presentable, I pat down the hem of my floral dress before exiting the washroom. Like they do *every* time I'm in their vicinity, the men of my uncle's crew wolf-whistle and call me derogative names. A handful of them even go as far as fanning up my dress like I have no rights whatsoever.

I'd slap away their hands, but since that only ever encourages them to badger me more, I act as if they're not in the room with me. My focus is on one man and one man only, and when I reach him, I'm reasonably sure even more unwanted attention will be directed my way.

"You're early," my uncle says with a disgruntled grunt. "Is he done with you already? Why am I not surprised?"

"Can I speak with you? I-In private, please." The stutter of my words is understandable. It isn't every day a woman puts herself in this predicament, much less with a man who has the same blood as her. "Perhaps in your office? It's quieter there." I gather his hand in mine like mine aren't shaking a million miles an hour before peering at him like he's a saint, and I'm a sinner willing to do anything to be granted a stay of execution. "Please. I'm sure it won't take more than a minute."

Fear encroaches me from all angles when he drags the back of his index finger down my bruised cheek. He isn't remorseful he hurt me. If anything, he's turned on by the fact he marked me so well, my welts are still noticeable twenty-hours later.

Hurting women is a favorite pastime of his. It also explains where I went wrong last night. I exposed that my biggest fear isn't him hitting me. His gentle touch is what scares me the most because I know it will only be gentle for so long before it jumps to maiming.

I don't know whether to barf or silently cheer that my plan is working when my uncle mutters, "Everything with me, dear, takes longer than a minute."

"Then perhaps you can grant me two?" I talk as if I'm a regal princess even with me feeling anything but regal. I feel dirty and disgusting, a stark contradiction to my emotional state most of last night.

Maddox. *Oh.* I never realized how much the world spun until the wee hours of this morning. The Walsh brothers are known for their playboy ways. They have a reputation almost every woman on the planet would happily ignore for a chance to occupy their bed, and after last night, I can confidently declare I'm now on that list.

Maddox was attentive, gentle, sweet, and mind-blowingly skilled. He heightened my sexual palate to a level I didn't realize it could reach, then he catapulted over it with a second round that was even better than the first.

I don't have much experience, but that won't stop me from saying last night was perfect. It was brutally beautiful. A true occurrence I'd give anything to be a part of time and time again.

Sadly, mafia princesses don't wear crowns.

We destroy them.

"Two minutes," my uncle grunts out, drawing my focus

back to him. "Then I must get back to work. Money waits for no one, not even someone as forbidden as you."

His inappropriateness today is off the Richter scale. He's always been a little perverted, and I often wondered why Ophelia feared him as much as she did, but I had no clue his level of sickness extended this far. Either Dimitri is closer to overruling him than even he realizes, or the agents Maddox mentioned are homing in on charges not even a dead spouse will stop from occurring. He's making mistakes, many of them, and this one is about to cost him his life.

When we enter his office at the side of his compound, Col locks the door before he spins around to face me. "Where do you want me?" His tone is low and gravelly. It makes it hard for me to speak, but I push through, aware this must occur.

"In your chair." When he moves toward his office chair, I push out, "Not that one." I nudge my head to the two sofas in the corner of the cigar-hazed space. "One of those. We'll have more room over there."

It takes a conscious effort to move my feet when he plops onto the sofa closest to me. I'm not second-guessing my decision. I'm horrified when his hands automatically move for his belt. I'm his niece, for crying out loud. His flesh and blood, yet he still sees me as an object of pleasure.

My lips quiver when I say, "Let me."

I brush away the invisible tear I stupidly believe is rolling down my cheek before pacing to his side of the room. There's no stopping this now. His responses the past five minutes assure me I have no other option but to continue with my plan.

"Close your eyes," I suggest, confident a normal man would struggle to maintain a rational head when their niece kneels between their splayed thighs to undo the zipper in their trousers. "It will be more enhanced this way."

I beg my eyes not to let any tears fall when he does as requested. They'd be more in relief than dismay, but I still don't want them to fall. I refuse to let him win.

After swallowing down the bile surging up my throat, I ask, "Are you ready?"

When my uncle hums out an agreeing murmur, I raise to a kneeling position, creep my hand into my bra, remove the boxcutter I borrowed from Caidyn's Jeep, flick it open, then slash it across my uncle's jugular from one ear to the next.

His eyes pop open in an instant, and his hands move even quicker than that. One shoots up to caress the wound that's no more than a papercut while the other one backhands me hard across the face. I fall to the floor before instinctively rolling into a ball to protect my face and body. In my shock, I forget about the hair I purposely left down. My uncle likes his women to look feminine. All his whores must wear their hair down. If they forget, he shaves it off before he hands them to his understudies for a month. They never make it out of that punishment the same woman. They're beyond scarred.

"You ungrateful little bitch," he sneers in my face after he drags me from the floor by my hair. "I fed you, clothed you, and kept my hands to myself even when the scent of your needy cunt begged me not to, and this is how you repay me. I should cut you up into little pieces. Hack you so badly, no one will care how sweet your cunt tastes. Or better yet, I should leave you in a room with my dog. I'm sure he'd do more damage than the knife you borrowed from..."

Shit, shit, shit, I inwardly scream when he reads the name engraved on the boxcutter. "Walsh Construction and Architectural Design."

After roaming his eyes over my face, I'm no longer worried about his dog ripping me to pieces. I'm petrified his teeth are about to get in on the act.

My worries are left unfounded when he drags his nose down the throb in my throat. His growl is immoral, so I won't mention his tone when he says, "I thought you smelled different."

While grinning like a madman, he pushes me back until I'm at an arm's length. "He got it out of you in one night."

He isn't asking a question. He's summarizing.

"I don't know if that makes you easy or if he's now at a point he'll do anything to stop you from getting hurt." The air in my lungs leaves in a grunt when he tosses me onto the sofa across from him as if I'm a rag doll. "I guess we only have a couple of hours to find out."

When he shouts his second-in-charge's name, Mario enters the room a couple of seconds later. He must have a key as he didn't kick open the door. "Watch her. If she gets out of line, pretend that's a dildo." My uncle's eyes drop to the box cutter at his feet during the last part of his statement. "I don't care how fucked up you make her, just ensure she's alive. Some guys get off on scars."

While smiling like I just made his life a shit-ton easier, he paces out of the room, his steps swaggered and slow.

Col Petretti is on a warpath, and I just put Maddox's family at the top of his list.

17

DEMI

I should be dead. My plan was to murder my uncle, then turn the knife on myself if his goons' bullets race across the room weren't fast enough.

Instead, I'm sitting across from him in an SUV careening down a dusty road.

In a way, I'm upset my plan didn't work, but I'm also content. Once Maddox fails to arrive tonight, I'll go to heaven instead of hell. Surely, God can forgive me for a measly paper cut. I've been to hell and back. That alone deserves a little bit of forgiveness, doesn't it?

My grin is way too smug for a woman about to be tortured to death, but what can I say? I get cocky when my greatest wish comes true. There isn't a single motorbike in the parking lot of an abandoned warehouse on the outskirts of town. Nor is there any sign of Caidyn's flashy Jeep my uncle's goons dumped a few miles out of town. There are Bentleys, Porsches, a handful of Audis, and many other foreign cars of which I don't know the names.

The richest of the rich are here to watch the ultimate blood sport.

Fight-to-the-death boxing.

"Stay at my side." My uncle's voice exposes he too has noticed an absence of regular folks. "If you so much as move half an inch from me, the first cut I make will be to remove your clit."

"Like you'd know where that is."

It dawns on me I said my comment out loud when he grips my face and thrusts me backward until my back is one with the SUV we just exited. "You're just like your fucking mother. Give you a little bit of dick, and you think you rule the world."

He digs his fingernails into my cheeks so firmly I'm certain he will leave a mark when defiance darts through my eyes. Nothing about Maddox was 'little,' and I was seconds from announcing that.

"Don't make me show you what it took to bring her into line. It drove your father so crazy, he walked straight off a fucking cliff."

I'd spit in his face if he weren't holding mine so firmly I can't get my lips apart. His rough handling is nothing new, but he's never taken it this far in public before. You can't emulate a man in control if you don't have your subjects scared enough to follow your every whim without prompting.

"Stay. At. My. Side," he reiterates, speaking slow.

He doesn't wait for me to nod. He simply walks away, leaving the heavy lifting to his men.

"Move it."

"I'm going," I assure Mario when an inch gap between my uncle and me sees the muzzle of a gun being shoved under my ribs. He's pissed I didn't give him an excuse to hack me up with the boxcutter. He's a sick fuck like that. He'd rather my uncle's seconds than an untouched woman because he knows they're already half-broken.

Several eyes shift our way when we enter the warehouse. It's set up similar to the underground fight circuit my uncle runs with the only surviving member of his family, Dimitri, but the clientele is sleazier-looking, and the smell of corruption almost outranks the scent of death lingering in the air.

I'm shocked by the number of revered stares my uncle is being given. It's rare for him to be admired. He makes these fools money, but more times than not, it costs them just as much in respect. You can't side with him and expect to come out with your dignity intact. If you want to deal with the devil, you better be willing to face the consequences of your actions.

My heart plummets into my stomach when it dawns on me why we've secured the eyes of many. They're not peering at my uncle in awe. They're struggling to work out why his inflamed knuckles are the same size and width as the bruises on my cheek. They're evidence my uncle is an abusive tyrant and the very reason he is being gawked at from all sides.

It's rare for my uncle to leave evidence of a crime. His slip-up this weekend shows how unhinged he is becoming. Hopefully, when he kills me tonight as punishment for Maddox's no-show, the evidence Maddox captured before I fled will see him convicted of murder. The Petrettis never leave a body—corpses talk, even the mutilated ones—but you can convict a man without a body. I overheard my uncle mention that only last month.

My eyes float up from the floor when my uncle's deep Italian timbre fills my ears. From what I learned from my father, the Petrettis haven't lived in Italy since the thirties. However, their accents are as thick as foreigners. They'd hate to be mistaken as the American now running their sanction. Henry Gottle, Sr., the boss of all bosses, is of mixed race. He has inky black hair like mine, eyes just as blue, yet, my uncle treats him as if he's a fraud.

"How much?" my uncle repeats when my eyes land on his face. "I don't usually bet on the underdog, but tonight, I can't lose." The crowd mingling around us hovers in close when he digs his finger into the cut in my cheek. He wants the world to know he hurt me, and he refuses for a little bit of foundation to steal his victory. "If he dies, I lose money but gain *so... much... more.*" His last three words are expressed in a way that makes my stomach recoil. "If he wins, which I highly doubt, I pocket a nice bit of coin that will have no issues finding me a young cunt to keep me warm for the night."

He speaks so poorly of women, I have to force my reply out of my mouth. "And if he doesn't show up, what happens then?"

The dress I wore to look 'pretty' for him is ruined when he yanks me forward with a brutal clutch on the dainty material. The top two buttons pop open, exposing the cleavage he swears I inherited from my mother.

"You don't want me to answer that." He waits for me to absorb the threat in his tone before he drags his eyes over the men loitering even closer. "Or perhaps I should tell you. The men are so eager, they might spoil the surprise."

"I'm your niece," I remind him like he may suddenly grow a conscience. "Your flesh and blood."

"I know." He taps my nose before he brings out the smile that shows blood will never come before his bank balance. "Why do you think they're so keen? It's not every day a civilian gets to bed a princess."

I scoff. *There's nothing regal about me.*

It appears as if my uncle heard my inner monologue when his grin turns blinding. "Right now, your blood is nobler than mine." He steps so close, our noses almost touch. "Because I've granted them permission to spill yours. They can't touch mine."

He chuckles at the paling of my face before he places a five-thousand-dollar bet on Maddox on my behalf. When he takes a seat ringside, wordlessly announcing that the event is about to commence, bids come in hard and fast. The money tossed into the bookie's hat exposes why my uncle was so desperate to sign Maddox as his fighter. Just his surname scribbled at the top of a portable blackboard fills the front row of seats that usually sit half-empty during the regular Friday night fights. They don't come cheap in a standard exhibition, so I'd hate to think how much these suit-clad men have forked out for an up-close visual of a murder.

I shouldn't smile at the fact they're wasting both their money and time, but I do. Even if Maddox has a photographic memory, he'll be a no-show tonight. I ensured the card my uncle scribbled on was out of Maddox's sight at all times, even going as far as asking if I could store it in his wallet for 'safekeeping.' I felt horrible when he granted me his trust without so much as a second blink, but the moment he entered me the first time, I knew I had made the right decision.

The Walsh brothers protect those they love, and the consummation of my relationship with Maddox placed me high on their list. Since that wasn't a part of my plan, I was forced to make another. Was it stupid of me to do? Most likely, but when you've got more to lose than you ever thought possible, you must think outside the box.

"You should watch," my uncle suggests when two women in gold spray-on bikini's announce the first fight is about to commence by prancing around the ring like their knees aren't knocking. "Then perhaps you can give Maddox some tips when he arrives." He bounces his evil eyes between mine. "You've watched him enough times the past year to know his strengths, so you can either help him benefit from that or let him die. The choice is yours."

I don't retort his comment that I've done everything in my power to keep Maddox and his brothers off his radar the past two years, but I do accept his invitation to sit in the seat next to him. I'm shaking so much I can't trust my legs to keep me upright.

Over the next several minutes, the first two fighters keep the men ringside entertained. From what I took in before I diverted my eyes to my feet, the fighters stand at a similar height, and they look as rough and ready as the other. The knowledge they're fairly matched won't have me watching the sickening event unfold, though.

Just knowing one of them will leave the ring in a body bag makes me immensely ill, so I won't mention the sickening crunches and grunts that come from their part of the warehouse over the next forty minutes. It's horrific, although it has nothing on the flip my stomach does when I spot a man who should be far from here entering the west entrance of the warehouse.

"Ha!" my uncle pushes out with a chuckle when he too spots Maddox. "I didn't think you had it in you." He isn't referencing Maddox. He was glaring at me when he said his comment. "Your mother should have taught me otherwise." I don't realize I'm crying until he wipes the salty blobs off my face with a rough scrub and a smile. I hate that my tears are making me look weak, but I'm too shocked to hold them back. "I should have killed her like I did your sister. Alas, I have an addiction for needy brunettes with fuckable lips."

Sister? What sister? I'm an only child, aren't I?

I lose the chance to ask my questions out loud when Maddox arrives ringside three heart-thrashing seconds later. He's dressed to fight in black running shorts and a white sleeveless tank that showcases the cut ridges in his arms. He'll be forced to take off his running shoes if he's here to fight. All parts of his body must bc up for manipulation in the ring.

My uncle tugs me behind him when Maddox's flaring nostrils announce he spotted the marks my face didn't have this morning. He isn't protecting me from Maddox's wrath. He's announcing to Maddox that he will have to cross more than a line to reach me.

"Nine o'clock on the dot. Lucky you weren't a second later. The men are so thirsty, they spent most of the fight watching *her* squirm instead of the bloodbath." My uncle laughs. No one joins in. The derogative way he articulated 'her' would make the hardest criminal grimace.

It takes Maddox working his jaw side to side three times before he can respond. "You said nine o'clock. I don't show up early for anything or anyone." His tone is way too calm for my liking. Not in a million years should he be here. Win or not, he won't walk out of this warehouse the same man. "*Except* her. I would have been here hours ago if it were my choice."

Even though I have no issue reading Maddox's underlying message—he's disappointed I took the decision to fight out of his hands—it won't stop me from trying to persuade him otherwise. "You need to leave." Ignoring my uncle's brutal clutch on my wrist, I step around him so Maddox can feel the urgency beaming out of me without interference. "Go now before it's too late."

His family won't survive my uncle's fury, and neither will I. Maddox loves his family. He wouldn't be the person he is if it weren't for them. I don't want them taken away from him because we create fireworks when we fuck.

"*It's all right,*" Maddox mouths to me like he does his brothers when he thinks no one is looking. "*We will be out of here before you know it.*"

When he winks at me, forever cocky, I sigh. He's walking into this blindly. He has no clue what he's about to face since they removed the deceased man from the ring and mopped up the blood during his race across the dusty warehouse floor.

"Maddox, please—"

"Ten, twenty minutes tops, then you'll never have to come back here."

"Spoken like a man with a bucket-load of confidence." My uncle shrugs before he twists his torso to face the bookmaker. "But cockiness only goes so far in the ring. Put fifty thousand on Igor. I feel like playing the field tonight."

I feel the blood drain from my face. Igor is who the men were bragging about when I was held captive in my uncle's office. He's undefeated in this tournament and known for killing men just for fun.

"Go, Maddox, please," I beg, my voice a roar.

He stumbles backward when I push him, but he doesn't get anywhere near as close to the exit as I'm hoping.

"It's okay." He promises when my wish to force him to leave sees a gun butted to my temple. "I swear to you, it'll be okay."

Droplets of salty water stream down my face when I shake my head. I want to believe him. I want to grant him the trust he so blindly gave me last night, but I can't. The world my uncle rules wasn't made for men like him. It will destroy him long before his time and crush his spirit even quicker than that.

With the crowd on their feet clapping and cheering about the commencement of the feature round, it takes Maddox climbing through the frayed ropes of the ring before our eyes lock and hold. He watches me when the roar of the crowd announces the entrance of his opponent, unfazed about Igor's large frame and killer demeanor. He's tattooed head-to-toe, even his scalp, and he's wearing the white cloth sumo wrestlers regularly don. I heard that's his trademark because he uses his size to crush his opponents to death.

"Don't let him get ahold of you!" I scream to project my voice over the uproarious crowd, adding to my warning by pretending to hug myself. "You need to move fast and time your hits."

I can't believe I'm coaching Maddox like I'm his trainer. Will I be able to do the same when he's killing a man with his bare hands? Or worst, summarizing ways to get him out of the danger zone? I honestly don't know.

After removing his shoes at the referee's request, Maddox jerks up his chin, advising he heard me. It should weaken the knot in my stomach. It doesn't. He isn't warming up his muscles for the exhaustive activity they're about to endure, nor is he prancing around the ring like Igor, feeding off the hype of the boisterous crowd. He's staring at the door he walked through only moments ago like he's hopeful the match will be called off before it begins.

"Protect your face," I scream at the top of my lungs when Igor creeps up on Maddox unaware.

The referee didn't announce the start of the fight.

Igor is just super eager for the bloodbath to begin.

"No!" I scream when Igor's fist collides with the side of Maddox's head so brutally, I'm shocked blood isn't pouring out of Maddox's ear. "Move off the ropes!"

I race for Maddox just as the light inside his head seemingly clicks on. While I'm yanked onto my seat by Mario pulling me back, Maddox ducks, missing Igor's second swing before he slams his fist into his ribs three times with the hope a fractured ribcage will slow him down.

When Maddox's plan comes up trumps, he moves to the other side of the mat. His hands are up, protecting his face, but his eyes continually stray to the door.

Anyone would swear he was waiting for someone to show up.

"I think we underestimated him," my uncle says to the bookie in a low, shallow tone. "He should have gone down after that hit."

After watching the bookie hand over a chunk of money to my uncle he's yet to earn, I shift my focus back to the ring. Igor is marching Maddox's way. He's pissed Maddox got his fists on him once, let alone injured him, and if the murderous gleam in his eyes is anything to go by, he's about to take all his annoyance out on Maddox.

"Aim for his legs!"

Maddox strays his eyes from the door to me, then to Igor before he bobs down low to swipe Igor's legs out from beneath him. Igor's thunderous crack with the canvas sends a collective hiss racing across the room. The shouts grow more rampant when Maddox's fist ramming into Igor's nose is even more brutal than his collision with the springless mat.

"Get up!" my uncle roars at Igor when Maddox's punishment of his face makes him slow to his feet. Unlike the demands of the men seated around the ring cheering for bloodshed, Maddox climbed off Igor after only half a dozen hits. He didn't pummel his face in until his mother wouldn't recognize him.

"Focus!" I demand when Maddox's eyes once again drift to the entryway door.

I don't care if my coaching gets me shot, raped, or any of the other horrible things my uncle is planning for me. If it gets Maddox out of this alive, I'll face the injustice because he won't be *anything* if he doesn't start paying attention to what he's doing. He isn't merely facing a killer in the ring. All the men surrounding him are also murderers.

"No, no, no, no, no!" I scream on repeat when Igor wraps Maddox up in a bear hug.

Igor is so tall, Maddox's feet immediately lift from the canvas. His arms are disabled, so only his head and legs are at his disposal to maneuver out of his attacker's hold.

"Throw your head back. Headbutt him in the nose!" I do the same to Mario when the crowd's shouts become too loud for Maddox to hear me.

When Mario stumbles back with a groan, his hands shooting up to protect his gushing nose, I race for the ropes. "Scramble! Use his woozy head to your advantage," I command when the vibrant shade of red on Maddox's face weakens by a smidge. "You need to bring him down. Make him drop. He is slower when he's closer to the canvas." For professional fighters, the opposite is usually true, but Igor is so large, he can't get any power behind his swings when he's on the floor.

I fight my uncle with as much gusto as Maddox does Igor when I'm pulled away from the ring by my hair. It's wrenched from my scalp, but the pain is barely noticeable. My heart is in too much agony to give a little bit of discomfort any attention. I can't see Maddox, but the horrendous crunches coming from the ring are enough for me to understand what's happening. Someone is being beaten to death, and it's all my fault.

"Let him tap out," I beg my uncle when he throws me onto a chair at the back of the bleachers. "Please. I'll do anything you want. A-a-anything at all."

His smirk would have you convinced I'm a comedian. "Even all these men?"

I drag my eyes over the men surging toward the ringside seats they can't afford. They're enjoying the bloodbath so much they're willing to risk being banned from next month's match for a better view. The number of men who pay top dollar to watch a man be killed is sickening. As far as I'm concerned, that makes them as corrupt and immoral as my uncle, but the knowledge they'll hurt me purely because I'm mafia royalty won't stop me from nodding.

The instant I slipped my uncle's business card out of Maddox's wallet, I signed my death certificate. Maddox's unexpected arrival hasn't changed that. I'm dead no matter what. My agreement to my uncle's terms just means I have to take the long way to hell.

"Please," I try again when I appear to be getting through to him.

My tears aren't convincing him, and neither are the uncontrollable shakes hampering my body. It's the mental calculation he did in his head when it dawned on him how many men were eyeballing me before Maddox arrived. They were hoping he'd be a no-show, so they could have their way with me, and my uncle is planning to cash in their wishes like he's a genie with an unlimited number of wishes.

When a gurgle I've never heard before rumbles in my uncle's chest, I stray my eyes in the direction he's peering. I prepare my stomach for the horrifying image of Maddox lying lifeless in the ring, so you can imagine my absolute shock when the only motionless thing hanging over the edge of the blood-stained canvas is Igor. His head is contorted at a weird angle, and although his eyes are open, they show no signs of life.

I suck in a shaky breath when my eyes finally land on Maddox. He isn't dead. He's barging his way through the crowd flocking him to issue their congratulations. The disdain on his face hardens with every step he takes. He killed a man for me, and now he looks set to murder another.

I should let him. I would if I weren't aware of the repercussions he'd face. There are rules this industry not even I can break. If Maddox kills my uncle, he won't make it out of this warehouse alive. Considering that's been my *only* objective the past twenty-four hours, I have to step between him and my uncle like protecting my family is more important to me than breathing, even when it isn't.

"Well done," my uncle gabbles out, humored by the rage in Maddox's eyes when I stop his charge by splaying my hand across his sweaty, blood-dotted chest. "You beat the beast and made me a bucketload of money."

When he attempts to hand some of that so-called money to Maddox, Maddox shoves it back into his chest, seizes my wrist in a firm hold, then tugs me behind him like my uncle did when he arrived. It's a clear sign to the men circling us that he only fought tonight for one reason. Me.

For the next several long seconds, my uncle gauges the reaction of the men eyeballing his exchange with Maddox like this is the real reason they fork over thousands of dollars every month. Some are enemies, some are allies, but without a doubt, all of them are sick fucks he wants to impress so badly, he goes off-script.

"Very well. You've earned it."

By it, he means me.

After clicking his fingers two times, he digs a gold pen out of the breast pocket of his suit jacket. It's the same pocket he put the boxcutter in that would have claimed his life if it weren't blunt.

"With the holiday season approaching, we have a delay between contests." When the crowd boos, he waves his hand through the air like he's a king. "I know, I know. Cry me a river."

While the crowd laughs as if he is hilarious, my uncle jots down the time and date for Maddox's next deathmatch onto the business card Mario handed him. "You will be forwarded the location the day before the next fight."

This kills me to admit, but my uncle isn't as stupid as he looks. There's no way the death matches could take place in the same location more than once. It's hard enough keeping the authorities away from his standard Friday night feature. I'm sure their interest in this type of circuit would be enough to have it immediately shut down.

My relieved sigh hits Maddox's sweat-drenched neck when he screws up the card within a nanosecond of my uncle handing it to him, tosses it to the ground, then spits on it.

My uncle throws back his head and laughs. I have no clue what he thinks is funny. I'm far from amused, even more so when he swings his eyes to me. I assume he's about to reference something along the lines of my mouth not tasting as sugary as my mother's, but I forget we're in public. He can't share his incest inclinations here.

"Do you truly think one fight gives you unlimited access to my niece? She's mafia royalty. Her blood is worth something." He stares me straight in the face while adding, "As is her cunt." He smirks at the narrowing of my eyes before continuing, "This is a month-to-month agreement." He *tsks* himself before stating again, "Or should I say match-to-match agreement. You have her until the next round. If you win that fight, she's yours again until the next round. And so on, and so on, and so on, until you get so bored of her, you'll beg me to slit her throat."

Maddox's words sound like they're delivered straight from hell when he spits out, "I'm not playing your games, Col." It's a throaty, heated reply that reveals his persona changed the instant he snapped Igor's neck.

"You're not?" My uncle steps up to Maddox until the thrusts of their chests compete for space. "Because to me, it looks as if you walked straight into my trap." His smug grin doubles when he drifts his eyes to the door Maddox was staring at most of his fight. He stares into the pitch-black night, laughing as if he has the world at his feet before he eventually returns his focus to Maddox. "You now know what I'm capable of. Don't underestimate me again."

When he tilts in to whisper something into Maddox's ear, I miss the majority of what he says, but I'm confident it's something along the lines of Maddox being a snitch since 'snitches' was vocalized loud enough for everyone to hear.

The tension in the room turns ghastly when Maddox and my uncle stand across from each other for several long seconds. I want to say something, but I can't get the words out of my mouth. I'm not only shocked by the turn of events tonight, I'm stunned by Maddox bobbing down to collect my uncle's business card from the floor. He doesn't hand it back to him as I'm hoping, he slides it into the pocket of his gym shorts before he heads for the exit that was nearly responsible for his demise. Since he's clasping my wrist, I fall into step behind him.

"I guess we're done?" my uncle says, his tone pompous. "Her cunt is yours until the next round. Who knows whose it will be after that?"

After coming to a dead halt in the middle of the eyeballing crowd, Maddox drags his eyes over my face. His pupils are massively dilated, making his eyes appear as deadly as the South China Sea in the middle of a typhoon, but they darken even more when his baby blues drink in the fresh bruises on my face.

"One last thing," Maddox eventually replies, his voice unlike anything I've ever heard.

Before anyone has time to respond, Maddox releases my wrist from his grip, takes one step back, then plants a perfectly structured right-swung hit to my uncle's cheek. It jolts my uncle back so forcefully, even with Mario always at his six, his tumble to the floor is brutal. He hits the dirty concrete with a grunt so loud, it projects over the shocked hisses of men who have wished to do the same but will *never* have the courage.

"Stay the fuck away from Demi," Maddox snarls over my uncle lying flat on the floor, dazed and confused, and quite possibly knocked out. "I earned *her*, that makes *her* mine."

I've previously said I don't want to be claimed, but I'm okay with it this time around. Maddox killed for me. He went against everything he's ever believed in and turned them on their heads for me.

That makes me his.

With my uncle too bewildered to order otherwise, Maddox regrips my hand, then recommences our exit. Shockingly, it's done without any interference.

I don't see that being the case when my uncle comes to.

18

MADDOX

I killed a man.
Me.

I snapped his neck.

Don't let the simplicity of my statement fool you. His murder wasn't easy by any feat. It isn't like you see in the movies. To snap someone's neck, you have to do more than contort their neck. The body usually follows any twisty movements you do, so you have to torque the neck away from the body before snapping it.

When the body is as big as the brute I was fighting, it would have taken everything I had to do that, so I went for something simpler—an age-old trick. I used force instead. I won't give you all the details. It isn't something that will leave me anytime soon, so I have plenty of time to share, but it also isn't something I want publicly acknowledged.

I didn't have a choice. Demi had a gun pointed at the back

of her head. Her uncle looked seconds away from murdering her, and from what the brute was spurting while crushing me like I was a bug, murder would have been the only kind thing to happen to Demi tonight.

Once he had me wrapped up in a bear hug, he told me how he dibbed Col's seconds, that he was going to rape Demi *after* she was sodomized by her uncle in front of the men surging toward the ring, chanting for more blood.

His confession caused something inside me to snap.

I held off for as long as I could. I tried to be the bigger man, but as I'm learning faster than I care to admit, there are barely any decent men in the world anymore. I put my faith in one far too much tonight, and my hope he was a decent man swung back and hit me square in the face.

I'm riding away from a crime scene with the girl I've had a crush on for over a decade on the back of my bike. Some would say that's a victory. To me, it isn't close to the truth. I should have never been in the predicament I was in. Demi should have never been in the predicament she was in. Yet, we were both there because of one man.

That's all set to change now.

I can't hold in the rage anymore. I can't brush it off with a cocky grin and a couple of well-rehearsed lines. I'm a murderer. Those advantages are no longer mine to use. I can only hope my new title won't change how Demi looks at me because, if it does, I may as well have let my opponent kill me. I was only there for her, just like I'm only here for her now too.

"I need you to wait here, okay?" I say to Demi after parking my bike at the side of a rusted bar on the outskirts of Hopeton.

It's attached to a twenty-four-hour service station that looks like it went out of business in the eighties.

Before Demi can answer me, I lift my shirt to my midsection, stealing her words. She isn't just gawking at my bruised abs, she's stunned into silence by the wires strapped to my chest.

"You were wearing a wire?" she asks after a couple of hearty swallows. "Oh my God, Maddox, if they find out you were wearing a wire, they'll kill you..." The stomping of my boot into the recording device steals the rest of her reply.

The ancient equipment agent Moses wired me with should have been the first indication I was being played. Regretfully, Saint was right when he said I have tunnel vision when it comes to Demi. That was his excuse for keeping us apart this long. He thought it was the only way he could protect me.

If the last twenty-four hours are anything to go by, I hate admitting he was right.

Does that mean I'll go back and let Demi leave when she raced out of the restaurant last night? No fucking chance in hell. My dad fell in love with my mother in under an hour. I think I broke the family record with Demi.

After removing the stolen plates Saint hooked me up with, I dump them into a bin at the side of my bike before cupping Demi's cheeks in my hands. It kills me that her face is more banged up than it was last night. I'm dying to ask her what she endured during our absence, but I can't just yet. If I know the full extent of her injuries, I'll be on track for my second murder tonight.

"No matter what you hear, I need you to stay here, okay?"

She looks like she wants to deny my request, but instead,

she awards me the blind faith I gave her last night when she asked to store Col's card into my wallet. She could have found anything in there—condoms, hotel room receipts. Hell, I'm reasonably sure there are a handful of numbers tucked away for a rainy day in my wallet, yet I gave her unhindered access like I did my cell phone. "Don't be long."

"I won't," I assure her.

It only takes two seconds to kick a man's ass, so Agent Moses should take half that since he isn't close to being a man.

I press my lips to Demi's like they have the power to switch me back from a murderer to an everyday civilian. Although they do lower my anger by a smidge, it isn't enough to alter my plan of attack. I was fucked over tonight, in more ways than one. I can't ignore that.

Old-town blues music blasts into my ears when I push through the swinging door of Charlie's Pub. It isn't the place you'd expect to find a bunch of federal agents. I guess that's why they frequent here. They take up more of the floor space than the regular folks, and the wisdom frustrates me to no end. If they had done their job, my hands wouldn't be stained with another man's blood. They let me down, and the weasel at the back of the group was the main culprit.

"I can explain," Agent Moses blubbers out when I join him at the end of the bar, away from prying eyes. "I took it to my supervisor. He said there wasn't enough to work with. I tried to call you. Your cell rang out."

A fool would believe him.

I'm no fucking idiot.

I only left his side when I commenced the hour commute to

the warehouse where the to-the-death fight was being held. He said a crew was on standby. They were supposed to raid the warehouse before I got close to the ring.

He left me hung out to dry.

Now he's about to be hung by the same wire.

I kick up a barstool in a way Saint would be proud of at the same time I fist Agent Moses's preppy-boy shirt. When the top two buttons in his shirt pop from my brutal clutch, I imagine Demi being grabbed in the same manner. The neckline of her dress goes down to the wire in her bra because her buttons were forcefully removed from her clothing. They're no longer there to fasten.

Acting oblivious to the number of weapons on me, I snarl out, "You said you had a crew in lockdown. I only had to prove the matches were taking place, then you were gonna get us out." Those were the exact words he spoke to me when he flagged me down half a mile out from Dimitri's private residence this afternoon. He said if I knew the location of the fight, he had a way of getting Demi out uninjured.

I stupidly believed him.

That isn't happening this time around.

"You fucked me over, Arrow."

He signals for his fellow agents to stand down before returning his eyes to me. "I called you, Ox. I told you to pull back, that we didn't have the resources. What more could I have done?"

He tries to weasel his way out of my hold like words alone will suffocate my anger. His misjudgment only makes me clutch him even firmer. "A lot more! That's what you *should* have done. I can't come back from this! Demi can't come back from this! You fucking ruined us!"

His terrorized eyes bounce between mine. "What happened to Demi? Did something happen? Did Col *hurt her?*" My stomach gurgles during his last question. Even if I hadn't seen the exchange between Demi and Col in his Audi, his tone ensures I'd never be uncertain as to what his question is referencing.

The genuine concern for Demi in his eyes sees me breaking the barstool over the bar instead of his head. Just like earlier, don't misread my actions. I'm fucking ropeable. I want to beat him until his eyes blacken with death, but my focus needs to be elsewhere right now.

I killed a man to save Demi, but I have no clue if I was too late. Was she hurt before I arrived? The relief in her eyes when I made a beeline for her after breaking the neck of my opponent has me skeptical, but I'll never know if I stay here.

The fret in Agent Moses's eyes when I grabbed him doubles as I end his bullshit with a handful of words. "I'm done. Whatever this is, was, or could have been is done." I clutch his shirt for a few more minutes before I push him away from me with a grunt.

Like a fool not in fear for his life, he straightens his disheveled shirt and tie before he attempts to barter with me, "You need to think about this, Ox. My recommendation will get you in the door. If you don't have it, you may not make it through the initial interview process."

"It's not like the Bureau hires murderers," I mumble before I can stop myself.

Agent Moses replies, but I miss what he says since I'm heading for the door. Even with Arrow demanding for his colleagues to stand down, our exchange has gained too many onlookers for me to feel confident I'll make it out of this bar without handcuffs circling my wrist. Considering Demi's well-being is at the forefront of my mind, I can't let that happen. Not even the manifestation of the badge he's been promising me the past seven months can detract from that.

I work my jaw side to side when Agent Moses halts my exit with a snarled comment. "You either continue doing as requested or face life behind bars."

"Life for breaking the buttons on your shirt?" I ask with a laugh. "Send me your tailor's bill. I'll pay for the repairs."

"You wrecked more than a handful of buttons tonight. An entire family's life was upended in an instant. Perhaps even more than one."

I don't need to spin to know what he's referencing. I can hear the sickening details. The squeak that popped from Demi's mouth when she was dragged away from the ring by her hair. The crack of Igor's neck. His final breath. I hear it all, and it's coming from the direction of the cell phone in Agent Moses's hand.

"Where did you get that footage?" My voice is thick with anger. He could have only gotten that footage two ways. He was either at the event that changed me in an instant, or he knows someone who was. Either way, I'm pissed as fuck he has proof of how far I'll go for a girl some may believe I've only just met.

"Where I got it from isn't the issue." He saunters my way, all pompous and shit. "*Who* I give it to should be your sole concern."

"Being in possession of such evidence and not handing it to the authorities is a crime in itself. If I go down for this, so the fuck will you." I could be way off the mark, but I've got to try something. If I don't, who will defend Demi when her uncle comes to?

When Agent Moses doesn't bother with a reply, acutely aware he has me backed into a corner, I open and close my fists two times before asking, "What do you want?"

"The same deal we already have," he replies without pause for thought. "Just on a bigger circuit."

I scoff, confident my fists won't make him enough coin he's willing to lose himself in the process. There has to be more at play here than I'm seeing.

My inner monologue trails off when a disturbing thought enters my mind. He had images of Demi schmoozing men who lost their lives in the ring. That means he's known of Col's operation for months, and he's done nothing about it. That makes him as corrupt as Col, and in a way, he's partly responsible for my opponent's death tonight. He has the resources to stop Col, yet he doesn't. If that isn't proof I can't trust him, nothing will convince me.

Needing time to work out a plan of attack, I mutter, "You have my number."

Agent Moses bobs his head like a bobble-head toy, unaware I'm not straight-up agreeing with his plans. "You made the right decision, Ox," he shouts as I push through the swinging entry door.

Just as I'm about to round the corner I left Demi on, my path is blocked by a man I'd guess to be mid-twenties with blond hair, a wiry beard, and icy-blue eyes. The fact he steps back in my way when I try to move past him reveals he bumped into me on purpose, much less what he says next, "What happened to your knuckles? They look a little busted up."

Even without him carrying a weapon, I know he's an agent. They have a scent I plan to scrub from my skin the instant I get home. A smell that makes me as pissed as fuck I *ever* thought I wanted to be a part of their operation.

"It's nothing," I reply with a smile, acting as if his narrowed gaze isn't bouncing between my bloody knuckles and swollen cheek. "Some dude was sniffing around my sister. I told him to back off with more than words. I'm sure you'd do the same for your sister."

He lets me sidestep him this time around, but I only make it two steps before a name stops me in my tracks. "Justine?"

After wiping the riled expression off my face, I spin back around to face the unnamed agent. I'm pretty good with faces. If I've seen his before, he must have had plastic surgery. That's how unrecognizable he is.

I jerk up my chin as if my blood isn't boiling. "How do you know Justine?" Since she's the only common denominator we have, I work with it.

"I don't know her," he replies, way too cockily. While smirking at my stunned expression, he digs a photo out of his pocket like it's a portrait of his family, then unfolds it. "I'm just surprised the guy you beat up doesn't have a single mark on his face." He waits for me to absorb Justine sitting across from

Dimitri Petretti in an intimate setting before he adds, "If she were my sister, I wouldn't have let him get that far." When I snatch the long-range photograph out of his hand, he mutters, "You can keep it. I've got plenty more where that came from."

He hits me with a cocky wink before he saunters away. As he breaks through the front entry door, I stumble upon Demi being held up by a tall man with a shiny head. He isn't holding her up with any part of his body. He's talking—a lot.

"I-I-I'm sure," Demi stutters out when I join them next to my bike. "But thank you for the offer."

I picture the horror on my mother's face if she ever discovers what I did tonight when the man in a plaid shirt shifts on his feet to face me. He doesn't say anything, but the look on his face reveals he thinks I'm responsible for the marks on Demi's face. In a way, he's right. If I hadn't fallen into Agent Moses's trap, Demi would have been uninjured, so every mark on her face is my fault.

The agent's Russian accent is thick even with the gun on his hip being government-issued. "Enjoy the rest of your evening."

Demi waits for him to join the other agents in the bar before she updates me on what their conversation was about. "He's a federal agent, Maddox. He wanted to know who hit me and asked if I'd like to press charges." After shoving a card for Special Agent in Charge Tobias Brahn into my hand, she scrubs a hand down her face like it isn't battered. "Jesus. If my uncle finds out I spoke with *anyone* in the FBI, he'll—"

"He won't find out," I assure her, confident the men she thinks are her uncle's enemies aren't. "But you need to be careful who you talk to. It's just you and me, all right? No one else."

Her brutal swallow reveals she understands my underhanded request. I don't want word getting out that I'm a killer.

"I won't tell a soul. You have my word, Maddox."

Some may say I'm a fool for believing her.

I'll tell you it's a Walsh trait.

19

MADDOX

As we reach the road my family cabin is on, I lower the revs of my motorbike. I've taken every back road known, whizzed past the main entrance three times, and rode the last two miles without headlights, hopeful our arrival would occur without fanfare. I should have realized Sloane would detect Demi's presence half a mile out. She barrels down the front stairs of the cabin before we're halfway down the driveway, and even quicker than that, she tugs Demi off my bike before removing her helmet.

"He's dead," Sloane states matter-of-factly after taking in the bruises on Demi's face. "Saint, get my gun. I'm going to fucking kill him."

"You have a gun?" Demi and Saint ask at the same time.

Before Sloane can answer, her focus shifts to the set of keys Caidyn hands me. They were passed over with two overflowing suitcases of clothes. "What's that? Were they clothes? I've told you before, you don't need to pack clothes for a weekend trip. My parents have everything we need at my family's country estate." After bouncing her eyes between a silent Caidyn, Saint, and me, she locks them with Demi's. "We're not going to my family's estate, are we?"

The fact she thinks a couple of days at a country manor is a solution for our predicament shows how little she knows about Demi's family. Saint didn't question me when I requested for him to pack Demi's things. Caidyn was a little more vocal, but more on the location of our hideout than the fact we need to bunker down while planning our next move.

Gratitude smacks into me when Demi slips her hand into mine before she tilts into my side. I thought seeing me kill a man would have her pulling away, not drawing closer. I'm as grateful as fuck it seems as if nothing has changed. "Maddox and I need to get away for a couple of days." She wets her dry lips before forcing out a set of words I'm certain will hurt her friend but must be said. "I want to go with him. I feel safe with him. He will protect me."

"Okay," Sloane replies, her one word groggy. "Then why don't we come with you guys? We can pretend we're ranchers living off the land. I've got my boots. I'll go grab them. Anything else we need, I'll buy on the way."

Demi stops her dart up the stairs by shooting her hand out to caress her arm. She doesn't speak. She doesn't need to. Her best friend can see the pleas in her eyes, so I won't mention the constant shake of Saint's head.

With her lower lip protruding, Sloane asks, "Can we at least text?"

Demi throws her arms around her neck and hugs her tight. "Every single day. I promise."

While she adds additional words to her pledge, I jerk my head to the side, wordlessly requesting an impromptu Walsh family meeting. We're missing Landon, but considering he'd spend the next three hours lecturing me on responsible decision-making, I'd rather he be absent. I don't have time to burn.

"Has Mom and Dad gone to the Four Seasons?" Our parents have had a timeshare in a two-bedroom condo for over a decade. They usually only visit in the summer, but Saint has the gift of the gab. He convinced them there's no such thing as too many vacation days.

Saint lifts his chin. "And Landon promised to take Justine back to school this morning, but I still have a bad feeling about this." He joins me near the trunk of his car. "Running won't change anything. If you made a deal with Dimitri, then go against it, you'll have *all* sides coming at you."

"I don't have much choice, Sebastian. I can't stay here." The fact I use his real name exposes how blurry my head feels.

"Why not?" Caidyn intervenes, unaware of the full story. He knows I fought tonight, but he has no clue it was a death-match. None of my brothers do. I kept that snippet of information solely between Demi and me. Well, so I thought. My altercation with Agent Moses this evening exposed tonight there's a massive leak in my boat.

With my head still in the disbelief stage of my remorse, I give a less murderous excuse for my cowardice. "I hit Col Petretti. It wasn't a fairy tap. I'm reasonably sure I knocked him out." For the first time in my life, my voice doesn't have an ounce of cockiness to it. "I think I broke his nose."

Saint hisses out a cuss, whereas Caidyn straight up shouts his. Their responses expose I was right to hold back all the details of my night. If they think hitting a mobster is bad, imagine their reaction when I tell them I killed a man.

Although I'm riddled with guilt that I ended someone's life, there's no denying the truth. "He was hurting Demi. I had to stop him."

Caidyn freezes with his hand suspended mid-air. "He didn't... it wasn't like..." He does a movement with his hands that shouldn't speak on his behalf, but somehow does. "Right?"

The lost expression on Saint's face exposes Caidyn kept matters we discussed last night under wraps. I'm not surprised he didn't rat me out. He's good like that.

"He didn't do... *that*," I answer, gritting my teeth. "But if I hadn't arrived, there were no guarantees. It was fucking horrific." When the crack my opponent's neck made replays in my head, I involuntarily shiver. "I couldn't make the shit up I saw tonight."

Mistaking the shakes of my body as me being cold, Saint tugs off his jacket and hands it to me. "Maybe talk to Dimitri? Things aren't tight with him and his father. He may help you if it benefits him."

"Maybe," I parrot, my head too muddled to think of a better reply. "But for now, I need to get her off her uncle's radar." I shift on my feet to face Demi during the 'her' part of my comment. She's still talking to Sloane, but I feel her eyes constantly drifting to me. I don't know exactly what her plan was when she ran this morning, and in all honesty, I don't want to know because if it's anything like I'm thinking, I would have made the scratch in Col's neck an inch deeper. I'm not a killer, but I'd kill again for Demi without a single thought crossing my mind.

When the innocence in Demi's eyes prompts me on what my family meeting was about, I dig the photograph I snatched out of the blond agent's hand earlier tonight before thrusting it in Saint's chest. Justine's welfare isn't solely his responsibility, but since he seems to know a heap more about Dimitri than he's letting on, I'll pretend as if it is.

"When was this?" Saint's voice is as rough as mine, his suspicion just as high.

"I don't know. I was planning to ask you the same thing."

Caidyn gives me a look, warning me to tread carefully but remains as quiet as a church mouse.

"Why the fuck would I know they went on a date?" Saint asks when my glare becomes too much for him to bear. "They could be friends."

"Friends? *Right.* 'Cause we all look at our friends like that..." My words trail off when I tap on Dimitri's face in the obvious surveillance image. He isn't looking at Justine like I do Demi. She's getting more attention from the men surrounding her than Dimitri.

What the fuck?

Caidyn unearths the reason for my quiet when he peers down at the photograph Saint is clutching for dear life. "Leave it with me," he says a couple of seconds later. When I attempt to fire off an objection, he shifts my focus back to Demi. "You've got more pressing matters to deal with than who our little sister dines with." With the photograph shoved into his pocket and his hands on my shoulders, he guides me to Saint's ride. "Get her out of here before they come looking."

I fucking hate that we're running like cowards, but sometimes running is the only solution.

Halfway into the driver's seat, I call Demi's name. When I'm awarded her eyes, I nudge my head to the passenger door Saint is holding open for her. "Are you ready?"

After nodding, she hugs Sloane like it could be the last time she'll see her, then she does the same to my brothers. It's stupid of me to feel jealous, so I won't mention it.

"Look after him, Demi," I hear Caidyn say a mere second before he closes the passenger door of Saint's car, trapping Demi and me inside. "He isn't the only brother I have, but he's the only one I like."

His mumbled comment swipes the uncomfortableness of our departure. It seems as if we're going on vacation instead of hiding from a man who will torture me for hours before killing me, or worse, force me to watch him do the same to his niece.

"It's really nice out here," Demi mumbles on a yawn when I pull Saint's car into the driveway carved along a mountain an hour out of Ravenshoe. "Has your family owned it for long?"

"This cabin doesn't belong to my family. A friend of Caidyn's said we could stay here as long as we need."

"Oh." Heat flashes across her cheeks like she suddenly feels stupid. "That's smart. We probably shouldn't stay somewhere associated with your family."

Hating that she feels responsible for anything happening, I gather her hand in mine, raise it to my mouth, then press a kiss on the edge of her palm. "My brothers aren't walking into this blindly, Demi. They know everything."

She forcefully swallows. *"Everything?"*

With the ground dewy because of the late hour, it's foolish of me to remove my eyes from the dirt road. I wouldn't if I didn't think my comfort was more vital to Demi than air in her lungs.

After tracking my index finger down her bruised cheek and across her plump lips, I mutter, "They know enough to know we made the right decision to get away for a couple of weeks. I'll tell them the rest when the time is right."

As much as I'd like to shelter her from her uncle's world forever, I don't see how I can do that and remain sane. My family is so close, I often forget we don't come as a package deal.

I park Saint's car next to the wood cabin's front porch before switching off the ignition. "How about we talk about this more in the morning? I'm wrecked." Emotionally more than physically, but I keep that to myself.

When Demi nods, I jog around to open her car door. I lost a part of who I am tonight, but that doesn't mean the morals my parents instilled in me are forgotten. I can still be a gentleman.

"Thank you," she whispers, shocked by my chivalry but also pleased.

Her bewilderment discloses I made the right decision putting her first. She's never been given a single thing without an expectation attached to it. Not even the hours she put in at

Petretti's Restaurant were compensated. Col has her convinced even things that should be given willingly come at a cost—even love.

I'm just praying like fuck that isn't the only reason she's here. I killed for her, but it wasn't because I want something in return. I did it in compensation for the years she was in the ring, fighting alone. I protected her from a bully once. From what I learned from Dimitri earlier today, she kept my family off her uncle's radar for years.

My reimbursement is far from over.

How could it be when it's only just begun?

20

DEMI

My mouth falls open when I walk into the cabin hand in hand with Maddox. It isn't the two-bedroom wood cabin that popped into my head when Maddox said it was secluded and off the grid. It has a large porch with a swinging chair hanging at one end. The grand staircase is the pièce de résistance of the entryway, and several carved wooden doors sprout off it in all directions. It's breathtaking. I just wish we were here under different circumstances.

I feel as if I've been forced through a grinder, so I can only imagine how Maddox feels. My father kept me out of the 'family' business as much as possible during my childhood. Excluding the bullies who were happy to announce their dislike of my surname, I had no idea where everyone's anger stemmed from. I thought it was jealousy-based since Dimitri was extremely popular with the female half of his school, but it only took minutes after my father's death to learn otherwise.

When I was called to the principal's office, I thought I was there to be congratulated for explementary attendance and grades. My every hope vanished when I entered Mr. Hardy's office. There weren't just two police officers in attendance, my uncle was there as well. Although I rarely interacted with him, there was no denying the gleam in his eyes. His brother was dead, and he knew all too well that his sister-in-law was incapable of taking care of a child.

The commencement of the downfall of my relationship with my uncle occurred when I begged Mr. Hardy to call child services. Like any teenager, I had heard horror stories of children in foster care, but I would have been free the instant I turned eighteen. My uncle doesn't give a single thing without expecting reimbursement for it. Just a roof over my head for four years would have seen me in his debt for the rest of my life. I didn't want that. I wanted a life far *far* away from him, so I did what every teenager would have done. I begged.

Mr. Hardy did the right thing when he went against my uncle's wishes by calling family services. I thought I had it all figured out. I should have paid more attention when my mother spoke about her brother-in-law.

I didn't last longer than a week in the foster families assigned to me. I was the perfect child. I rose before the sun to prepare breakfast for my host family, cleaned, cooked, and babysat the children younger than me, but without fail, I'd arrive home from school Friday afternoon to discover my bags packed and a child services agent waiting for me.

I would have continued shifting from place to place for the next four years if Dimitri's friend hadn't advised me my room would be right next to Dimitri's. "He's a light sleeper," he promised. "He hears everything."

Rocco Shay had a bad reputation, but there was nothing but unvoiced promises in his eyes that afternoon. Putting my faith in him could have ended disastrously, but for the most part, it worked in my favor. The first time I was slapped by Col was years after I was placed under his guardianship. It was also the very same day Dimitri moved out.

"Do you know if they have a first-aid kit?"

Maddox stops partway to the kitchen before he floats his eyes over my face.

"It isn't for me," I whisper. "It's for you."

"I'm fine." He stops, shakes his head like dry blood isn't pooling out of one of his ears, then starts again. "I will be fine."

When he recommences our trek to the kitchen, I dig my heels into the plush carpet. "Please. I want to take care of you..." When he attempts to interrupt me, I talk faster, "... like you did me."

Several seconds pass in silence. It isn't awkward. There's too much chemistry crackling in the air to represent anything close to awkward.

The knot in my stomach loosens its grip when Maddox mutters a couple of seconds later, "If you're doing this to get into my panties, you are off the hook. I'm not a third-date type of guy."

He jokes when he's snowed under, but I'd rather it than him completely closing off.

"I'm not trying to get into your panties," I reply, struggling not to smile. "I'm hoping it will get you into mine."

Needing to occupy my hands before I fist his blood-dotted shirt and drag him toward the closest bedroom, I enter the kitchen, praying like hell the heat from the fireplace roaring in the living room doesn't stretch to the back of the house, or I'm about to combust. That's how hot Maddox's grin makes my veins.

My eyes drift from my empty plate to Maddox when he asks, "Do you want to talk about what happened tonight?"

I've been anticipating his question for the past several hours. I could tell he was holding back when I cleaned his bruised and scuffed knuckles before dabbing them with antiseptic ointment, and the evidence was still apparent when we worked side by side in the kitchen to make another one of our famous early breakfasts. He has a knack for waiting until the time is right to commence an interrogation. I'm less hostile when I am overcome with tiredness.

"What do you want to know?" When a panicked glint darts through his hooded gaze, I wet my dry lips. "He didn't touch me. N-not in the way you're thinking."

"Has he previously?"

His exhale fans my cheek when I shake my head. As I said previously, my uncle's inappropriateness is at an all-time high right now. He's hinted about hurting me many times, but he's never followed through as he made out he would this weekend.

The ache in my chest reduces when Maddox treks his finger

across the fresh welt on the side of my face. "What was this about?"

"I... ah..." I pause, unsure how I can explain I tried to kill a man without making it seem as if I'm a murderer in the making. I guess I shouldn't worry since Maddox asked the question. He may have ended Igor's life, but he isn't close to being a killer, so I'm sure he'll understand.

I begin to wonder if I was sucked into a time warp when Maddox reads the truth from my eyes like we've been a couple for years. "You scratched Col's neck?"

"It wasn't supposed to be a scratch. The boxcutter was blunt," I confess before I can stop myself. After a quick swallow to moisten my throat, I say, "I took it out of Caidyn's Jeep. I thought if I dealt with my uncle first, you wouldn't have to, but I probably made matters worse. The boxcutter had Caidyn's firm printed on it."

"Ah."

I wait for him to elaborate. When he doesn't, I blurt out, "Ah? That's it? I confessed my biggest, darkest secret, and all you say is 'ah.'"

Maddox laughs like our conversation is nowhere near as serious as it is. "I wasn't leaving you hanging. I was just taking a moment to absorb how kickass you are." He scoops my hand in his, then tugs me to his side of the sofa. "You went against your blood for me. I fucking love that."

"You won't when he bites back. Col has been at this years longer than us. He knows what he's doing." Maddox shrugs like my worry has no steam. "We can't go into this blind, Maddox. I won't allow your family to be affected by this."

"I know," Maddox replies without the slightest bit of hesitation in his tone. "That's why I'm not worried."

My chest thrusts up and down when he pulls me to sit on his lap. He's been unusually quiet the past three hours. It's understandable. He was pushed to the brink, and although his body came out of the carnage relatively unscathed, I can't say the same for his insides. The Walsh brothers are protective, cocky, and extremely lovable, but that isn't where their skills end. They're also master crafters at hiding their emotions.

The fact Maddox waited years to make a move is proof of this. Only days ago, I had no idea my crush was mutual.

After slinging my arms around Maddox's neck, I lower my forehead to rest against his. His eyes are so dilated, I can see my cut cheek and swollen eye in his pupils. Lucky for me, they're barely noticeable through the admiration shining in them. Tonight should have torn us apart, but for some strange reason, it made us even closer.

"Do *you* want to talk about what happened tonight?"

Maddox takes a moment to consider my question before he shakes his head. I'm disappointed, but I am also aware it will take more than an offer to listen to get him to open up.

"When you are, I'll be right here, ready to catch you."

The past thirty-six hours seem like barely a blip on the radar when he jerks up his chin. To most, my offer would be worthless, but to Maddox, it's priceless.

The tension in the air shifts to lust when Maddox mutters out a couple of seconds later, "But until then, how shall we occupy our time?"

I twist my lips like the innuendo in his tone has no meaning.

It also conceals the fact it's three in the morning. "We could play a board game?" While fighting to hide my grin at the disappointment crossing Maddox's face, I wave my hand over the stack under the coffee table. Once I'm certain his frustration is at a pinnacle, I add, "I've heard naked Twister is a lot of fun."

"We can't keep doing this," I push out breathlessly when my overstretch for the red dot sees Maddox and me tumbling to the floor in a twisted mess of hands, lips, and tongues. "If we want any chance of making it out of the carnage unscathed, we need to add words in between the sex and flirting."

I'm telling him we should stop at the same time I'm yanking his shirt out of his trousers. I'm dying to scrub my hands over the bumps in his midsection before dropping them to the much larger one sitting behind the zipper in his pants.

Much to Maddox's disgrace, we fought our attraction as long as we could. I'm unsure whether I should be pleased or disgusted to announce we lasted a measly twenty minutes.

"Do you want me to stop? If you want me to stop, say so right now, Demi. I'll stop as soon as the 's' leaves your mouth." Maddox slips a hand under my shirt and bra, groaning when he feels how budded his gravelly tone made my nipples. "It'll fuckin' kill me, but I'll do it. I will stop this right now if that's what you want."

I answer him by tugging his pants down to his knees. "Sweet Lord," I whisper to myself when his cock springs free from his trunks. I felt it in all its glory a little over twenty-four hours ago, but it's thicker now, angrier.

Spirals of pleasure coil around me when I crawl down Maddox's body at a slow, teasing pace. He made sure he landed on the floor, so I wouldn't be crushed by him when my elbow began to wobble, so I have unimpeded access to his delicious body.

"Oh, fuck, Demi. I don't know if I should let you do that," Maddox says as he wets his suddenly bone-dry mouth. "I'm no longer wearing any trunks, but my family's reputation is still at stake."

I kiss the sixth, seventh, and eighth bump in his stomach before I drop my lips to the cropped blond hairs spread across his pelvis. "You're not going to do a Flint or a Ramsey because you can't come in your pants if you do it in my mouth."

He falls back onto the Twister mat with a groan before throwing a hand over his snap-shut eyes. Worry would blast through me if I weren't confident he wants this as bad as me.

"You'll want to watch this," I parrot, speaking the words he said to me when he made me ride his face. "Everything is better when you witness it firsthand."

I don't wait for his heated gaze to warm my face before swiping my tongue across the slit in the crest of his cock. I devour him without the slightest bit of hesitation. Talking can wait. My desire to taste him for the first time cannot.

"Fuck me," comes out of Maddox's mouth in a husky groan when I take his dick between my lips for the very first time. "This is even better than in my dreams." He props his elbows onto two different colored spots before he raises his ass off the mat.

He didn't change his position so he can feed his impressively thick shaft in and out of my mouth. He did it to ensure he can see exactly how far I take his cock down my throat.

"Fuck, Demi, fuck," he curses when his engorged knob reaches the very back of my throat. "You can't be as insanely sexy as you *and* know how to deep throat. You've got to give the competition something to strive for."

His praise has me taking him into my wet, heated mouth faster. The strain it causes my cheeks is almost unbearable, but I soldier on, determined to show chemistry will always outrank skill level. I wasn't eager to return the favor of my previous sexual partners since they mostly left me high and dry. I can't use that excuse with Maddox. He's brought me to climax more times than I've climaxed in my entire sexual history.

Suck after suck, I take him deeper and deeper. The moans simpering from his mouth encourage my relentless pursuit. I flatten my tongue, swivel it around his knob, and trace it along the veins feeding his magnificent cock over and over again until his balls draw in close to his body.

I'm wet just from the way he watches me drive him to the brink one needy suck at a time, so I won't mention how delicious he tastes. This isn't supposed to be about me. I want to thank him for what he did and express that I'll completely understand if he wants to take it all back once he realizes exactly *what* he did. I won't hold it against him at all. Just the past two nights of freedom make up for a lifetime of injustices.

My nipples pucker against my lace bra when the salty goodness pumping out of Maddox's cock thickens. He's close to the edge, and I'm about to take him there.

"What..." I push out in disbelief when he withdraws his cock from my mouth just as the veins keeping it hard match the frantic rhythm of the throb of my clit.

"I want to be inside of you when I come." Maddox pounces to his knees, flips me over, arches my back, then enters me from behind.

I call out. Screaming my only response since I have nowhere to grab, and I'm being filled by a dick that deserves an upstanding applause. With my hands slippery from the heat bouncing between Maddox and me and the Twister mat being made out of plastic, I'm going down no matter how hard I fight. The floor gets closer with every brutal pump Maddox does, but I keep the knowledge of my soon-to-be collision to myself, preferring to die being fucked like I never thought possible than stop him now.

"You... oh God... yes..." I say through frantic breaths when Maddox grips my throat. His hold isn't close to painful, but since he had to weave his arm through the gulley of my breasts to do it, I'm no longer concerned about faceplanting onto the hard floor. He has me. He has me so fucking good. "Oh God... oh. I'm going to come."

I power through the sheer insanity engulfing me when Maddox grunts out, "Good, 'cause I'm right-fucking-there with you."

He pumps into me over and over again until my screams turn earthshattering, then he buries himself balls deep, grunts my name, and spills his load inside of me.

21

DEMI

I stare at the bathroom door, unsure whether I should knock or not. Maddox has been in the shower for the past thirty minutes. For someone like Sloane, that isn't a big deal. She only ever leaves the bathroom once the water runs cold. But for Maddox, a man who was pushed to the absolute brink long before I took his dick between my lips, it seems a little obsessive.

He was handling things better than expected. We ate, talked a little, then we fucked like what happened last night wasn't real. Even with the hour being early, I was hoping to get back to the talking part of our recovery, but Maddox's phone had other ideas. He had only just finished cleaning his cum from the inside of my thighs when it buzzed on repeat. Since it was barely five in the morning, I encouraged him to answer it, panicked it might have been important.

The expression on Maddox's face when he read his messages revealed that was wrong of me to do, but instead of telling me the reason for the deep groove between his brows, he announced he was going to take a quick shower.

You know the story from there.

I could ask him through the door if he's okay, but that seems a little impersonal, especially considering he's the only person who truly knows me since he was forced to walk in my shoes only hours ago. Furthermore, the battle he's facing is solely my fault, so shouldn't I be the one to guide him through it?

Confident that is the case, I exhale a big breath, then push down on the handle.

"M-Maddox?" I hate the stutter his name is delivered with, but it can't be helped. I'm genuinely petrified my uncle has forced him to become a shadow of himself. It didn't seem like that when we fooled around on the Twister mat, but what else could be the cause for his unusually long shower? "If you stay in the shower much longer, you'll turn into a prune."

The cabin's water heater must be massive. There's enough steam to assure me the water pumping out of the showerhead is still scalding. It takes three lengthened strides to part the steam enough to spot Maddox in the shower, and when I do, my heart sinks to my feet. He's seated on the floor, his back is resting on the marble tiles, his head is flopped backward, and his eyes are closed. The knuckle-busted hand he gripped my throat with earlier to save me from tumbling to the floor is resting on his bare thigh, and it's uncontrollably shaking.

Even with his hands being pelted by a healthy spray of water, they're more battered than they were only an hour ago. I'd say his new welts are complements to the grout brush dumped next to his thigh. Its white bristles are stained with blood and flecks of skin.

"Maddox..." If there weren't a massive groove between his reddish-blond brows, I could pretend he's fallen asleep. Unfortunately for all involved, I know that isn't the case. "Is everything okay?"

When he pops open his eyes, the pain in them cuts through me like a knife.

He's hurting—badly.

Past pretending this is okay, I tug off the jeans I placed on before we ate, throw open the glass shower door, then step into the steam-filled space. I hiss through the shock of the high temperature of the water while moving Maddox's hands off his thighs. Once I have them at his sides, I straddle his lap, curl my arms around his stiff shoulders, then bury my head into his neck. Even with him remaining as stiff as a board, I hold him tightly while repeating for him to breathe through the dread crushing him.

This is the exact reason I ran yesterday. The Walshs have a reputation, but it isn't one built on fear. Their parents raised them with respect, values, and love. That makes them incapable of killing without feeling an ounce of remorse.

"It'll be okay," I whisper into his neck, my lips quivering. "I promise you, I will make things right."

I'm anticipating for it to take more than a few measly words to drag Maddox off the edge he's precariously dangling on, so you can picture my utter bewilderment when he tugs me in closer after banding one of his arms around my back. He draws me in until my chest is flat against his and his nose is buried into my hair.

When I tug the ponytail holder out of my hair, wanting absolutely nothing between us, his exhale ruffles more than my partially soaked locks. It kickstarts my heart as well. He should hate me for what I forced him to endure. He should despise me on sight. Instead, he acts as if I'm the only person capable of saving him.

"I'll make this right, Maddox. I'll fix the mistakes I made."

We sit in silence for several long minutes. It hurts knowing he's hurting, but it also feels good that he can accept my comfort without it making him feel weak. Only brave men are in touch with their emotions. The others are usually the villains of the story.

"He had a family," Maddox confesses a short time later, his voice croaky and distant. "A wife and daughter."

I pull back, the pain in his words too profound to disregard. "You didn't have a choice."

"His daughter is only three. She's a baby."

"You didn't have a choice," I echo, my words spaced by big, determined breaths. "If you hadn't done what you did—"

"He would have hurt you." I nearly shake my head, but his next confession steals more than words from my mouth. They pinch my resolve as well. "He was married, his wife gave him a daughter for fuck's sake, so why did he torment me with how he was going to rape you?"

I knew there was more to his snapped response than first perceived.

Now I know what it was.

Maddox didn't just protect me from one monster. He went against an entire warehouse of beasts.

"Igor tormented you because he wasn't you, Maddox. He knew the difference between good and bad, but he didn't care. He had no morals... *none*. He killed because he wanted to. You did it because you *had* to. It was you or him..." When he shakes his head, I talk faster. "It *was* you or him, and you made the right choice when you picked you. He was a monster, so for all we know, you could have saved his daughter from a lifetime of suffering."

In an instant, it is as if a lightbulb switches on in his head. I don't know if my words switched it on or my bruised face. Whatever it is, it clears the remorse in his eyes even quicker than it lowers the severity of the groove between his brows.

"She could have been you," Maddox whispers as his eyes float over my face. "She was his blood, but your uncle proves that doesn't matter to those men. They take what they want, and they don't give a fuck about who they hurt in the process."

When he briefly touches the marks on my face like he did earlier in the car, a tear topples down my cheek. I hadn't thought about Igor's daughter's life replicating mine during my reply. I was merely trying to ease Maddox's guilt. But when I truly think about it, he's right. Anytime I saw Igor's wife, her chin never left her chest. I thought she was shy. Now I feel like an idiot. Keeping quiet on abuse is almost as bad as being an abuser.

If Igor hurt the woman he apparently loved, how cruel was he to the girl he was told he must love? I never doubted my dad loved me, but he loved my mother more. You can't choose your family. You're stuck with whomever you get. My relationship with my uncle is sure-fire proof of that.

"One man's life ended tonight, Maddox, but so many more were most likely saved... including yours, the most important of them all."

He chipped away a massive chunk of concrete from my heart on a freeway two nights ago when he told me I mattered. Now I've done the same for him. There's just one difference. I truly believe what I am saying. I wouldn't be who I am if I hadn't occasionally pretended to be a Walsh during my youth. I was too flabbergasted by Maddox to want to be his sibling. I simply wanted to be a part of something that mattered.

Maddox made my wish come true when he stood up for me in the second grade, then he completely knocked it out of the park when he took care of me while I cried. He didn't do that because he felt obligated, he was there for me because he wanted to be.

Confusion blasts through Maddox's greenish-blue eyes when I say, "I was wrong to run. I thought you wouldn't get hurt if I left, that there was no way you'd miss me since we had only been together the one time. In the end—"

"You hurt me more?"

It takes everything I have not to let my tears fall when I nod.

Maddox gives me a moment to compose myself before he confesses, "You didn't physically hurt me, Demi. You hurt me here." He gathers my hand in his before he places it over his chest. "I had no clue where you were or what he was doing to you." His eyes float over my face as he says, "He did *that* in less than five minutes. You were gone for hours." I choke when he chokes. "I thought he had—"

I kiss him before he can say another word. It's stupid of me to do. Things are tense, and he's baring his soul to me, but I can't take another second of wondering what went through his head when he walked into his empty room. It kills me thinking about how things could have ended if he hadn't found Igor's weak spot, so I can only imagine the torment he endured during our nine-hour separation.

"Forgive me," I beg over his kiss-swollen lips after kissing him senseless. "I ran because I thought things were moving too quickly, that you'd be better off without me. I was wrong. Things may be new between us, but they were—"

"Years in the making," Maddox interrupts, soothing the pain of my aching heart with four little words.

"Yes. Perhaps even decades." As my eyes dance between his, I nod. "A second feels like an hour when I'm with you, but it felt even longer when we were apart. I promise to remember that the next time I get scared."

"I'd rather you not be scared." I nuzzle into his hand when he curls it over my unbruised cheek. "But I understand I haven't given you much choice." When confusion blasts through my eyes, he treks his finger across my lips. "You saw me kill a man. It's understandable you'd look at me differently."

The confusion on my face jumps onto Maddox's when I shake my head. "I didn't see what happened. I was behind the bleachers." He sucks in a relieved breath that is quickly withdrawn when I add, "But even if I had, I wouldn't have looked at you any differently. You're not him, Maddox. You're not a selfish prick." I'm not against using his words on him if it helps him see sense through the madness. "He hates from the get-go. You do the opposite."

He angles his head to the side, his smile too content for someone whose sanity was hovering above extinction only minutes ago. "Are you saying what I think you're saying? Are you implying that I... I—"

"No, that isn't close to what I'm saying." It is, but it's way too soon to let my ridiculous notions speak for themselves. "I'm just saying your wired differently than the men in my uncle's industry. In a better way." My last sentence is pushed out in a hurry from the raising of Maddox's brow. "I don't want you to *ever* become like them. It would kill me to see you like that."

"I won't ever become them, Demi."

"How can you be so sure?" I ask like there was no actuality in his tone.

He pulls me in closer until it seems as if not even my soaked shirt is between us before he replies, "Because I have you, and they never will."

22

MADDOX

For the past six days, I've awoken coated in sweat. It's winter, so I shouldn't be as sweaty as I am. It just seems to be one of the penalties for being a murderer. Some mornings, I wake up on the verge of screaming. Others, I stare at the ceiling, wondering what went through Igor's head in the seconds leading to his death. Did he know he was about to die? Or was he as shocked as me I could end someone's life?

No matter how I wake, every single morning without fail, Demi is at my side, promising me it will be okay. She's never once made me feel guilty about what I did. She barely brings up that night almost a week ago. She just curls her arms around my sweat-drenched body, burrows her head into my neck, then reminds me to breathe through the torment tearing me in two with shallow, perfectly-timed breaths.

That isn't happening this morning because I haven't awoken in a cold sweat. I'm clutching a tattooed hand, squeezing it so tightly, I'm certain I am seconds from breaking several bones. I don't know if it was instincts that woke me in the middle of the night or the fact I'll never truly settle until Col is dead, but whatever it is, I'm glad I stopped the stranger before his hand got to within an inch of Demi's cheek. She promised me she's never been touched sexually against her wishes before, and I want to keep it that way.

The breathy chuckle of the man who almost got within touching distance of Demi reveals he isn't a threat, much less the words he whispers, "If you think I'm gonna hurt your girl, you obviously haven't heard the stories about me."

Rocco was only released from prison a few months back. He was serving a second seven-year sentence for manslaughter. Why such a small sentence for such a horrendous crime, you ask? His first 'murder' was in defense of his mother. He was only fifteen and walked in on his father beating his mother to within an inch of recognition. His second stint was when his sister attracted the same type of scumbag as their mother.

Some people say his reduced sentences were thanks to his friendship with Dimitri. I'm not so quick to jump onto that bandwagon. The judge assigned to both of Rocco's cases came from an abusive background. He understood that sometimes the only way you can end the domestic violence cycle is with a bullet. He couldn't exactly say that to Rocco, but everyone knew what he was thinking when he sentenced him to seven years behind bars with eligibility for parole in three. He was an adult during his last three court appearances, but he didn't have the book thrown at him. People can be excused for being a little fucked up when they come from a childhood like that.

Rocco's misdemeanors are easily brushed off, and so are Demi's.

"Wanted to see the damage firsthand," Rocco informs while taking in the rapidly healing marks on Demi's face. Compared to what they once were, they're barely noticeable. "Dimi's decision makes sense now." His words are barely whispers, but they're loud enough to send an involuntary shiver rolling up Demi's spine. She whimpers in her sleep before she rolls onto her hip, her hand instinctively moving to find me under the sheets. We've only been hiding out for just under a week, but it truly seems as if we've been together half a lifetime.

After tossing the sleeping pants Demi pushed down my thighs with greediness last night into my face, Rocco nudges his head to the door leading to the living room, wordlessly requesting to have a word out of Demi's earshot.

Curious as to what he meant about Dimitri's decision, I jerk up my chin. Rocco does one quick final sweep of Demi's face before he gives us some privacy. After tugging on my pants under the sheets, I push Demi's hair back from her face, then whisper in her ear that I'm going to grab a glass of water.

Her eyes pop open in an instant. "Are you okay?" The hand she crept across the bedding to find me unknowingly traces the bumps in my midsection. She isn't teasing me. She's seeking hints of the nightmare that usually clings to my skin long after I've awoken.

"I'm fine." I inwardly curse before correcting myself, "I'm thirsty as fuck. Thought I better replenish some of the fluids you sucked from me last night in case you feel the need to suck me dry again in the morning." When I hit her with a frisky wink, her smile shines brighter than the moon peeping through the cracks in the wooden shutters. She doesn't just hold me when I'm reminded how far I'll go for her, she occupies my thoughts in a way only she can. "Go back to sleep. I'll only be a minute."

My nostrils flare when I lean across to press a kiss to her temple. Our hook-up last night occurred in the shower, but the location did little to lessen the smell of my skin on hers. It's an intoxicating scent I'd strive to recreate if I knew there wasn't a mass murderer waiting in the living room for me.

I wait for Demi's breathing to indicate she's asleep before slipping out of bed. Even knowing Rocco is rarely seen without a gun, I ball my fists before entering the living room. I hate that he found us so easily, but I'm not surprised. I saw Dimitri's hacker's skills firsthand. He unearthed the location of the death-match within a couple of keystrokes.

My arrival in the living room reveals even mass murderers still have integrity. It gives me hope I didn't completely fuck up my life last week. "How are you handling things, Ox? Bet it took a lot to stop at one hit."

I had wondered if news was circulating about me striking Col.

Now I know without uncertainty.

Although Rocco's smug expression is stroking my ego, I get down to business. "What decision did Dimitri make?"

"That's it?" Rocco replies with a laugh. "You're just gonna leave me hanging without any details. Not cool, man, not fuckin' cool." As he rubs his hands together, his lips curve into a mammoth grin. "Dimitri has kept your runs local, then you'll be close by for Demi..."

"And?" I ask when his question seems unfinished.

"And..." I don't know if he has a barbell in his tongue or if he just likes swishing it around his mouth when he's teasing. Whatever it is, I wish he'd get to the fucking point. I've got packing to do. If Dimitri has located us, it will only be so long before Col's crew comes knocking. "... you won't have any issues competing in the comps each Friday night."

"I can't fight for Dimitri, Rocco. His father is a part-owner of that comp."

He *tsks* me as if I'm being eccentric. "Dimitri has it handled."

"*Handled?*" I scoff. "How the fuck is that handled?" I point to the room Demi is sleeping in. "*His* cousin was assaulted by *his* father!"

"Yet, you're still breathing after making Tweetie birds fly around his head," he fires back. "Do you think that was by chance?" He doesn't wait for me to answer him. "Smith found your hideout in under two minutes. If Dimitri hadn't intervened, Col's men would have arrived a day or two after that." When my confusion remains paramount, he pulls off the Band-Aid in one quick motion. "Your brother paid your debt. You're not on Col's ledger anymore."

"You torched my brother's business." The night after the deathmatch, both Caidyn's Ravenshoe office and site office were torched. Since it's believed to be the act of an arsonist, investigators were brought in. It will delay the insurance claim process, which means he'll be out of business for months if not years. That might be okay for established businesses, but Caidyn's was only just getting off the ground. I don't know if he'll come back from that.

"Arson doesn't get me off," Rocco pushes out with a laugh like our conversation isn't half as serious as it is. "But I guess that doesn't matter when you're desperate, does it?"

He steals my chance to reply by handing me a tablet. It must be a prototype as it's nothing like any I've seen at the shops. "Caidyn torched his business?" I half question, half confirm after taking in the surveillance video playing on the tablet. "Why the fuck would he do that?"

"Same reason I popped a bullet between my sister's punk-ass boyfriend's brows. Sometimes you've got to take shit into your own hands."

I get what he's saying. I also understand it, but if this footage gets out, Caidyn is up shit creek without a paddle. His insurance company will never payout, and he doesn't have the capital to start afresh.

"Now, I bet you're more than interested in what's in the bag." Rocco prances on the spot like he belongs on one of the Backstreet Boys' reboot videos before he pulls open the zipper of my gym bag sitting on the coffee table. It isn't brimming with smelly gym socks and badly in need of a clean clothes. It's lined with Benjamin Franklins. There would have to be at least one hundred thousand in there.

"Ten percent of it is yours. The rest needs to be delivered to this address." Rocco hands me a device similar to the one showing Caidyn's firebug skills. "The message will remain until nine o'clock. After that..." He makes an explosive noise with his lips.

"It will blow up?"

Rocco almost falls to the floor, laughing. "Nah, man. This isn't *Mission Impossible*." He continues chuckling while saying, "Smith will perform a magic trick." Smith is the hacker I mentioned earlier. "No trace of that address will be found once he's done." He nudges his head to the tablet in my hand when he says 'that.' "So all you need to worry about is ensuring the goods are on site before each fight. Do that, then you won't need to worry about Col."

I don't need to ask him what happens if I don't.

"What are they supplying me with for this much money?"

Rocco gives me a look that verifies I don't want him to answer my question. "The less you know, the less chance you'll get prosecuted." He jerks his head to the main room of the cabin. "Do you have a babysitter for her? I could pop over around six if need be."

The riled expression on his face reveals he's being playful. Unfortunately for him, I lost that side of myself when I killed a man. "I've got it sorted."

I forcefully walk him to the door, my already-slow pace slowing even more when I spot the butt of a lit cigarette in the corner of my eye.

"Sniper," Rocco says, all calm and collected. "Dimitri put one on the front and back entrances, and two on the road leading to the cabin." He shrugs. "It's a little obsessive, but you kinda got to be with Col." He gallops down the front three steps of the cabin before tossing me a set of keys. "Take her. She'll make you less suspicious." He isn't talking about Demi. He nudged his head to a 1987 Buick GNX. It's been lowered and is painted matte black. "And she's got a good size trunk for the goodies."

Not speaking another word, Rocco signals to a man with a clover tattoo on his cheek to move out before they slide into the back of a single SUV. I wait for the taillights of his ride to sink into the abyss before shifting my eyes in the direction I saw the amber of a cigarette. I don't like being in favor to Dimitri, but I prefer it over being in his father's shit book.

After a few deep breaths, I pace back into the cabin. I'm not surprised to find Demi leaning in the doorjamb of the main bedroom. I've been gone longer than necessary for a glass of water, and she's more clued in than people give her credit for.

"You okay?"

The worry etched on her face clears away when I jerk up my chin. "Was just getting some fresh air."

She pushes off her feet while saying with a yawn, "I'll join you."

Her already wobbly strides shake even more when I shout, "No!" She's wearing one of my shirts as a nightie. It shows way too much leg, and I'm far too jealous to let anyone see how delectable she looks in a STEM Academy shirt. "Both my lungs and veins are replenished, so how about we deplenish them?" *Is deplenish even a word?*

I shrug off my confusion when Demi asks, "What do you have in mind?"

With my grin as bright as the twinkle in her eyes, I wave my hand over a stack of board games on my right. "We could always play a board game."

23

MADDOX

Six weeks later...

C*rack!*

While lurching into a half-seated position, one of my hands claws at the blankets while the other endeavors to remove the vice-like grip around my neck. It's been almost two months for fuck's sake, an entire forty-eight days, yet I still wake up most mornings coated in sweat and struggling to breathe through the guilt suffocating me. I thought the guilt of ending a man's life would have weakened by now. I assumed it would have up and left the instant I stood across from Col without a bullet being lodged into my brain. I had no fucking clue I'd still be grappling with remorse weeks later.

I guess I shouldn't be surprised.

Some people are born killers.

I am *not* one of those people.

I've played the actions that night in my head on repeat. Considering how the law works, my downfall that eventful day should have commenced right around the time my chest was lit up with two assault weapons.

That's far from gospel.

I fucked up by believing Agent Moses was an honorable man.

I don't have any proof to back up my claims, but I'm reasonably sure Agent Moses and Col are working together. Col called me a snitch while reminding me what happens to them if they run their tongues to the wrong people. As far as he was aware, I turned up that night to fight as requested. There was no snitching going on.

Well, there wasn't.

I've shared a tale or two the past couple of weeks. It isn't to who you're anticipating. Agent Moses can burn in hell as far as I'm concerned. My thoughts on Dimitri Petretti aren't much better, but I'd consider pissing on him if he was on fire. His father and Agent Moses wouldn't be so lucky. I'd watch them both burn with a smile on my face.

While 'working' with Dimitri as part of our agreement, I've reached the conclusion he's suspicious his father is coercing with a side of the law his family hasn't sided with before, but since I'm eager to keep my dark side a secret, I've kept my stories on the slender side. Dimitri knows I fought for his father last month. He's aware Demi was put up as collateral and that I showed my dislike of that by knocking his father the fuck out, but he has no clue the fights have a man stretched out of the ring in a body bag every single match. Will I update Dimitri on my knowledge once my conscience doesn't feel so guilty? Probably not. Dimitri isn't a good man. The shit I'm helping him get onto the streets is sure-fire proof of this. I may not be murdering men with my bare hands, but I'm sure the goods I am driving from town to town is slowly killing them.

The goons I deliver a bag of money to every Friday morning explicitly told me not to open the packages they load into the trunk of my car, but only a moron would act as if the brick-size packages are flour.

When I realized what I was distributing, I tried to back out of it. I made it all the way to the street that Dimitri's mansion branches off when I was stopped in my tracks. It wasn't two armed men with machine guns strapped to their chests slowing me down this time around. It was Agent Moses and a threat I'd spend the rest of my life behind bars if I didn't continue following Dimitri's orders.

He didn't want to bust Dimitri with a bigger haul. He wanted to make sure his cut of the profits remained high because the more drugs I move for Dimitri, the bigger payouts law enforcement officers like Agent Moses receive to turn a blind eye.

I'm being fucked in the ass from both sides of the law, and there isn't a damn thing I can do about it.

Upon noticing my breathing pattern regulating as it shifts from remorseful to angry, Demi's hand moves from the bumps in my midsection to my face. "You good?" Her voice is groggy, revealing it is still early.

I hum out an agreeing murmur before scooting up the mattress, so my back braces my pillow and the headboard. My nightmare must have gone longer in my head than realized because my pillow is almost soaked through.

"Take mine." My lips barely twitch when Demi squashes her index finger to them. "I've drooled on your chest *every* night the past six-plus weeks. I don't see tonight being any different."

Her comment about it still being night has my eyes straying to the clock on my bedside table. It shows it's a little after eleven. We're not usually early-to-bed people, but my agreement with Dimitri sees me needing to rise earlier than the sun every Friday. I told Demi her cousin wants me to squeeze in a pre-fight workout before each match. I'm unsure why I lied. She witnessed me kill a man. I can't shock her any more than that. I just still believe some things are better kept under wraps until the timing is right.

"Aren't you tired?" Demi asks a few minutes later. When I peer down at her, shocked she's aware I was still awake, she murmurs, "You only ever do a maximum of six figure-eight patterns on my back before you zone out. You went well past a dozen."

My heart does an elongated beat when she switches on the lamp on the bedside table. It's the same bedside table that got me in all types of trouble two short months ago. Caidyn dropped it off last month when he tried to return the bundle of money I left in the glove compartment of his Jeep. We're staying at his friend's house for free, Demi can whip up a feast fit for a king with the most basic ingredients, and when Rocco arrives with a bag of money each week, he ensures the fuel tank in the

Buick is also chock-a-block full. Other than putting away a good chunk of coin each week with the hope I'll soon get Demi as far away from here as possible, I don't have any other needs, so why not help my brother who bankrupted himself for me? I owe him more than a ton of dirty money, but at the moment, it's the only thing I can give him.

"It's barely there," Demi reminds me when I trace my finger over the slither of silver in her right cheek before I tuck a lock of hair behind her ear.

She's been safe here with me for a little over six weeks, but I can't help but wonder if that will still be the case when I fail to show up for the next deathmatch next week. I need to get her out of the firing line, I simply have no fucking clue how to do that. I don't trust the law. Her flesh and blood see her as a commodity, and although my brothers adore her, I see weariness in their eyes any time her name is mentioned lately. I changed for Demi. They just have no clue how widespread the leap was since I've kept my murderous ways between Demi and me.

"It's the scars we can't see that take the longest to heal."

I don't get the chance to contemplate what she means. My focus is far from misery when my girl is tugging my sleeping pants down my thighs. There's no time for sadness. The only ache I'm feeling is the throb in my cock when I try and talk her out of sucking me off.

"Thought you said we can't keep using sex as our vice when we're feeling snowed under."

Demi takes my dick in her hand before raising her eyes to mine. Fuck, she's beautiful. All her bruises are gone, and her eyes are bright. If you excluded the faintest scar from the gash

Col caused her cheek when he punched her in the face, you'd have no clue she was assaulted seven weeks ago. Even with her grin being hidden by my rapidly rising cock, I'm confident in declaring I made the right decision when I put her first. She comes before anything and anyone. My studies. My brothers. Even my family. She will always come first.

"I also thought you said you'd talk to me when you're struggling." My thigh muscles bunch when she swipes her tongue over the crest of my cock like we're making out instead of arguing. "Doesn't look like you're willing to maintain your side of our bargain yet, either."

"I was going to talk to you." My last two words come out rough, inspired by the rumble of a man in need from his woman curling her lips over his knob. "I just thought you were asleep." My dropped eyes pop open when Demi suddenly yanks back. "What the fuck? You can't do that to a man. My God, Demi. You never, I repeat, *never* de-suction mid-suck. I could suffer permanent erectile damage." I whisper the word 'erectile' like I'll jinx myself with a dysfunction by saying it out loud.

I angle my head to the side and peer down at Demi with her lips a mere inch from my now aching cock when she asks, "More damage than lying?"

"I'm not lying to you." I fucking am, but that's a story for another day. "I was sweating too much to know if the wetness on my chest was you or me." Since most of my reply is honest, it comes out sounding that way. She wasn't lying when she said she drools. It's one of her talents that reminds me she isn't a goddess. She's fucking close, she just needs to dampen down the amount of drool she disperses each night to fully accept the title.

When Demi's lips remain hovering above the crest of my cock, I crumble like a narc being offered a deal. "What do you want to know?"

Most men would run for the hills if forced to have a heart-felt one-on-one conversation mid-blowjob. Demi's ability to suck the marrow from my bones would have me agreeing for a shrink to sit in on our escapades if it guarantees my dick will still be sucked.

Demi awards the absolute honesty in my eyes that nothing is off-limits by taking care of the droplet of pre-cum pooled on the end of my cock. Her lick sends a pleasing zap straight to my balls and has my head falling back so I can voicelessly thank God for bringing her into my life. Our relationship is messy and complicated, but her smile alone makes up for a lifetime of injustices.

While stroking my cock to restock the pre-cum she lapped up, she asks, "Where do you go every Friday morning?" She drags her tiny hand to the base of my dick, squeezes it a little, then returns it to the crown. "You have everything you need to train out back, so why attend a gym for an extra session?"

"Competition is stiff." Not as stiff as my dick, but not a complete lie. "I've got to make sure my cockiness isn't seeing me walk into this blind."

I hadn't really considered that the past month and a half. I've been victorious each week, but it hasn't come without consequences. I sported a black eye for two weeks after my first bout, fractured my pinkie finger the week after that, and last week, I not only bruised my ribs, I cracked a couple of them as well. The longer I fight for Dimitri, the fiercer my competition is becoming. "My competitors' 'owners' now know I'm not just a pretty face. I need to back up their claims with an impressive skill set as well."

"Can I watch you fight this week?"

A stern "hell to the fucking no" sits on the tip of my tongue, but my mouth refuses to relinquish it. Demi isn't stupid. She knows there's no chance in hell I'll say no to her when she's lowering her plump lips down my shaft.

"Fuck, Demi, fuck!" I grunt out when her lips come to within an inch of the cropped hairs splayed across my pelvis. I'm not bragging when I say it isn't logical for her to fit so much dick down her throat. I've got length—*notable length*— and girth, yet she sucks me down like she wants my load dispersed directly into her gut. "Just a little more."

I grunt when my greediness for her to take *all* of me sees her releasing a gag. I know I'm packing heat, but unvoiced acknowledgment is so much better than spoken truths. That's what my relationship with Demi is founded on. She knows I care like fuck for her. I'd put her above anything and anyone, but I don't need to shout that from the rooftops for her to know. I merely have to show her, which I've done every day for almost two months.

"It's not safe for you there, Demi. I'm not willing to risk it." Do you have any clue how hard it is to talk when you're being driven to the brink of ecstasy by delicate lips and an adventurous tongue? Take my word for it. It's almost fucking impossible.

"I can't stay here forever, Maddox. It'll drive me crazy." Like she is me when she swivels her tongue around my knob. After dragging her teeth over the tip ever so gently, she does a second prolonged lick. "Besides, Rocco said my uncle is away, so there's no reason for me not to come."

"Fucking Rocco."

I realize I said my comment out loud when Demi murmurs, "He's offered. I declined. I'd much rather fuck you."

She thinks she's being cute. I'm seconds from going on a murderous rampage—*after I come.* I'm a good fighter, but I am no He-Man.

I push Demi's head back toward my dick before saying, "You shouldn't be talking with Rocco. He isn't a good man." She greets him when he drops me off after every fight. She has no clue about his middle-of-the-night visits each Thursday. "But I'll ask him what he thinks when I see him later today." This kills me to admit, but Rocco is somewhat protective of Demi. If he thinks she'll be in any danger, he'll tie her ass to a dining room chair to ensure she stays out of the firing zone. "Until then..."

I don't have to speak another word. With a smile that exposes she knows she's won this battle, Demi swipes her tongue across the slit in the crown of my cock, then devours me like she's never been fed.

It's a highly-craved forty minutes.

"I don't see an issue with it. Col is out of town. Dimitri is occupied. It might be a good opportunity to get her out and about for a couple of hours." Rocco tosses a gym bag full of cash into the trunk of the Buick before slamming it shut, forgetting Demi isn't aware of our morning rendezvous. "Shit, sorry. I forgot you're keeping things from her."

"I'm not keeping things from her. I'm..." *I've got nothing.*

"Telling porkies, pulling her leg, keeping it on the down-low. However you Irish fucks say it, you're doing it."

Despite what my pasty-white skin tells you, I'm only part Irish. I probably have as much Italian blood running through my veins as Dimitri. "Why is Dimitri occupied? He hasn't missed a feature the past six weeks." I can't say I blame him. From the quick calculations I've done, each Friday night schedule pulls in an easy one hundred thousand.

"He's... ah... got some family shit to take care of."

In case his blubbering didn't clue you in, Rocco is a shit liar.

"Fien?"

"Who?" Rocco fires back, once again showcasing his horrendous skills.

I don't know who the fuck Fien is, but it's clear she's important to Dimitri. He could be in the middle of negotiating a record-breaking deal, and he leaves within a nanosecond of Rocco whispering her name into his ear.

Eager to end our conversation before he puts his foot in his mouth, Rocco nudges his head to the hanging open driver's side door of the Buick. "Why don't you get a head start, then you'll be back in time to make your girl breakfast in bed." I shake my head, the tingling in my balls from the best blowjob of my life still not enough to convince me to leave Demi in Rocco's care. Furthermore, Saint is already on his way. He buzzed me thirty minutes ago, but before I can announce that, Rocco's next set of words steals more than words from my throat. They wind me as well. "It's the best way to start her big b-day."

"It's Demi's birthday?" I was meant to articulate that in my head.

When Rocco nods, I snatch up his wrist to check the date on his watch. I knew Demi's birthday was approaching, but with everything going on, I didn't realize it was this close.

"Fuck!" I curse when Rocco's expensive timekeeping contraption announces it is the twenty-first. It's Demi's first birthday as my girl, and I completely fucked it all up. "I'm a fucking asshole."

"Relax," Rocco says with a laugh. "Last year, she got a double shift at Petretti's. I'm sure you can't do worse than that."

"She deserves better than some fucking eggs on toast, Rocco." He lifts his chin but remains quiet, leaving me plenty of time to devise a much better plan. "Do this run for me—"

"No can do," he interrupts before I can state all my terms.

"Then I'll do a double run next week."

Rocco shoves his tattooed hands under his arms before he arches a brow. "Who says there's more than one run a week?"

I jog around the trunk, lean into the Buick, then pull on the trunk latch. "I've seen Dimitri's crash pad. I know you've got more than a two-bit operation going on." After removing the gym bag full of cash from the trunk, I shove it into Rocco's chest. "Do this for me, and I'll do two runs a week from here on out."

A half wolf-whistle, half chuckle vibrates his lips. "Dimitri said you were gone. Yowie, motherfucker, you're full-blown in love."

His comment has my fists itching to smash his teeth in, but I hold back when he lowers my gym bag from his chest, but he doesn't let go of it. "Two runs a week. I'll be back Tuesday." The urge to smack him into the middle of next week returns full pelt when he adds, "Give the birthday girl a kiss for me," before he slides into the back of an SUV, leaving me with a plan but no way of implementing it without freeing Demi from the trap I caught her in seven weeks ago.

24

DEMI

Nerves are in abundance in my stomach. I'm so excited, I feel the need to pee for every minute of every hour. Today I am twenty-two. I never thought I'd reach this day, much less have a reason to celebrate it, yet here I am being driven to a secret location by my boyfriend, who also happens to be the only guy I've ever crushed on.

I'd pinch myself if I weren't afraid it would wake me up.

I haven't left the cabin in a month and a half. It was stocked with supplies before we arrived, and anything we've used, Rocco turns up with like magic each Friday afternoon like he scoured our pantry before his arrival. I have no reason to leave, but I'm still grateful to be out of there. Claustrophobia makes no sense until you stare at the same walls day in and day out.

When Maddox pulls his bike down a dusty road many miles from the cabin, he squeezes my hands wrapped around his waist, drawing my focus to him. "This is going to be as tacky as fuck, but I hope you still enjoy it."

I assume the unease in his voice is because he had to project it over the healthy rumble of his motorbike engine but am proven wrong when a large wooden building comes into sight over the horizon. It's a big old barn in the middle of nowhere. There could be a fancy ranch attached somewhere, but since most properties this far inland come with thousands of acres, I could be wrong.

After parking at the side of the barn, Maddox dismounts his bike, removes his helmet, then helps me with mine. Once he has them stored in his saddlebags, he shifts on his feet to face me, smiling at the shock on my face. "Have you ever heard of Troy Gentry?"

"The highest-scoring player in the history of the NHL?" I roll my eyes. "Never."

His smile doubles before he nudges his head to the barn. "He thanks this for his high-goal tally."

Still confused, I remain quiet. It's for the best. If I hadn't kept my mouth shut, I might have missed the springs of curly blonde hair pushing open the barn doors to reveal an almost full-size hockey rink hidden inside.

"Sloane!" Maddox wiggles a finger in his ear, wordlessly protesting my girlie squeal that just burst through his eardrums, before he joins my race across the dewy grass to Sloane and Saint. I've seen Saint a handful of times the past six weeks, but I've only communicated with Sloane via phone and text messages. I've missed her so much.

"Happy birthday!" She returns my fiercely protective hug

before pulling me back so she can drag her eyes over my flushed face and wide eyes. "A six-week romp-a-thon has made you all types of nasty." Panicked that I look like a wreck stops filtering through my head when she adds, "Hook a girl up! I need recommendations on guys up to the task. You look *smoking!*"

My eyes shoot to Saint, stunned Sloane is seeking reps. Her texts made it seem as if she and Saint were still going strong like Maddox and me. Clearly, I read her messages in the wrong manner. There's so much tension brewing between them, I'm shocked the ice rink hasn't melted.

Although Saint acts as if Sloane's comment isn't grating his last nerve, his tight jaw tells another story. He's pissed as fuck, but he refuses to nibble at the bait Sloane dangled in front of him. I guess I shouldn't be surprised. His signature move isn't well known because it's a rarity.

Eager to ease the tension suffocating the air, I ask, "What are you guys doing here? I thought you had a big exam coming up?" My final question is solely for Sloane. Although Maddox is also attending university, he does a majority of his studies at home. Since she's prelaw, Sloane doesn't have the same leeway.

"Stuff exams. It's your birthday. That's far more important." After slinging her arm around my waist, Sloane nuzzles her nose into my neck. "I'm also dying to see your reaction to your very first snowstorm."

Maddox waits for my confused gaze to shift to him before he motions up his chin, signaling to someone in the shadows of the barn to switch on the lights. When the hockey rink illuminates, I'm torn between sobbing and smiling. Foam snowmen dot the ice rink, and fluffy white froth is falling from the sky.

When I step closer to the rink, needing a moment to gather my composure, Sloane's arm falls from my waist a mere second before Maddox's torso warms my back. "The ice under your feet is real, but unfortunately, the snowmen are fake, and the snow is made from dishwashing liquid. I'll take you to see real snow one day, but for now, this will have to do."

"It's beautiful," I say, mesmerized how the lights high-lighting the rink make the bubbles pumping out of the machines above our heads shine like real snowflakes. "I love it."

Needing an excuse for the wetness about to fall onto my cheeks, I rest my head onto Maddox's chest and tilt my chin so the 'snowflakes' can land on my face. A smile curves my lips when blobs of teeny tiny bubbles splat onto my cheeks. They're a little chilly, making it seem as if I am truly in the middle of a snowstorm.

I remain in my peaceful bubble for nearly ten minutes before the chill projecting off the rink becomes highly notice-able. Maddox moved away, lowering the heat roaring through my body by an easy twenty degrees. "Now it's time for the true snow-day experience to begin."

When he pulls a sheet off a snow sled, I giggle like my heart isn't racing a million miles an hour. I'm not scared. I'm petrified I am seconds from blurting out three little words I swore I wouldn't express until Maddox does first.

"Come on, Demi. Climb aboard. Once you've mastered the wimp whistler, we'll move up to the big one." Maddox thrusts his hand to an inflatable slide at the side of the rink. It looks like it should be hanging over the ledge of a swimming pool, but it's lumped onto a massive circle of ice instead. "The Mad Max Mount."

With memories of my past on lockdown and my mind ready for a new vault-load of better memories, I thrust my arms into the winter coat Sloane is holding out for me before shuffling across the ice.

One day of good memories won't alter the horrible things of my past, but today's moments are tomorrow's memories.

Note for future self—*ice-skating is harder than it looks.*

My backside is bruised, the tip of my nose is red, and for once in the past six weeks, Maddox only gets some of the credit for my damp panties. I wore the pants and jacket kindly supplied by Mr. Gentry, but I landed on my ass so many times, the wetness of the ice eventually seeped through.

Did it make my smile any smaller the past two hours? Not at all. I loved every single minute at the skating rink. It was a true highlight of my life. I could easily go to bed now and say this was the best birthday of my life. But as luck would have it, Maddox still has a handful of activities for us to undertake today.

Stop number two is forty miles from the skating rink. It will occur without Sloane and Saint, who are currently enduring an awkward eighty-mile trip back to Hopeton on Maddox's bike since he asked Saint to borrow his car. His poor planning exposes he was in the dark about Sloane and Saint's switch from lovers to friends as much as me.

Sloane tried to secure herself an invitation for our next activity, but Maddox was quick to shoot down her endeavors. He said the rest of the day was solely about us, so you can imagine my confusion when he lowers the revs of Saint's car so he doesn't miss the turn-off for a shooting range in a country community many miles from Hopeton.

The chill of my hands weakens when Maddox curls his hand over mine before giving them a little squeeze. "The best protection a woman can have is the courage to protect herself."

His words sting my eyes with moisture. They were beautiful and so very much on par with his personality. He wants to save me from the world, but he also recognizes he can't do it alone.

"So, what do you say, birthday girl? Want to blow some guy's nuts off?"

Laughing, I nod my head. "Does he have to be a paper silhouette, though? I know a few guys who need dismembering, starting with your brother, Saint."

"Deserving, but still... ouch!" Maddox groans with a chuckle before he jogs around to open my door for me.

He's seen me naked more times than I can count, brought me to ecstasy with his brilliant tongue only hours ago, and whispers dirty, wicked thoughts into my ear every single time we fuck, but today I blush.

What can I say? His old-school gentleman ways turn me on.

"This place isn't free carry, Demi, so unless you want me frisk-searched, keep that grin on the down-low." He grabs at his crotch in case his teasing tone didn't get the point across. "Or I could strap you to my front and tell them you're napalm."

He kisses me before I can answer him. I don't mind. I'm always up for being kissed, especially when it's by him.

Maddox waits for the tingles in my pussy to extend to my toes before pulling away, then he drags his index finger down my nose, curls his hand around mine, then guides me inside.

We're greeted by a lady with a thick accent and super cute pigtails. "Hey, y'all. Welcome to Allabee's." She bounces between rows of guns like she's a murderous Barbie doll. "Are you here to purchase or fire?"

I'm about to say fire when Maddox shocks me for the second time today. "Both."

I don't want a gun. I don't know why. I've just never had a good vibe about them.

"All righty, then. Well, come on over and take a look. Perhaps you can test a few models in the range until you find your fit." After gesturing for us to follow her to a counter with guns more suitable for novices, the clerk says, "I'll need to see ID, though. Protocol and all. We can't hand guns to any ol' fool."

The hits keep coming when the slip of my hand into my purse is halted by Maddox producing two identification cards. They're driver's licenses for New York State. One for me and one for him.

What the hell?

"Perfect," the gun stockiest breathes out with a purr. "Now let's get you weaponed up, Mr. and Mrs. Noble."

"Please, call me Richard," Maddox suggests, stoked our fake IDs passed the test.

"Or Dick," I add on, ensuring Maddox knows I'm not

comfortable with this. "He much prefers when people call him Dick."

"Fake IDs, gun purchasing. Jeez, Maddox, were you at any time planning to update me on your 'supposed' plans?" He follows me into the firing range before guiding us to the booth Brittney assigned to us. My gun is pink and lightweight, but it still looks wrong being gripped by my hand, so I won't mention the beast of a gun Maddox chose to test. "I understand where you're coming from, and I get we joked about leaving this life behind many times the past six weeks, but we're supposed to be a team."

"We *are* a team, Demi. The licenses and guns are to ensure we *stay* a team." After placing our guns onto a table behind our booth, he tugs down the earmuffs meant to protect my hearing from the gunfire booming around us until they circle my neck, then he secures my hand in his. "The licenses are new. I figured it would be best to test their authenticity somewhere less obvious."

"Gun purchasing isn't less obvious."

He continues talking as if I never spoke, but the tugging of his lips gives away that he heard me. He likes when I'm sassy, which sees it occurring more times than not. "What's the one thing you want more than anything in the world?" I'm about to say my dad, but he beats me to the punchline. "Excluding your dad." When the hope in my eyes answers his question on my behalf, he whispers, "I can't give you that if we stay here."

"But your family." I want to say more. I should say more. I just can't. If I talk, my voice will crack, and then I will cry. I cried on my last seven birthdays. I don't want to cry today.

Maddox brushes my dry cheek, expressing that he understands my struggle before he pulls me into his chest. "My family will understand, Demi."

The way he says 'will' exposes his family is unaware of his plans. If they were, I doubt they would help him as much as they have. They're close because no one has intruded on their dynamic as I have. Caidyn will never say anything, he's too polite, but I've noticed the more times he 'babysits' me, the shorter our chats are becoming. Even Saint was a little reserved today. I could blame the conflict between him and Sloane for that, but that would be the cheat's way of explaining the knot in my stomach.

When silence reigns supreme for several long seconds, Maddox says, "Will you at least think about it?"

I take a moment to contemplate a reply. When several seconds of deliberating get me nowhere fast, I take the coward's way out. "We will talk about this more when we're not paying ninety dollars an hour for a booth at a firing range."

"Sounds like a solid plan." Maddox kills me when he drags his index finger down my nose for the tenth time the past two hours. "It's your birthday. We can do whatever you want on your birthday."

It's wrong to admit my first thought is to take him up on his offer, so I won't mention it. Maddox is who he is because of his family. I don't want to force him to learn who he is without them. It will kill him more than the other title he doesn't deserve to have.

————————

Waterworks fill my eyes for an entirely different reason when Maddox whispers, "Make a wish."

We resembled novices at the skating rink, pros at the firing range, purchased boots and cowboy hats at a real-life working ranch on the way to a late lunch, then ate at the cutest little diner in the middle of the boondocks after skimming rocks across the freshwater creek at the back of the café. It has been a perfect day, and Maddox has made it more divine by finding the only cupcake in a hundred-mile radius with a candle on the top.

The trickling of diners in the café breaks into rapacious applause when I blow out the candle as requested. I think that's the end of the embarrassment, but Maddox has other plans. With him taking the lead on vocals and the dining staff harmonizing his ballad, he commences singing happy birthday.

I wish I could declare the Walsh brothers can do anything. Unfortunately, Maddox must be tone death. Otherwise, what excuse does he have for his horrendous singing voice?

"Okay, okay," I say with a laugh when Maddox's fourth 'hip, hip, hooray,' thunders through my eardrums. "That's enough." I drag him into our booth before planting my mouth on his. "Thank you," I whisper over his quirked lips. "Today has been perfect. My best birthday by far."

He nips at my bottom lip before muttering, "But..."

I hate doing this, but I don't have a choice.

My uncle's schedule waits for no one.

"We have to go."

"We don't have to go." Maddox inches back before he drifts his baby blues between mine. "We could stay here forever. Can't you see it?" He drags his hand across the funky-looking café. "You could be the head chef, I'll be your apprentice, and everyone will soon learn to only dine here on the days you're rostered on."

I laugh even when I shouldn't. "You're not that bad of a cook."

I toss a dirty napkin into his face before barging him with my hip, demanding he scoot out of the booth. Even with a much bigger fight on his agenda at the end of next week, his fight tonight is the feature. If he's late, there will be no chance we'll escape with a set of fake IDs and the hope for a fresh start.

"When you win, dinner is *on* me."

The sexual innuendo in my comment guarantees Maddox won't deny my underhanded demand I attend tonight's match. It's my birthday. He said I can do whatever I want on my birthday. Although I hate the idea of seeing him get hurt, I want to support him as he has supported me for the past six weeks. He's a fighter, so my 'job' as his girlfriend is to be a ringside cheerleader.

"Last chance, Demi," Maddox says when we reach the dusty lot at the front of the café. "Demi's café is for sale. Who knows how long it will remain on the market?"

After taking in the 'for sale by owner' sign stuffed in the front window, I drag my eyes over the delipidated building, tube-lighting that no longer works, and the wonky 'D' at the front of my name on the sign hanging above the entryway door before lowering them to Maddox. It is ridiculous for me even to contemplate what he's suggesting, but I'd be a liar if I said it hasn't piqued my interest. "Can I sleep on it?"

"That's close enough to a maybe for me." With his smile as big as the low-hanging sun and his arm wrapped around my shoulders, he guides me back to Saint's car. I won't lie. I wish we were still on his bike. His hand barely left my thigh during the second half of our travels today, but there's nothing like snuggling up to his back and cocooning him with my warmth.

I smile like a fool when the reasoning behind Maddox's thirty-minute bathroom break between lunch and dessert makes sense. He picked wildflowers for me. They're spread across the bench seat in Saint's car, along the dashboard, and a handful of wayward ones made their way to the floor.

"The day's got away on me. I didn't have time to get you a pres—"

I stop his apology by kissing the living hell out of him. He has nothing to be sorry for. My day has been perfect. He woke me up by going down on me, cooked me an amazing breakfast I only cringed at twice while eating, spoiled me at the rink, then showed me that although he can protect me, I can also protect myself.

He was right. I feel safer knowing that.

"Thank you. I love them." I almost tack another three little words onto the end of my statement, but mercifully, the lemonades I downed with lunch catch up with me. "Do I have time to pee?"

"Again?" Maddox laughs before he nudges his head to the outside washrooms.

If that isn't proof how crazy he is thinking we can restore this place, I don't know what will convince him.

"You good?" I stray my eyes from Maddox making his way to the ring to Rocco, who despite his constant stirring, was requested to stay by my side by the very man he uses me to annoy. "You keep wiggling and shit. Like you're not a big girl who knows how to use the potty."

My eyes roll skyward. "It's nerves. I'm nervous."

"Nerves... *right.*" Rocco scrubs a tattooed hand over his bristle-covered jaw while asking, "Who gets nervous when they're backing a winner?" Before I can tell him to shut up, the expression on his face shifts from teasing to shocked. "Do these nerves make your stomach a little queasy? Are you super tired? Or better yet, can you remember the last time you had your period?"

"What the hell, Rocco! Why are you asking me that?" My words have barely left my mouth when the truth smacks into me. "No... I'm not... *pregnant.* Why in the world would you think that?" I pant even faster as a confession I shouldn't be telling anyone tumbles out of my mouth. "We've never used protection. Not once."

When my endeavor to fill my screaming lungs with air overtakes the crowd's chant excited the fight is about to begin, Rocco gives lying a try, clearly unaware he's crap at it. "All right, calm down. It could be nerves." He bumps me with his shoulder before smiling a huge grin. "When I cruise by on Tuesday, I'll bring some *special supplies*." He whispers his last two words. "They'll tell you one way or another if it's nerves in your stomach or something else."

I'm grateful for his assistance. However, I'm still confused. "Tuesday? Why are you coming over on Tuesday?"

"Ah..." His jaw hangs long enough for the referee to announce the commencement of Maddox's fight without interference. "It's the only day I have free. Thought I'd help a girl out." He pivots me to face Maddox prancing around the ring before muttering, "How about you coach your boy. The crap you ate at lunch will make him a little slow off the mark."

I'm not going to ask how he knows what we ate. Maddox spent the thirty minutes before his fight warming up while glaring at Rocco, so there's no uncertainty in my mind that he didn't update him on what we ate for lunch.

Rocco is a snoop, and I'm reasonably sure I know who he's snooping for.

Dimitri became more family-orientated a couple of months back. Not enough to give me the full pardon I'm seeking, but sufficient for him to stick his nose where it isn't wanted.

"Come on, Maddox. It's late, the restaurant is almost empty..." *And I know the perfect recipe that will suffocate your urge to have a panic attack when I tell you we may have created more than fireworks the past six-plus weeks.* "My uncle is in Europe.

He can't come back in an hour." When pleading doesn't work, I remind him of the fantastic day we had, which grew even better when he took down his opponent in the second round. Although the loser's 'owner' refused to hand over the money he lost when he placed his fighter against Maddox, it was a lot of fun seeing Maddox in his element. It reminded me he isn't as saintly as his brother's nickname and that the Walsh brothers have a reputation for a reason. "It's my birthday. I want to cook for my boyfriend in my favorite restaurant for my birthday."

"Jesus fucking Christ, Demi. When you say it like that, how can I say no?"

I scoop his hand that should be more battered than it is into mine before replying, "Don't say no. Say yes. I'll make it up to you. Remember that kiss we almost shared in here? It won't be an almost anymore."

"Bribing me with sex. I should have known." While smiling to assure me his tone has no malice whatsoever, he leads me into the back entrance of Petretti's.

A sense of coming home filters through me when the sound of overworked staff booms in my ears, and the sweet smell of tomatoes and garlic lingers in my nose. My dad loved this place. That alone means I'll never see it in a negative light.

"Demi!" Ty wraps me up in a hug before half my name leaves his mouth. "Where the fuck have you been? We thought you had dropped off the face of the earth." He stops, arches his brow, drags his eyes up and down Maddox's body three times in slow motion, then whistles air between his teeth. "Can't say I blame you." He twists his torso to face Jude, who's preparing the last of the meals. "What did I tell you, Jude? If only he were gay."

Jude doesn't deny Ty's claims. He just shifts the focus by asking if we are here to eat.

"I was hoping I could whip something up for old time's sake. If that's okay, of course?"

"Sure, it is. This kitchen was yours long before it was mine." He nudges his head to the industrial fridge. "Fresh snails just arrived. From what I've heard, they were a fan favorite."

I laugh at both Jude's witty comment and Maddox's screwed up face. "Thank you. We will stay out of your way as much as possible."

When I twist to face Maddox, I can't wipe the smile off my face. In a weird way, today has been almost an exact replica of what I envisioned my life would be once I left this place, except it's occurring here, in the last place I thought possible. "Anything in particular you feel like eating?" I smile wider when his sultry grin answers my question on his behalf. "You can have *that* later, for now..."

"What about that dish you whipped up almost two months ago?" Maddox fills in when I leave my reply hanging wide open. "The Maddox special."

"Okay," I mumble while wracking my brain to remember exactly what I put in his dish that night. I went all out, hoping to impress him even when it should have been the last thing on my mind. "One Maddox special coming right up."

I don't even make it two steps away when Maddox seizes my wrist and tugs me back. "If I recall correctly, it's *your* birthday, right?"

"That it is," I reply, even knowing too well he's aware today is my birthday.

Tears mist my eyes when he says, "Then aren't *I* supposed to cook for *you?*"

Torn between smiling in excitement and cringing with worry, I ask, "Under my guidance?"

"Of course," Maddox replies as he paces us toward the large industrial refrigerator he crowded me against all those weeks ago. "I don't want you dying on me."

Many *many* hours later, I breathe through the ache of an overstuffed stomach while dragging my tongue across my suddenly bone-dry mouth. Maddox and I cooked, flirted, and ate more carbohydrates than I've consumed in my life, then we washed up like a regular, everyday couple.

It was only when Maddox handed me the final dish to dry did the simplicity of my life the past six weeks smack into me hard and fast. I've craved this very thing for so long, knowing my every wish had been granted saw me muttering three little words I never thought I'd say to anyone. You can love in my family industry, but you must *never* openly express it

But I did.

I declared my love out loud for the world to hear.

And for once, not an ounce of fear encroached me. It actually felt relieving, which is stupid when you truly think about it. We've been together almost twenty-four-seven for over six weeks, and we dealt with the good and bad within the first three days of our relationship, so telling Maddox I love him was the next logical step.

I'm pleased as hell to tell you he responded better than hoped. He didn't immediately say it back. He whipped my backside with a damp tea towel, made a remark about how hard I made him work for it, then he pinned me to the fridge that tried to commence my downfall weeks ago before he kissed the living hell out of me.

Only once he had me on the brink of climax did he say it back—multiple times. In my ear, along my collarbone, and as he trekked his succulent, kiss-swollen lips over the thrusting curves of my breasts. He even says it now while kneeling before me, drinking in the damp panties his last five minutes of attention caused.

We're in public, in the very town my uncle makes sure women feel worthless in, yet I feel as if I have the entire world at my feet.

"Ohh..." I gargle out with a long breath when Maddox's impatience gets the better of him. He didn't wait until he had my panties pushed aside to drag his tongue along the crevice in my pussy. He did it through the moist, cotton material, causing it to cling to my aching pussy even more than it already was.

"Put your leg over my shoulder, then bring that sweet pussy to me."

I do as instructed without additional prompting.

"Now tilt your hips forward. Show me how bad you want this."

My pussy is practically shoved into Maddox's face when the heat of his breaths cause my hips to naturally gyrate. Their movements can't be helped. I'm not in control of anything when his head is between my legs. Mercifully, I somehow have Maddox convinced I'm a pro in the bedroom. He has no clue I watch him for prompts.

I bite back a groan when his tongue circles my clit. There's no doubt it is extra sensitive. I just have no clue if that's because I'm pregnant or because of the fantastic day we've had. With his hands gripping my ass, he plants a bunch of sloppy kisses on my pussy. He's teasing me, taking it slow, knowing I'll soon beg him for more. I love making love to him, but I also like when he loses control.

"Please," I beg a short time later. The pressure he places on my clit with his tongue is perfect, and my knees are shaking from his tongue exploring every inch of my dripping vagina, but I need him to loosen the reins to lose control. I need him to eat me how only he knows how.

"Yes..." I hiss out with a moan when my every wish is answered with only one plea.

Maddox buries two fingers inside of me before slowing curling them, finding the spot only he can. He flicks the sensitive bud in my clenching pussy while his tongue hits my clit with rapid-fired hits.

When my thighs shake, I brace my back against the fridge. I feel like I'm spiraling. My head is dizzy and filled with a crazy lust haze.

"Come on, Demi. Give it to me. Come on my face."

His voice, the scruff on his chin, and his heavenly fingers are the perfect trifecta. I shimmer and shake as tingles activate over every inch of me. "I'm so close."

Maddox is so focused on me, I've completely forgotten where we are, how we got here, and why his knuckles are red. Nothing but climaxing is on my mind.

"Rock against me, Demi. Take what you fucking need. I'm right here to catch you when you fall."

The roughness of his voice has me imagining how hard he is. He's wearing jeans. The zipper is still done up. His cock must be in agony.

"You, Maddox, please. I need you." The sensation is overwhelming, I can feel myself coming undone, but I still want more. I need his thick rod filling me with the heat of his cum. I want it all, and I want it now.

"Whoa, slow down," Maddox pushes out with a chuckle after rising to his feet. After wiping away evidence of my excitement from his lips with the back of his hand, he says with a smile, "Your legs are a little unstable."

His smirk during his confession unleashes a side of me I've never seen before. I yank at his shirt like a madwoman, uncaring that I pop several buttons. "You... in me... now!" Big, needy breaths separate my words. I'm panting out of control, my body equally pissed with the intermission and thrilled by it.

My begs turn greedy when the removal of his cock is quickly chased by my thumb lapping up the droplet of pre-cum pooling on the tip. He's heavy in my hand, pulsating with unquenched desire. "I want you to fuck me, Maddox. Hard and fast. I want you so bad."

When our eyes catch, something alters in his. "Show me just how bad."

I hook my leg around his waist like I'm a gymnast before

grinding my aching clit on the crown of his fat cock. The grunt that rumbles up his chest is enough to pull my legs out from beneath me, so I won't mention the sensation that overwhelms me when he spins me around, curls me over the large bench in the middle of the kitchen, then drives home. "Yes... fuck me, Maddox. Fuck me hard."

As he fills me to the hilt, my hands dart out in search of something to tether myself to. I'm freefalling hard. My limbs are heavy and unmovable, and I'm chanting Maddox's name on repeat, but I don't need to anchor myself down. Maddox catches me as he always has—*as he always will.* He won't let me fall because, unlike every other man I've come across, he loves me for me and not what I can offer him.

25

MADDOX

While struggling not to give myself a pat on the back for a job well done, I hand Demi her panties I managed to salvage this time around, tuck my still half-mast cock into my jeans, then spray the kitchen counter at Petretti's with disinfectant spray. Even if I hadn't spilled my load into Demi's snug pussy, it would be hygienic enough to eat off within the hour.

I'm exhausted from a huge day, my muscles are screaming in pain, and we're in a place I will forever despise more than I'll ever relish, yet I'd be lying if I said I wouldn't do it all again right now. And no, I'm not solely mentioning my public romp with Demi.

We don't just gel together beneath the sheets, we're so on par that the first thing I felt when she told me she loved me was relief. I was getting worried she was immune to the Walsh charm. The cabin doesn't give me many opportunities to showcase it, but I gave it my best shot tonight.

I think our sweaty fuck on a stainless-steel bench announces just how suave my skills are, but just in case, I'll give you an idea of the absolute bliss on Demi's face. Her eyes are bright, her cheeks are a hue of pink, and her luscious lips are pulled high at one side. She can't stop smiling, and neither the fuck can I.

My plans today went off without a hitch. Nothing will bring me down from this high.

Except perhaps him.

"Landon, what the fuck, man?" I stand in front of Demi, not only blocking her from his view but subjecting myself to the full fury of his narrowed gaze. He's pissed. He isn't the only one. "Have you heard of knocking? It's in the bro-code. Perhaps you should take a look at it."

"Perhaps you should," he fires back, his voice unlike anything I've heard. "If you know what the fuck it is anymore." He steps closer to me, his chest thrusting. "Where the fuck have you been, Maddox?" He knows exactly where I've been, but he doesn't give me the chance to answer him. "Saint has been calling nonstop. Caidyn drove out to the cabin. We've been trying to reach you for hours, and where do I find you?" He leans to the side so Demi not only hears his reply, she can also spot the disdain in his eyes. "In the last fucking place you should be."

"That's enough, Landon. Leave her out of this."

When Demi tries to walk away, equally horrified and embarrassed she's the sole focus of Landon's anger, I snatch up her wrist before she can get two feet away from me. Landon may be my brother, but Demi is my girl. She comes before anyone.

"Apologize to Demi, then tell me what the fuck has you so riled up."

"Apologize? You want me to apologize?" When I jerk up my chin, his face goes as red as a beetroot. "Apologize for what?" He once again doesn't wait for me to answer. "That *nothing* has been the same in our family since Saint let slip neither her nor her friend was on his radar."

When he nudges his head to Demi partway through his comment, her scoff is quiet, but her swallow is loud enough for two blocks over to hear. "That you're being led by your dick instead of your head."

The sex-scented space won't help my appeal, so I keep my mouth shut.

"That it's *your* fault Caidyn's insurance claim fell through and that he could face prosecution for attempting to defraud an insurance company."

Air evicts from my lungs in a hurry.

That was a jab below the belt I wasn't anticipating.

"Or how about the fact you're not the only Walsh fooling around with a Petretti?" I try to talk, but nothing will come out. "But you wouldn't know about any of that, would you, Maddox? Because you don't give a fuck about anyone but her."

"That's not true." Even if he weren't my brother, he would still have heard the deceit in my voice. It was laced with it. "I can help Caidyn." I don't mention it will be with dirty money because that would give Landon more reason to clench his fists. "Saint isn't a fucking saint. Everyone knows he's plucked the occasional random out of a crowd." I take a mental note to apologize to Demi for dissing her friend when I feel the increase of her pulse through our joined hands. "And I'll talk to Justine." Landon didn't straight up mention she is the one messing with a Petretti, but with Demi being the only female Petretti left standing, I put two and two together remarkably quick.

"Words? That's your solution?" When I nod, Landon tightens his jaw. "You need more than words to deal with vermin. The Petrettis are evil. Their blood is pure poison. The kindest thing anyone could do for mankind is to stop them from procreating—"

"Maddox!" Demi shouts at the same time my fist makes a cracking noise with Landon's nose. Violence shouldn't be the solution for anything, but I am as sure as fuck not going to sit by and watch him insult Demi like that, especially on her birthday.

"Go the fuck home, Landon." When his hands ball up, ready for a fight, I reiterate, "Go. *The fuck*. Home."

Landon works his jaw side to side before he spits out, "When your sister ends up in a ditch, and your brothers are in jail, remember this conversation. I'm warning you things are going to end badly. What you choose to do with that information *solely* falls on your shoulders."

26

DEMI

I've patched up Maddox's knuckles every fight for the past six weeks. Tonight is the first time I'm clearing smears of his eldest brother's blood from his hands. He didn't split Landon's cheek like my uncle did mine, but he did whack him hard enough to cause blood to dribble from his nose.

I'm not shocked Maddox responded to Landon's taunt, I just wish it could have been for any other reason. I can change my name, cut my hair, and wear contact lenses, but no matter how much I alter my looks, my DNA will never change. I am a Petretti, there's no denying that, and if my intuition is anything to go by, Landon's niece or nephew will be as well. They may not have the title, but they will have the blood.

After locking my eyes with Maddox's, I blow cool breaths onto the iodine ointment dotted across his knuckles. Usually, when we reach this stage of our exchange, my gentle breaths are soon switched to needy pants. That isn't happening tonight.

Maddox is so deep in thought, he isn't in the cabin with me. His mind is far from here.

"Why don't you call Justine? Get her side of the story." I dump the iodine-soaked cotton balls into the bin at the side of the bathroom before pacing toward the door, eager to give him some privacy to work through his confusion.

I could use a couple of minutes as well.

Unlike many times tonight, Maddox doesn't halt my retreat by grabbing my wrist. He uses words instead. "Landon didn't mean what he said."

"Yeah, he did," I reply after spinning around to face him. "I just really hope you don't feel the same way."

"I don't." His tone isn't close to being confident. "But she's my sister, Demi. My *baby* sister. I can't let her..."

"End up with a Petretti like you?" I fill in when words elude him.

I silently beg for him to shake his head, so you can picture the devastation on my face when he bobs his chin instead. I understand his objective and comprehend he's programmed to protect his sister, but not even recalling the world's best day can harness my disappointment.

"Demi—"

"It's fine." I grit my teeth, silently warning nothing will be off-limits if a single tear falls from my eyes. "I'm fine. Call your sister."

I dart out of the bathroom as quickly as Landon stormed out of Petretti's Restaurant earlier tonight, and for the first time in ages, I don't shame my tears when they soak my pillow.

"Shh, stay asleep. I'm just grabbing a glass of water." I balk more from the dishonesty in Maddox's tone than recollection he finally came to bed. I've watched the clock for the past three nights. Not once has he come to bed before the little hand reaches one.

Things have been awkward between us. It isn't uncomfortable enough to have me worried we won't come out the other end shaken but okay, but it has ensured I haven't shared news about a possible stowaway with him.

Not all the awkwardness is Maddox's fault. We've barely had a moment to talk. Saint and Caidyn have been blowing up his phone since news of his exchange with Landon hit their ears, and Sloane's issues with Saint have kept the battery on Maddox's laptop at a constant low. We have so many other people's problems coming at us from all angles, there's no time for us to mull over our own issues.

My heart breaks when Maddox runs his fingers through my hair as he has a minimum of once a week for the past six weeks. It usually lulls me to sleep within a couple of seconds. It doesn't have the same effect this morning. There's too much tension in the air for any amount of nurturing to work.

Once I settle my breathing to indicate I'm asleep, Maddox sighs heavily before he clambers out of bed. The disappointments keep coming when he fails to tug on a pair of pants. He usually sleeps naked. He hasn't done that since Friday night. We haven't been sexually active since our sweaty romp in

Petretti's kitchen. I guess confirmation from your big bro you're sleeping with the enemy is enough to turn any man off.

I wait for the hinges on the front door of the cabin to creak open before I slip out from beneath the sheets. My tiptoe across the floorboards is done in silence. Not even my tug on the old wooden shutters Maddox has kept closed the past six weeks makes a peep. It's as quiet as a graveyard at midnight, meaning I have no troubles overhearing Maddox's conversation with Rocco.

"You knew he was going out with her, didn't you? That's why you said Dimitri was occupied."

Rocco doesn't balk at his accusation. That's a clear sign Maddox is on the money.

"Your sister is an adult, Ox. Who she dates is none of your business." He opens the hatch at the back of an SUV before pulling out a gym bag. If my blurry head isn't leading me astray, I'm reasonably sure it's Maddox's gym bag. "Furthermore, he has no interest in your sister."

"Ha!" Even with Justine being his sister, Maddox's rejection of Rocco's claim isn't odd. Justine is beautiful. She has exotic eyes, pure, untouched skin, and hair the color of lava. Saying Dimitri is disinterested is the equivalent of saying he's going on a sabbatical from sex. Never going to happen. "If he isn't interested, why fucking bother? Guys only bring out the charm for one reason, to get into a chick's pants."

Ouch.

One little sentence and all the good memories from the past six weeks are pushed to the back of my mind.

When Rocco remains quiet, having no plausible excuse to

deny his claims, Maddox hits him with a stern finger point. "Tell Dimitri to stay away from my sister or our deal is off."

Rocco shakes his head like Maddox's comment didn't have half the steam it did. "No can do. This is bigger than you and a half-assed threat, Ox."

"It won't be half-assed if he doesn't step the fuck back."

With furled lips, Rocco forcefully shoves the gym bag into Maddox's chest. "How about you remember who the fuck you work for?" I step back when his eyes stray to the window I'm camped behind.

I can't hear anything Maddox or Rocco says next. The large wooden pillar holding up the cabin's roof is too thick. I can assume it isn't pleasant since they get into a bit of a tussle. It isn't violent enough for me to intervene, but it's clear neither of them is willing to back down from their beliefs. They're as hotheaded as each other.

I hear my pulse in my ears when Maddox's final shove is chased by him sliding into the driver's seat of a midnight black Buick. He floors the gas. Even if he still believed I was asleep, he couldn't anymore. That's how brutal the tires on his ride flick up the rocks in the driveway.

Once the taillights of the Buick disappear, Rocco drags his fingers through his hair before shifting on his feet to face me. He stares straight at the slat I was peering through earlier, announcing my watch has been busted before he digs a white paper bag out of his jacket and places it on the top step of the porch.

He farewells me with a bob of his chin before he signals for the brute who watched the exchange between Maddox and him with a smile on his face to join him in the SUV.

I wait for the taillights of their car to disappear before collecting the package on the porch. I know what's inside. It's confirmation I can't hide from the truth a second longer. I'm moments away from either ruining the Walshs' reputation or saving it.

Maddox's behavior the past couple of days has me unsure which result I should root for. Both have the potential to end one way—disastrously.

27

MADDOX

My back molars smash together when I take the corner Dimitri's compound is located on too quickly. The back tires of the Buick slip out, dragging me and $100K worth of coke toward the slippery rock-edge. This is my last run. I'm fucking done with Dimitri and his family's shit. It's time for me to take Demi away from it all.

The ten thousand I earned tonight on top of the fifty thousand I've put away the past couple of months doesn't seem like much, but Demi's birthday celebration proves she doesn't need expensive things to be happy. She simply needs to be anywhere but here. My brothers constant interference the past three days assures me of this, much less Rocco's threat that if I don't jump on cue, he'll advise Dimitri to leave me defenseless to Col's wrath.

I was so fucking ropeable, I told Rocco to bring it on, confident Col couldn't make matters any worse. Demi has been unusually quiet, my sister is acting like a brat, and even the seclusion of a cabin in the middle of nowhere hasn't given me a single minute to sit down and take a breather. It's been one thing after another, and I'm about ready to snap.

Lucky for me, I know the perfect person to take my anger out on.

"Is Dimitri in?"

A brute with a skull full of tats notches up his head before he requests for me to pop open the Buick's trunk. When he twists his semi-automatic weapon around so it hangs off his back, I remove a gun from the glove compartment. It isn't the one I purchased on Demi's birthday. I borrowed this one from one of Dimitri's crew during my first stop this morning.

Only a fool enters a gun battle with his fists at the ready.

I'm not surprised to find Dimitri seated behind a big desk, wrangling paperwork. Drug lords don't sleep during peak business hours.

After taking in my balled fists, Dimitri locks his eyes with my face. He knows why I'm here, but he acts as if he doesn't. "The funds from last month's fights will be deposited into your account by the end of business Friday. I don't have any intel on the fighters being brought forward for next month."

"I'm not here about our arrangement." Hoping there's some kind of man hidden beneath his grouchy exterior, I slot into the chair across from him before hooking my right ankle onto my left knee. "Is it true you're using my sister as bait?"

His scoff is silent but oh-so-fucking gratifying.

His ship has a leak because I just removed the first plug.

"Whatever do you mean?" Dimitri asks, acting stupid.

"Don't play the dumb card with me, Dimitri. You might have all the stupid fuckers around here believing you've got the hots for my sister, but I know there's more to it than you're letting on. You paid the dessert menu more attention last week than you did Justine, yet you're trying to organize another date. Why?"

Even before Rocco let slip during our tussle this morning that I have nothing to worry about because Dimitri has no desire to bed Justine, I had an inkling Dimitri's interests weren't as they seemed. Caidyn said over and over again during a three-hour-long teleconference yesterday that Dimitri drooled over the dessert menu more than he did Justine last week, yet we still needed another two-hour-long conversation about it. I'm fucking wrecked, and all I've done the past three days is talk.

Dimitri slightly tilts to his left. A telltale sign he just drew his gun on me. "She isn't in any danger."

"That wasn't what I asked."

I wink, then lean forward, my composure too frayed to feel fear. In the heat of the moment, I slid into the driver's seat of the Buick and took off like a bat out of hell. I wasn't bolting from Demi. I was eager to get this stage of our life over and done with. I just really fucking hope she doesn't misread my disappearance in the wrong manner when she wakes up. Things have been tough the past three days, but knowing she's there, ready and willing to lend me an ear once the shit stops raining down on me made everything a little easier to swallow.

Although Dimitri is quick to shut it down, I still spot the shock that registers on his face before it fully disappears. He, like many other people in this shithole, underestimated the

Walsh reputation. We can protect those we love without machine guns, and even if they were required, they'd never know it.

"You're willing to die for your sister?" I don't need to answer him. He can see the confirmation in my eyes. "How does Demi feel about that?"

No number of swallows will lessen the gurgle of my stomach. Demi took the hit of a man without a single tear falling down her cheek. She's as strong as an ox, but I'd rather she didn't need to be.

Confident he has me right where he needs me, Dimitri sinks low in his chair. "If Demi were taken by your enemies, how far would you go to get her back?" Just the fact he asks that reveals he has no clue Demi's biggest enemy is the man who gave him life. "And what about that kid of yours growing in her stomach? The one you don't know about because you're ignoring all the signs."

I can't talk. My mouth gapes open and closed, but not a single word escapes me. I'm not just summarizing what he said, I am seeking the signs he's confident I missed. There is a handful of them, but that doesn't mean what I think it does, right? Girls pee more than guys, in general, and the extra sleep Demi has been getting the past couple of days is from sexual exhaustion, right?

Right.

Then why the fuck is the voice inside my head screaming the opposite?

"What if he or she were ripped away from you? How far would you go to keep her safe?" It dawns on me it isn't just

Demi being fucked over by her uncle. Not even his son is safe. "My daughter was cut out of my wife's stomach. They butchered her like a piece of worthless meat. I don't care who I have to trample, I won't stop until they're forced to pay for their mistakes."

Although I get what he's saying, nothing can alter the facts. "Justine is my sister. I won't have her used like this."

"And she's my daughter!" After tossing a photo of a dark-haired girl I'd guess to be around the age of two to my side of his desk, Dimitri stands from his chair so there isn't a chunk of wood between me and the muzzle of his gun. "She ranks higher than anyone."

His flaring nostrils double when I return his hostile stance with one just as aggressive. He's shocked I have the gall to pull a gun on him, but his surprise won't see him standing down anytime soon. We stand across from each other for the next several seconds, our stare-down only ending when a thick Russian voice booms across the room, "Lower your guns." Seconds feel like minutes when we ignore the stranger's directive. "Don't make me repeat myself. I'll shoot you both before leaving you here to rot. Trust me when I say two less criminals in a sea of many won't be missed."

Hating that he has me confused as one of Dimitri's goons, I lower my gun before ending our exchange with a final warning, "Stay away from my sister."

I dump the gun with the serial number scratched off onto his desk before walking away. My brisk pace slows when my eyes land on the person who interrupted us. He's the man who tried to convince Demi to press charges when he found her battered and bruised outside a rusty old pub. He's a fucking agent, and I'm once again close to being snared by a Bureau's trap.

While cursing my stupidity into the cool night air, I divert the direction of my course. Instead of heading back to the Buick to drop it off at Rocco's mansion-size home, I move into the street. Demi will never achieve the peaceful life she's after if I serve seven years behind bars for drug trafficking.

Upon noticing a van with a local pizza shop sign on the side door, I pull up the collar of my jacket. No pizza company in Hopeton has the funds to purchase a brand-new Mercedes Benz X-Class commercial vehicle. They pay Col far too much to keep their legitimate businesses off his radar to splurge. I wouldn't be surprised to discover half of the Hopeton businesses can't afford their staff's wages.

I keep my chin glued to my chest until I round the corner the van is parked on, then I prick my ears to ensure I'm not being followed. I walk almost eight blocks before I flag down a cab coming in the opposite direction. I could call my brothers to pick me up, but I'm already struggling to work out how I'll explain to Demi where I've been the past five hours. I don't need more controversy.

I'm confident Demi will understand my eagerness to get my final run done and dusted, I am just not keen to see her reaction when she discovers I'm more like her family than she realizes.

I didn't solely punch Landon because he insulted Demi. I did it for our future kids as well—children I always knew I'd have one day but never truly considered until Dimitri popped the idea into my head.

Demi and I are super relaxed with protection. By super relaxed, I mean we haven't used any. Truth be told, I assumed Demi was on the pill. When I discovered that wasn't the case, I should have manned up by gloving up. I don't know why I didn't. I could palm it off as that I've had her bare, so I couldn't go back, but if that were the case, why didn't I simply suggest she use the pill or get the implant? I keep my thoughts in my head for a reason. If the excited butterflies in my stomach are anything to go by, I'm reasonably sure I know why.

My relationship with Demi has occurred at the speed of lightning, so it's only fair babies and marriage are crossed off my list of accomplishments sooner rather than later.

"Are you sure this is the address you want me to take you?" asks the cab driver after pulling up to a set of lights. "There's nothing out that way but sticks and mosquitos."

"Yeah, that's right. I've heard there are good hiking tracks hidden back from the road." I didn't give him the cabin's address. I'll have to walk the final two miles.

The blond man with a reversed cap and a wonky grin hooks his arm over the passenger seat before cranking his neck to face me. He drags his eyes down my jeans, Vans shoes, and polo shirt before returning them to my face. "Hiking... *right.*"

With the cab driver's friendliness gobbled up by suspicion, we make the trip in silence. I don't mind. It gives me plenty of time to contemplate what to say to Demi and exactly how the fuck I should say it. I also take a couple of minutes to mull over the idea she's pregnant.

I won't lie, I'm hopeful.

My brothers don't understand my protectiveness of Demi.

They've never been in a serious relationship, so they don't understand my desire to keep her safe is more important than anything. I'm sure their opinion will change when they learn she's carrying their niece or nephew.

A baby will change everything, and for once, it will be a good change.

"Are you sure this is where you want me to drop you off?"

I answer the cab driver by handing him a couple of bills from the bundle of Benjamin Franklins left in my gym bag. The fare is already eye-watering, not to mention he needs to make the trip back to Hopeton alone. The money I gave him should cover both the fare and his time. It should also be enough to fill his tank with gas, lessening my guilt.

I peer at him like he's insane when he says, "I'm good." He nudges his head to the cash he pushed back through the gap in his window. "That there is blood money. No good can come from it."

Not speaking another word, he winds up his window, then pushes down on the gas pedal. With the sun in the process of rising, it takes ages for me to be confident the hues of orange bouncing across the landscaped plains aren't the taillights of his cab. I hate that I'm wasting time being cautious, but just like my earlier request for him to make a quick detour past a drugstore, I'd rather be safe than sorry.

After another twenty minutes standing by the side of the road, I push off my feet and head in the direction of the cabin. I

don't walk along the shoulder of the road. I keep my tracks
hidden by the dense forest bordering all the roads out this way.
The number of trees I have to veer past makes my pace a little
sluggish, but the lights of the cabin soon present on the horizon.
Its illumination advises Demi is awake. I'm not surprised, she's
been going to bed with the sun the past couple of days.

"Demi..." I remove my coat and mud-sloshed boots at the
entryway door before I enter the empty living room. "Are you
preparing breakfast?" *God, I fucking hope so.* I've missed her
cooking as much as the sugary taste of her lips the past couple of
days.

"Demi..." I call out again when I find the kitchen void of a
single soul.

I'm about to go search for her in the bedroom when a box on
the kitchen table stops me in my tracks. It's a box of pregnancy
tests—an *empty* box of pregnancy tests. All three sticks have
been removed.

"Dem—" This shout is higher pitched than my earlier two. I
don't know about you, but I don't see a woman taking three tests
to authenticate a negative result. It's usually the shock of a posi-
tive that sees them tearing through an entire packet. "Are you
sleeping?"

With a smile, I pat down the rumpled bedding in the middle
of the mattress before racing for the attached bathroom. My
pace slows when the noise of running water filters through my
ears. My girl is in the shower, and I'm more than ready for us to
wash off the dirt of this putrid life.

"I hope you didn't start without me."

I dump my jeans on top of Demi's sleepwear in the doorway

of the bathroom before I yank my shirt over my head. In my hurry to join her in the shower, I fail to notice there's no steam billowing under the bathroom door. The water has run cold, meaning Demi's been in the shower for hours.

"Demi..."

When I push open the partially cracked-open door, my heart drops to my stomach before a mangled roar leaves my throat. Demi is in the shower, but the sound of running water isn't from the showerhead. It is the horrific noise of the blood draining away from Demi's slumped body circling the drain.

"Demi!"

The End... for now.

Demi *is available now!*

Be sure to add my author page to your social media to remain up to date on all news relating to upcoming releases.

Facebook: facebook.com/authorshandi

Instagram: instagram.com/authorshandi

• • •

Email: authorshandi@gmail.com

Reader's Group: bit.ly/ShandiBookBabes

Website: authorshandi.com

Newsletter: subscribepage.com/AuthorShandi

** *If you enjoyed this book, please leave a review* **

ACKNOWLEDGMENTS

I can sit down and write a book without batting an eye, but this is tough for me. There are always lots of people to thank, but not enough page space to thank them adequately, so I'll keep it simple.

Thank you to those who inspire, encourage, and support me. Thank you for buying my books, reading them, and leaving reviews. Thank you for sending me messages of support, and telling me how much you love my characters. Thank you for being there when I wanted to walk away from writing. Thank you for taking a chance on a high-school dropout who can't string two sentences together without making a mistake. And last, but not at all least, thank you for seeing past the mess to understand the story beneath it.

Without you, there would be no me, so for that, I'm forever in your debt.

Much Love,

Shandi xx

ALSO BY SHANDI BOYES

Denotes Standalone Books

Perception Series

Saving Noah *

Fighting Jacob *

Taming Nick *

Redeeming Slater *

Saving Emily

Wrapped Up with Rise Up

Protecting Nicole *

Enigma

Enigma

Unraveling an Enigma

Enigma The Mystery Unmasked

Enigma: The Final Chapter

Beneath The Secrets

Beneath The Sheets

Spy Thy Neighbor *

The Opposite Effect *

I Married a Mob Boss *

Second Shot *

The Way We Are

The Way We Were

Sugar and Spice *

Lady In Waiting

Man in Queue

Couple on Hold

Enigma: The Wedding

Silent Vigilante

Hushed Guardian

Quiet Protector

Enigma: An Isaac Retelling

Twisted Lies *

Bound Series

Chains

Links

Bound

Restrain

The Misfits *

Nanny Dispute *

Russian Mob Chronicles

Nikolai: A Mafia Prince Romance

Nikolai: Taking Back What's Mine

Nikolai: What's Left of Me

Nikolai: Mine to Protect

Asher: My Russian Revenge *

Nikolai: Through the Devil's Eyes

Trey *

The Italian Cartel

Dimitri

Roxanne

Reign

Mafia Ties (Novella)

Maddox

Demi

Ox

Rocco *

Clover *

Smith *

RomCom Standalones

Just Playin' *

Ain't Happenin' *

The Drop Zone *

Very Unlikely *

False Start *

Short Stories - Newsletter Downloads

Christmas Trio *

Falling For A Stranger *

One Night Only Series

Hotshot Boss *

Hotshot Neighbor *

The Bobrov Bratva Series

Wicked Intentions *

Sinful Intentions *

Devious Intentions *

Deadly Intentions *

Milton Keynes UK
Ingram Content Group UK Ltd.
UKHW020834141124
451205UK00013B/882

9 781923 062795